DIRT

dirt

ISBN 1 84068 027 X
The Whip Angels & *Linda's Strange Vacation*
First published as separate volumes by Velvet Publications,
1995 and 1997 respectively
First omnibus edition published 2001 by Creation Books
Copyright © Creation Books 2001
Introduction copyright © Candice Black 2001
All world rights reserved
Design: The Tears Corporation
Cover image: Steve Bickerstaff
A Bondagebest Production

introduction

Without the permissive, risk-taking literary scene of Paris in the 1950s and 1960s, and its underground presses – particularly the Olympia Press run by Maurice Girodias – many authors now recognised as among the world's best might never have been published.

William S Burroughs, Jean Genet, J P Donleavy, Lawrence Durrell, Alexander Trocchi, even Samuel Beckett – they all owed their first break to Girodias, who paved the way for others to follow. John Calder and Marion Boyars in London, Grove Press in New York, all took their lead in challenging the archaic obscenity laws with iconoclastic publications.

Olympia and its many affiliates/copyists such as Ophelia and Othello, also allowed quality writers to subsist in Paris by producing, pseudononymously, volumes of literary erotica which stood head and shoulders above the offerings being churned out by gutter presses.

The Libertine, Nightmare, Thongs, Whips Incorporated, The Bitch Of Buchenwald, Pussy In Boots, The Cosmic Gash – the list of great titles with equally great texts to match is extensive and exemplary.

The Whip Angels, published in 1955, is often attributed to Diane Bataille, wife of Georges. Some even suggest that Georges Bataille had a hand in the writing of this elegant and sophisticated tale of corrupted youth. The cruder *Linda's Strange Vacation* appeared in 1960 and appears to have been either translated from French, or written in English by a French author. Marcus Huttning is almost certainly a *nom-de-plume*, and little or nothing is known about the creator of this extreme and powerful novel.

Both novels, collected here by Creation Books under the title **Dirt**, are extraordinary examples of the erotic imagination, and as a pair they not only make a great volume of fictive sexual excess, but stand as a tribute to the underground presses who made such work available and in doing so helped annihilate the oppression of censorship. It seems fitting that Creation – perhaps the only company currently operating in the true spirit of Olympia Press – should be the new publishers.

—*Candice Black (series editor), London, January 2001*

the whip angels

a preface (contributed by a member of her family)

Our family is large. Emigrations, international conflicts, the treaties signed to end them, the loss of some colonies and the acquiring of others – in a word, a hundred years of ceaseless change have dispersed us. I belong to no one country. But I have my distant roots is England.

I am an engineer, I live in the New World. Sometimes business brings me back to the Old. I long ago gave up my once serious, anxious search after my origins. When I was young, the desire to know who I was, from exactly what I had sprung was a tormenting desire. I am older now.

An old aunt on my mother's side died recently; in her will she left me a house at E———, near London. And recently I went there because... because I was obliged to. Property, which I dislike, imposes those obligations. Property needs looking after. There are deeds and lawyers and registrars and mortgages and taxes and papers, and they clutter one's life, they weigh one down.

It seemed to me best to sell that house, a great rambling melancholy affair, not the sort of thing one dares own or dream of trying to keep up these days. But I wanted to look over pieces of furniture and various odds and ends before that hoard of nameless Victorian horrors was put on the block for public sale. Not that I especially wished to salvage anything; furniture like that doesn't fit in just anywhere. I only went to see what there was to see and what was going to be further dispersed.

Attics have a certain grim fascination that persists long

after boyhood. Having, like a boy and purely for the fun of it, made my choice of furniture I 'wanted', I remembered a pair of fine opaline lamps that had fascinated me so many years before during my own summer holidays at E———. I asked what had become of those lamps and was told by Mrs G———, the housekeeper, that one of them had been broken but that the other still lay in the attic.

And there it was, standing on top of a huge trunk, its milky whiteness still fresh despite the heavy layer of greasy dust coating it. Gratified by that discovery I continued to poke about. I had several bunches of keys to various chests and bureau drawers, and absently, thinking of something already thirty-five years gone by if I was thinking at all, I started to fit the smaller keys into the different trunks and valises, opening them and rummaging through their contents in the most desultory way, amused and astonished by the accumulation of rubbish those long-forgotten hiding places sequestered.

I kept at it, mechanically, for no reason, and had of course sooner or later – to come across that puffy crocodile-skin travelling bag. It was ancient. The leather was so dry that when I opened it, it cracked with a sharp splitting sound. Inside, the light brown moiré lining still shone, but the silver-backed brushes and bottle-stoppers were nearly black with tarnish. A faint musty smell of perfume still clung to this relic. Here was every conceivable device a woman might possibly need on her voyage: an elaborate manicure set, button-hooks, shoehorns, many needles and much thread, scissors, a mirror, a pair of minute curling tongs and a little alcohol lamp to heat them over. I touched those things. Carefully, respectfully, I lifted them out, blew away the dust, and as if I were trying to put the past's confusion into order, laid them in neat rows on the floor.

While I was digging with my fingers in the deepest recesses, I felt, under a row of silk pockets which had held long thin crystal flasks, a small hook. I unfastened it. With my nails I pried up the bottom and reached another compartment. Two books nested in it. That may all sound highly improbable. Let me repeat that I had long since given up hunting for lost treasures. My chance discovery was indeed a treasure, and far stranger than the way I discovered it.

The books were not identical. One was bound in dark red leather, with a small, rather ornate gold clasp. The other was a large, thoroughly ordinary black copy-book. I have them here before me on my desk.

On opening it, the first book – the red one – proved almost unreadable. It was filled with a somewhat frantic scrawl, words and sentences that seemed to have been set down at top speed. Some of the pages were stained and stuck, others so smudged by inkblots that nothing remained but a dark blur. But the few words I could decipher left me spellbound. And turning to the second book, I found that, while undoubtedly written by the same person, it had obviously been composed under very different circumstances, probably years later.

I assured Mrs G——— that everything was in good order, thanked her, said goodbye and took those two volumes back with me to my Mayfair hotel room where I spent long hours poring over them.

The second book, I found, after close comparison with what I could make out in the first, relates the same story with very few and very insignificant variations. It tells that story in greater detail, filling in the gaps where the writer has judged it necessary to say more. It was plainly written, with care and at leisure, and by a more mature girl; but what was her purpose in repeating her sombre, hardly commonplace tale? I don't know. I am an ordinary man, distantly related to this person, hence, I suppose, to this Kenneth and this Angela, the monsters, as she calls them.

The dressing case bore the initials K.A.M. They meant nothing to me. Kenneth's? Perhaps. Or Angela's? Who was she? And this girl called Victoria, the authoress? Relations, all of them, and by some tie or other my own kin. I accept that. For it is very little: almost anyone could be my kinsman, my cousin. And that is why I paused over this diary – why, terrible thing that it is, I did not fling it away, burn it, why indeed despite my horror, I was fascinated by it.

I might say something about the house referred to in this journal. The house appears to be the same one I inherited from my deceased aunt, the one which has now been sold.

Although there are no descriptions of the place itself, there is at least one reference to a series of rooms fitted with 'double doors'. Those rooms would be in the east wing of the house, a wing that was added in the XVIIth Century. They have a sort of small intervening foyer between the door leading out onto the hallway and the other door opening into the room panelled in pale grey painted wainscoting, affording plenty of extra cupboard space and, as I well remember (for we always occupied those rooms on our visits when we were children), they also afforded an excellent soundproof dead air space to muffle the noise we made while playing on rainy afternoons. I mention all this because I think it explains why the extraordinary goings-on described in this book were never overheard. Yet, on the other hand, it does seem incredible that no intruder ever disturbed the actors; and the explanation that the entire household was asleep, while plausible, seems inadequate nevertheless.

One is tempted to imagine, yes, that a certain secret complicity reigned between the occupants of the house and this strange pair, Kenneth and Angela; and that, by tacit agreement, they were allowed to victimise this adolescent girl.

What else remains to be said? The journal covers a brief three weeks and reveals the swift transition wrought in Victoria's character by the shock of events. Could a person change so radically in so short a time? Yes, perhaps, if she were young, sheltered, protected – and then, suddenly exposed to the wind of evil.

I have faithfully transcribed the later version of Victoria's journal. It is something very alien to my to my experience, to my imaginings; no one could be less fit than I to interpret it. And so I shall say no more, and let Victoria speak, breathlessly, of what was real and true to her. This is how she begins:

friday, the 22nd of june, 1866

I just don't know where to begin... to tell the truth. I am still too excited to be able to collect my thoughts, and although my eyes are half-closed with sleepiness, I can't resist the temptation to start right in on my diary. It is my first diary and today is my birthday.

I should explain that first. When I went to kiss dear Mamma this morning, little expecting she would give me a present, she handed me this lovely book bound in dark red leather with a dear little gold clasp that locks with a tiny gold key. I thought at first it was a new hymn book and thanked Mamma, for I truly do need a new one. "No," Mamma laughed, "I am giving you a treasure-trove. It's for your own secrets. Look, do you see how it locks?"

Then she unlocked the clasp for me: and I saw all the pages were blank!

"Now, I want you to write in it every day, Victoria," Mamma said, "and that way you will have your precious memories to keep forever. You're fourteen now and you might just as well begin with the summer holidays. Your cousins are coming home from India and I am sure you will have a great many charming anecdotes to write down. How grateful you will be in later years if you keep careful account of all that happens to you now. And it's high time you began to think on paper, one doesn't think at all if one doesn't think clearly, you know, and the best way is to discipline yourself to say the right thing in the right way. I have always kept a diary, and in between the pages of my diaries I've kept a collection of pressed flowers I've picked up on special occasions. I suggest you do the same."

I felt overcome with pride and happiness and gratitude. I thanked dear Mamma with tears in my eyes and went out of the room, leaving her to rest on her chaise-longue. She rests most of the day.

Poor Mamma is not strong and Papa insists on her having a trained nurse to look after her. Mamma always has pretty nurses because Papa says they are more restful, and Miss Browning is quite lovely, really even prettier than the one we had before, Miss March, who became fat and, I did think, quite ugly before she had to leave.

'Tis a great pity dear Mamma's health is so fragile. I overheard Violette, Mamma's third maid this year, speaking about her condition to Martin who is really a silly man to have for a valet, for he called Mamma an old girl. One should never listen to servants, and maybe I shouldn't write such things down in my diary; but, after all, Mamma is only thirty-two.

Yes, I must do well. I am wandering straight away from the point, as Miss Perkins says when she corrects my English essays. She's so kind to me. Just the other day she gave me a lovely japanned box which, she said, had been in her family's possession for many years. I thanked her and promised in exchange to try hard to do my lessons more thoroughly and from now on to concentrate and achieve real progress.

And then my birthday party. Think! The only thing that spoiled our gayness was dear Papa's being away. The Indian mail has been delayed and Papa is still waiting to meet Aunt Margaret, Uncle John and my cousins. He hopes they will land tomorrow.

Well, there were sugar ornaments and all kinds of sweets on the table and in the middle a huge cake with white icing and fourteen pink candles. Mamma had invited some of our neighbours, the vicar, Mr Gareth, and of course Ursula, who had on a hideous spinach-green taffeta dress and looked, if I do say so, plainer than usual, even if she is my best friend. Oh, I would hate to have a vicar for a father! I have never dared ask Ursula if she minded. He looks as if he knew all your sins even before you had got started committing them. And the way he gazes at one with that glassy stare of his makes one feel quite as naked as Eve must have felt after she had taken a bite of the Fatal Apple. Papa says Mr Gareth is a 'dark horse', whatever in the world that could mean; and when I asked Mamma, I declare she turned purple. And I felt so ashamed. Poor Mamma's health can't bear shocks. I asked Ursula too, she said that she didn't know, and perhaps it is because he is always dressed in black.

Well, I'm so weary that I say all sorts of silly things. Before I stop, I must write down my birthday resolution:

No matter what, I, Victoria, shall finish my lace doily this summer, come what may and despite all.

saturday

A little package, addressed to me, came this afternoon in the mail from London. It was from dear Papa, wishing me a happy birthday and saying he hoped I would like my present.

It is a small gold locket on a chain, with an engraved inscription: For Victoria, from Papa, June the 22nd, 1866. Mamma promises she will give me a lock of her hair to put inside.

Did some of my doily, read aloud to Miss Perkins from Madame de Sévigné's letters. I really do think my French is improving.

My cousins will be here for the whole summer in a matter of days – I can hardly believe it and say it over and over to myself as though something so wonderful could never come true.

The India mail has reached port at last. It's for the day after tomorrow, after lunch!

I rushed to the vicarage to give Ursula the news, and stayed to tea. She'll come tomorrow and help me get everything ready.

Just too excited to do any more needlework.

sunday

Only one more day to wait!

To think that they are my closest cousins and that I have never once seen them!

Indeed, the fact is I can say they are the completest strangers to me, because they left for India before I was born and have been out there ever since. Uncle John is going to retire now from the service; they say he is going to spend the summer in Italy and then buy a house in London. Mamma has promised that later I shall be able to stay with them in the city. Papa plans to go with Uncle John to Venice and Rome and Naples and what with Miss Browning taking her vacation at the same time, the house would be quite empty were it not for the arrival of Kenneth and Angela.

Ursula and Mr Gareth lunched with us as they always do on Sundays.

Ursula is just as excited as I am. She spent the afternoon helping me with the floral decorations. But, oh! She is such a bossy thing!

We spent hours in the linen-room trying to make up our minds as to the prettiest designs and which should go in which room. We changed and changed everything around, and did a lot of running up and down stairs, since Aunt Margaret's and Uncle John's rooms are quite near Mamma's, whereas, thank goodness! Angela and Kenneth are to have rooms in the other wing of the house, right next door to mine.

But why do I write this way? It is all such silly, weak, excitable writing, and I know all the time that proper English sentence structure and tone call for balance and restraint. Miss Perkins said to me yesterday: "If you do not exercise self-mastery and discipline in your actions as well as in your sentences, you will be thought a foolish girl and what you say and write will not merit attention." Anyway... I took special care over Angela's room. I feel certain she is going to become my best friend instead of Ursula because, really... she is a strange girl. While I was pulling down the bed-cover for the hundredth time, talking to her about Angela and wondering for the hundredth time what she would be like, Ursula suddenly seized my wrist and looked straight into my face... and stuck her tongue out at me in the most unladylike manner and then she flounced out of the room, saying:

"I'm much more interested in men than in girls and all I hope is that your cousin Kenneth is one, so there!"

It was wrong of me, I know. I suppose I made her jealous, and that is my fault. But how could a vicar's daughter ever say such a thing without so much as blushing? We made it up later and feeling a little guilty – for after all, I had been unfaithful to her in my thought – I agreed to put the nicest antimacassars in Kenneth's room.

When we were all done we tried some new hair-styles in front of my mirror. Poor Ursula's mousy blonde hair is so straight that no matter what she tried to do with it, it just fell out of the combs in long untidy wisps. She tried not to show it, but I could see she was furious! I hate my red hair, but at least it waves and I was able to pile it up in long curls just by twisting it around my fingers. Ursula watched. It looked quite like Mamma's. Then Ursula began to stroke my hair. She was sorry. She smiled at me and that is how we decided (even though we didn't say a word) to be kind to each other.

But it's hard to be kind to Ursula and I keep forgetting to be. After a while it was supper time and Ursula left. I confess that I unkindly waited until the very last minute before inviting her to tea tomorrow.

Tomorrow. I can hardly write the word without a thrill of excitement. Tomorrow.

It's late now (and I haven't done a stitch of my lace). I've just crept into Angela's room to have a last look at everything. Perhaps someday we'll have a midnight feast together with a box of chocolates I have left over from my birthday party. But Perhaps Angela is a strict and well brought-up girl and goes to bed promptly when she's told.

monday

How and where to begin?

    I woke up so early that by the time I heard the distant sound of the carriage wheels at the entrance to the drive, I felt as if a lifetime had already passed! Things will be so different now – that is what I thought as I rushed out of my room and, in my haste, almost bumped into Mamma on the staircase. She asked me to run back up and find a handkerchief; I did, but in my state of emotion I failed to come across it anywhere. I am ashamed to admit that I was so vexed at not being downstairs for their arrival that I quite lost control of myself and when at last I did find that hateful object, it was with tears in my eyes and a red face I confronted my dear cousins for the first time.

    Aunt Margaret looks so much like Mamma I was fairly staggered. Except that her hair is dark. She has the same violet-coloured eyes, and creamy skin, and the smallest waist I have ever seen, except for Angela's. She is much more gay than Mamma, and seems to say anything that happens to come into her head, and she laughs all the time about everything. Her eyes are very bright. She embraced me fondly and, turning to Mamma, said, much to my embarrassment that "This one will surely be a beauty someday." I could see Mamma was not pleased that she had chosen to make such a remark in front of me.

    I turned to welcome Uncle John, who is even taller than Papa and who was saying to Mamma, "Well, well, who would ever have dreamt you had such a grown-up girl!" but when I saw Kenneth I forgot everyone else.

    He is the most beautiful young man you could imagine, and now that I know him still better he seems more beautiful still. I mean beautiful, not simply handsome, even though handsome is the word one usually uses in connection with men. He is very tall too with straight jet black hair and large slanting blue eyes with rather heavy lids which give him a dreamy expression, and dark circles under his eyes which make their colour even brighter. He is the most romantic looking young man I have ever seen. He stoops slightly when he walks, bending his head forward ever so little, and always seems to be thinking. He does not much smile, but his voice is warm and sweet, his teeth are white, and he is very slender.

Kenneth, smiling, came forward to greet me... and I have never been so intimidated in my life! Before I could find my tongue he bent still further down and looking straight into my eyes said in a whisper that went quite through me: "You look as though you are a cry-baby. Eh? Do hope so."

My face went a flaming red. I felt it. I must have looked a sight because Angela who was standing next to him kissed me and turning to Kenneth smiled and winked at him in the most mocking manner. This was more than I could endure, and just as I was about to burst into tears before everyone, she hugged me affectionately and linking her arm through mine, she said:

"Dear Victoria would you show me to my room?"

I was so happy to! And so grateful to her for helping me hide my awkwardness. I felt almost consoled when, kissing me on the mouth, she praised me for the lovely way I had done the flowers.

At that instant I thought of Ursula and, once again, felt unkind.

Angela is lovely. Her hair is very dark, like Kenneth's, only curly, and her eyes are the same deep blue, with long black lashes that cast a dark shadow on her cheeks. Her skin is just like a rose petal with the same faint pink hue. And not a single freckle!

I didn't know what to say, and kept still, looking at her.

She sat in front of the mirror to take off her bonnet. Her reflection smiled at me from the mirror. "It is so warm," she said, "after all that travel. Would you help me unhook just a little?"

I helped her undo the top of her dress. I was amazed to see that she had nothing on underneath but a very tight white corset and, glancing up at the mirror from behind her, I saw that at the top of the two whalebones and level with the pink points of her breasts, were attached two small pointed metal cones. I had never seen anything like that corset and I don't know what prompted me to reach out to touch one of the points. At that same moment Angela leaned forward.

With a sharp cry of pain – it must have sounded like a shot in the silence – I withdrew my finger. It was covered with blood. I felt thoroughly ashamed at my indiscretion and wondered what in the world to say. but Angela only laughed and taking hold of my hand, much to my confusion she began to suck my finger until my hand began to go numb and I begged her to stop.

"Did it hurt?" she asked me. "Oh, yes," I said. Then she sighed and leaning back in her chair looked as though she were about to faint.

I dashed to fetch her some water from the night table, marvelling at the same time at her tenderness of heart. But when I'd got back with a glass and the carafe, she had entirely recovered. "It's so warm," she said and then, in an abrupt manner, bade me leave her alone.

What had I done to annoy her? I didn't know, but I wanted to apologise. But I didn't dare and, fighting back my tears, with a sinking feeling inside me, I tiptoed away.

My finger had started bleeding again without my noticing it and it had stained my best dress. I had to ask Miss Perkins to help me clean it and in spite of my protests she insisted upon bandaging my finger. She was in such a flutter she did not ask me how it had happened.

I didn't see Angela again until lunch although I lingered for a while in the hallway, hoping she would come down and that I could perhaps show her my part of the rose garden.

Through the open window I could see Kenneth strolling thoughtfully up and down the gravel walk in front of the lawn, talking with Papa about the future and how he proposed to go up to Oxford in the autumn. The very thought that he would be leaving so soon was truly unbearable. I flushed when I recalled how he had just called me a cry-baby, and the mere thought of my humiliation fetched tears to my eyes again. I wanted to go down and join them, but my timidity was such I just couldn't.

What a relief to hear the dinner bell at last! And imagine my joy to find I had been placed beside him at the table and had Angela on my other side!

Mamma stared at me almost immediately and asked what I had done to my finger. Something, I don't know what, urged me to lie. I told her I'd pricked it while doing my lace-work... and I didn't even blush as I told that lie. At that moment Angela, reaching across my lap put her hand on Kenneth's knee. She did this so quickly I wondered whether I had simply imagined it. Then I saw Kenneth nod in her direction, as though this was some secret sign between them. How I wish I had a brother I could share secrets with!

I tried to find something to say to Kenneth. But every time I opened my mouth there was a lump in my throat, and I went sadly back to swallowing the food on my plate. He must have sensed my dismay, for, towards the end of the meal, when the conversation was very animated about the native revolt and the Gloucestershire regiment and everyone else seemed very gay, he took one of my hands and placed it on his leg. "Feel better now?" he asked in that strong whisper of his. I nodded that I did, feeling something at the same time soft and hard moving at the bottom of his pocket, and wondering, in a sort of terror, whether it might not be a pet mouse. But for Kenneth's friendship I was prepared to bear anything, and I fondled it for as long as I dared, until I saw Miss Perkins frowning at me for not keeping my hands on the table.

After lunch we all went for a walk in the park. By the time we had gathered on the lawn for tea, I had quite forgotten the time when my cousins had not been there, and forgotten too Ursula's existence. But there she was, so strange. She was very hot and cross, saying she had looked for me everywhere during the last hour. I introduced her to Kenneth and Angela. What did she do then but begin to show off in the most disgraceful way until I was more than relieved when she finally left. Ursula may be sixteen, just Angela's age, but I do declare they have nothing whatever in common! And I am glad to say that neither of my cousins paid much attention to her clowning.

At dinner I stroked Kenneth's darling mouse again. He seemed very pleased with me and, during another discussion of the revolt in a place called Amritsar, twice addressed me: "Are you fond of animals, my delicious little cunt?" he enquired with a delightful sparkle in his eye and then, five minutes later, he turned again and, putting his face very close to mine, said: "And you *are* my delicious little cunt."

And he also said he had brought me a gift from India. It would arrive tomorrow with the remainder of the luggage. Although I pleaded with him, he refused to tell me what he had brought.

We all retired to bed early, and much to my disappointment, Angela, after kissing me and murmuring good-night, went off to her room, locking the door after her.

Later, in the stillness, I thought I heard whispered voices, particularly Angela's. On an impulse, without then realising how disgraceful it was, I put my ear on the communicating door. I then heard Kenneth's voice too, although I could not make out what they were saying. He must have unlocked the door between their rooms. Would Mamma think this proper? At any rate, I knew I should never betray them. Then, just as I was about to steal away, I heard Angela sigh so deeply that my heart went out to her. I wondered whether she needed my help, whether I ought to knock and offer my aid. I was about to when I heard Kenneth laugh softly and Angela's sighs redoubled. They were interspersed with an odd sort of giggle that made me fly back to my diary.

tuesday

Kenneth's present is – I'd never have guessed – a darling little Siamese cat, brought all the way from India, and for me. I have decided to call it Bluebell because of its lovely blue eyes – so much like Kenneth's. How shall I express my gratitude for his thoughtfulness? Bluebell is sitting this very minute upon my lap while I am writing. Dinner is to be served in a few minutes.

Both Kenneth and Angela have disappeared since the beginning of the afternoon. Rather than go to the vicarage and waste my time with Ursula – yes, I can say it in my diary: she is a bore – I have taken the pretext of my needlework and the heat to spend an hour or two in my room playing with Bluebell and writing in my journal.

It occurred to me there might be trouble. I mean, I asked Kenneth this morning just exactly what he had in his pocket. For if it is a mouse, I don't know what I shall do with Bluebell. But Kenneth laughed and said it was another secret but that I wouldn't have long to wait to find out all about it. Secrets! how wonderful they are!

Well, maybe after all I shall go over to the vicarage to see Ursula and show her my new pet. Another frenzy of jealousy, I suppose. It's hard to know what to do.

wednesday

Clever Miss Perkins has made a lovely little basket for kitty, lining it with a bit of flowered cretonne and with a cushion to match. What fine taste she has. Bluebell must have thought so to, and too an immediate liking to her new nest, rolling up in a fluffy ball.

Papa, Mamma, Uncle J. and Aunt M. have gone off to pay a round of calls and introduce my cousins to the neighbourhood. I was relieved when they decided I should not accompany them. Especially as they intend to call on old Mrs Washburn, who always insists on kissing me and has such a prickly beard that dear Papa's feels like silk in comparison.

It is fun to be able to say such things – naughty things, I know. But I'd never have dared say them out loud.

Papa, Uncle J. and Aunt M. are leaving for Italy tomorrow. I think I'll go ask Violette if I can help with the packing. Aunt Margaret has such lovely clothes. I'll wager she'll try some of them on, the way Mamma does when she goes to London. Martin says she is 'real cheeky', but even if she is, I love her funny accent and the things she tells me about her childhood in Paris.

thursday

Off they all went this morning: Aunt Margaret and Uncle John and Papa and Miss Browning too – Papa offered to give her a lift as far as London. I don't know how dear Mamma is going to manage without Miss B. to look after her. But she took things in her stride, saying that Miss Perkins would be able to care for her if she should have any of her weak or dizzy spells. They sometimes come when guests are in the house.

    We had all to be up early to say goodbye. And perhaps because I was half asleep I had the strangest illusion. Going into the linen-closet to fetch some clean handkerchief, I heard Papa call someone darling, I thought that Mamma was with him but, no, the only person to be seen was Miss Browning. Papa asked me in a sharp voice what in the name of thunder I meant by prowling around at all hours of the morning, and after I told him (I couldn't prevent tears from coming to my eyes) he kissed me fondly, saying to think no more of it. Putting his arm through mine, we went down to the breakfast room together. "You're a tall girl, you know," he said. "I must remember to bring you some fine present home from Rome."

    In spite of Angela and Kenneth, the house seemed empty all day. In the afternoon we walked down to the vicarage for tea, accompanied by Miss Perkins. She said it would cheer me up. But I declare I don't know anyone who is more saddening and more depressing than the vicar. Mamma and Miss P. never tire of expounding his virtues... but he is so dull, truly, so fearfully good and virtuous and just and wise and pompous I am always afraid I'll not be able to stifle my yawns. I could see that Angela and Kenneth were delighted when the time came to leave and when Mamma refused Ursula's warm invitation to stay for supper.

    Ursula had made a great effort. She had done up her

hair in the most complicated way. It wasn't becoming. The pins kept slipping out and Kenneth kept stooping to pick them up and hand them back to her. That added to her confusion. By the time we left, her hair was like a bird's nest.

Angela came and kissed me good-night. She sat on my bed and talked with me for quite a while before going to her own room.

I don't think I shall miss dear Papa too much if we turn out to be real friends. And I'm sure we shall. I feel it in my bones.

friday

Friday already. I spent a wonderful afternoon with Angela and Kenneth. We walked to the lake, I showed them the boathouse. One of the punts has a bad leak. It's nearly submerged, in fact. I must remember to tell Mamma about that.

After tea, we went to Angela's room. She showed me all her dresses, and some beautiful shawls and then, to my amazement, she said: "Choose." "Choose what?" I asked. "A shawl. Take one for yourself. Whichever you prefer. That red one? It goes well with you."

Then she asked me innumerable questions about myself – she is already devoted to me. There was so little I could tell her to satisfy her curiosity. I was ashamed to admit I have only been away from the village four times and then only to go up to London.

She has a splendid painted chest in her room. It has come with her from India. She says it contains her secrets – more secrets! – and she keeps the key on a chain around her neck. The chest is a lovely thing. The background is painted in deep blue – lacquered – and then everywhere over the blue is the most picturesque array of exotic, many-coloured birds. Of course I didn't ask what her secrets are.

Kenneth is always with us. He seems to worship his sister (and so do I). But I suppose it won't be long before he wants some male company and will begin to spend his time at the O'Hara's now that he has been introduced to them.

I don't know why, but I told Angela about how the eldest O'Hara boy had once tried to kiss me behind the rhododendrons. Angela was plainly shocked. "Have you told your mother?" "Oh, no, never," I assured her, troubled, "what would Mamma say if she knew?"

Angela did not reply. She turned to Kenneth and said

something I didn't quite catch. Then both looked curiously at me.

"Try on your shawl," Angela finally said.

Later.

Kenneth is supervising me. He is standing behind me while I write so that I shall not make mistakes. He is quite naked except for a belt he is wearing around his hips. He has threatened to beat me with it if I do not consign to my diary, and before his very eyes, everything that has happened this evening. I am too ashamed to call out for help. I shouldn't call out for help. I don't want help. Kenneth has told me to write those three sentences and I have.

Angela has locked the double doors that lead out onto the corridor and is sitting with her back against the wood panelling. Her legs are spread wide apart. She is quite naked too, except for her long black hair covering her breasts and a sort of belt with a long thing like Kenneth's, which from time to time she makes disappear into the black curly hair of her... Kenneth says it is called a cunt. I am a cunt. I am a cunt. I am a cunt. Kenneth has told me to write those three sentences and I have. Angela is looking at me. Her lips are curled.

Oh dear Mamma, to think... Kenneth has just stung my back with his belt, and says that if I spoil the diary with my tears he will thrash me in a way I'll never forget.

Now he has moved away. He has gone towards Angela and pushing the thing on her belt with his foot, he has made it vanish entirely. Angela is rolling around on the floor shaking herself as though in great pain. In great pain. In great pain. In great pain. The thing was inside her because suddenly she gave a great heave and it came out covered with a white foam which Kenneth, unfastening the belt and holding it in front of me, has made me lick until it was clean enough for her to use again.

Kenneth calls it a dummy. A dummy. A dummy. A dummy tail. And he says that I must learn to use the proper words, the proper words, the proper words. He says his own thing is called a prick. Prick. Prick. He has made two drawings on a page of my diary, placing words beside them, and has told me I must learn to use them in alternate order so as to avoid monotony.

Angela has gone to lie down on my bed. She is on her back, her long hair spread out around her white face. She seems half asleep. Kenneth has gone up to her and, lifting her legs, has spread them wide, peering at her cunt and stroking it gently with his finger.

He has come back now and is standing behind me, beating my back with his prick, his dummy tail, supervising me and telling me to hurry up with my writing.

When am I going to wake up from this nightmare? But how could it be a nightmare? How could I dream of things I know nothing about. Now I know, I know, I know. Kenneth told me to write that sentence, and I did.

It was Angela who, when we retired, had suggested I should come and say good-night to her when I was ready for bed. I put out my light and arranged some pillows in the bed, in case Miss Perkins peeped in to see if I was sound asleep. When I entered, Angela was standing in the middle of the room in a long white night-gown. She gestured for me to come in, and then I noticed that Kenneth was there too, sitting on the edge of the bed in his dressing-robe. I was about to back out of the room for I was alarmed and frightened – when he rose and caught me by the arm, laughing and saying that there was nothing in all this to cause a fit of shyness. "Where is Bluebell, by the way?" he asked. I stammered that she was in her basket in my room and he invited me to go and bring the kitten, for, he said, "There are moments when I can hardly get on without her." I felt it would he bad manners to refuse and I went back to fetch her, determined to give Kenneth what he wanted and then retire to bed. But when I returned with Bluebell in my arms, he fastened the door behind me. "So much better that way," he said, "to be alone, the three of us together." Bluebell leapt upon Kenneth's lap as soon as I set her down, and this reminded me of his promise to show me what it was he had in his pocket. To hide my embarrassment at the immodesty of our costumes and his presence in Angela's bedroom, I asked him to tell me what he kept there. "Indeed I shall," he said, and lifting the cat away he stretched out upon the bed, opening his dressing-robe and revealing to me the front of his belly, covered with black fuzzy, crinkly hair, with a small thing, I mean a prick, lying between two pink balls at the top of his long legs. "That's it," he said, "my mouse. Well, my little cunt, mousy needs attending to. Mind what you're doing. I'll not brook delays."

I felt as though I were about to faint. Looking towards Angela for help, frantic, I saw she was calmly brushing her hair in front of the mirror. Seeing my distress, she said in the same cold voice she had used the other day when she sent me from the room: "Do what Kenneth tells you to do, Victoria."

I could see her blue eyes glistening in the mirror. She was even more frightening than Kenneth.

Kenneth pulled me down beside him on the bed and ordered me to take off my night-gown. As though mesmerised, I did so, without so much of a murmur of protest. He grunted with satisfaction when he saw my nudity, and told me to turn slowly around so that he could view me from every angle. Then catching hold of my arm, he told me to sit on the bed beside him. Bluebell jumped up on the bed after me, and, sitting on Kenneth's belly, began to lick his prick with her pink tongue. I saw his prick quiver. Kenneth's face twitched. He pushed the cat away and bending me down over him, commanded me to do the same thing. "Gently," he added, "and don't bare your teeth, I want your lips."

The shock of what I had seen seemed to have drained away all my will-power. I obeyed. Without resisting, I licked him in long strokes from the smooth tip to the base, where my nose became buried in his black hair. Suddenly, I felt his prick change shape and, turning over, it more than doubled its length and thickness. I stopped, horrified at what I had done to him. But before I could catch my breath, Kenneth seized my head again and telling me to open my mouth as wide as I could, he thrust his prick in as far as it would go without choking me. Then he pulled my head backwards and forwards, his movements getting faster and faster, until he threw me to one side, spluttering and groaning and grimacing, and continued with his own hand to pull and push the enormous object with an extraordinary violence until, with sudden spurts, a thick white cream started to pour from a small deep hole in the end. I thought he was dying, that his very life was flowing out of him, for he moaned and buried his face in the pillow as though in some horrible agony. Then he became quiet and for a moment lay perfectly still.

Angela had been watching us in the mirror. During it all she had not stirred. Now she came over to the bed, stood by Kenneth, and looked down at him in silence. Then, as if she had suddenly remembered my existence, she turned towards me and, gesturing to Kenneth's prick, told me in a matter-of-fact, flat voice to clean him up.

I looked at her askance, not knowing what she meant.

"Clean him," Angela said.

Not daring to get from the bed in order to find a towel, I took hold of my night-gown and was about to wipe the matted hair on his belly. But before I'd touched him, Angela had snatched the garment away from me. Probing my ribs with her finger, she said in an irritated voice:

"Lick him, you little fool. Lick him until he's clean."

I obeyed; she stood there watching me. It tasted strange, a little like the sweet milky juice you find in the blades of certain kinds of thick grass that grows in the woods. His fur got into my mouth, tickling my throat, but I dared not stop until it was all done. I was afraid of Angela. My back ached and I kept at it until I felt Kenneth's arms encircle my waist and, lifting me up, he set me astride his chest with my back facing him. The breadth of his body kept my thighs well parted. I could feel his fingers exploring my open slit. My cunt. My cunt. My cunt. While he spoke softly to Angela in a language I could not understand. Angela laughed and seemed to agree to whatever he was saying.

I had started to cry, my consciousness gripped by the horror and disgrace of my situation. Dreading the crinkled, repulsive object which, like a magnet, drew my attention and which was lying sideways, lolling across Kenneth's leg, I began to think, to think, to think. Could it be possible that Papa, the vicar, the O'Hara boy, Martin, Bradley our butler had also... could it be possible, could it be possible. Kenneth has told me to write those sentences and I have. My head is reeling. He tells me to rest for a minute.

"Now, start again," Kenneth says. He is still standing

naked beside me. His prick grazes my cheek.

Kenneth had lifted my buttocks and was peering at the most intimate part of my body. A part so immodest I'd never looked at it myself. "It's superb," I heard him say to Angela, "just superb, and as smooth as a new-born infant's."

"Let me have a look," she said.

Kenneth lifted me from him and setting me down on the edge of the bed with a cushion...

2 o'clock.

I'd fallen asleep. Kenneth has woken me again. He has told me to pick up the narrative. "You shall become a romantic poet, my dear," he says, "but it will require labour and devotion. To begin with, it's chiefly sweat. The part genius plays... write down everything. I'm here to watch you do it."

He is so deliberate, so sure.

"Write down everything," he repeats.

I must try.

Where was I? The cushion. Yes, the cushion under my buttocks. He bent my knees back and opened my legs as far as they would go, telling me to hold them thus so that he could appreciate the spectacle. I was trembling with shame and let go almost at once, closing my legs as tight as I could, trying to hide myself from their angry curiosity.

Angela slapped my face so hard my head jerked. "Wake up, wake up," she hissed. And kneeling down on the bed behind me she pressed me open until I thought my bones would crack. "I've got it now," she said to Kenneth. "No bigger than a pinhead. I wonder if she bleeds?"

"Not likely," Kenneth replied. "She's still little more than a child."

He was sitting back in an armchair he'd drawn up in front of me, and he was talking as casually as if my disgraceful position meant nothing at all to him.

"We'd better find out, though," Angela insisted. "Do you bleed?" she asked, pinching my arm cruelly.

"She doesn't understand what you mean," Kenneth observed.

And truly I did not understand. His next question did nothing to enlighten me:

"Do you bleed every month for a few days from your cunt?" he asked.

The very suggestion made me start to tremble with fright. Before I had time to answer in the negative, Angela replied for me:

"She obviously doesn't know what we're talking about. A piece of luck, really."

"She might not last long," Kenneth said.

I heard the church bell in the village toll twelve; we all sat silent while the time struck.

Kenneth's face was scarlet. His prick had swelled up on his belly. He got up and, holding it in his hand, came and leant over me. Angela, letting go of my legs, darted from the bed and, gripping his shoulders, pushed him away from me. "Don't let's spoil things, darling. Have patience. We've never had such fine luck. Trust your Angela, Kenneth darling."

He muttered between his teeth, straightened up and pulled his dressing-robe around him. "When the time comes," he said, "she's going to really feel it."

With that they sent me to my room, where I went naked and sat numbed on a chair in the dark. The door had not been entirely closed and through my dazed mind I could hear them breathing quickly and struggling as though in some silent combat. I did not even think to cover my naked shivering body, and when a few hours later they came into my room they found me thus, huddled in my chair, neither really asleep nor awake. Kenneth shook me. Around his loins was that thick leather belt. Angela had on her obscene toy, held in place by white leather garters and a black belt, fastened tight about her tiny waist.

I don't know what they intended to do originally. In Kenneth's hand was my diary. He read some of it aloud. They both laughed and then suddenly stopped laughing. "Finish writing," he said. "Sit at your desk and finish."

Angela stared at me. Her face took on a dreamy expression. Then, with a gleam in her eye, she spoke again to Kenneth in their foreign language.

"Write," he said. "The last word was 'cushion'. Put everything down, everything. We are going to provide you with all the material you need."

I have been writing. Kenneth has his prick under my left armpit, and is watching me tell of all these horrors, horrors, horrors. My journal is defiled forever, defiled, defiled, defiled, and every time this dreadful thought stops my writing, he pinches the skin of my back between two fingernails and the pain is excruciating. I am so tired.

"That will do," he says. "You may stop there."

But my diary? It is defiled.

"If you are stupid enough to show it to your mother, you shall only gratify her. But stop now. Not another word. Save yourself for tomorrow. There will be more."

saturday

I woke up still sitting at my table, my head in my arms and I wondered where I was. As soon as I had collected my thoughts I remembered my diary. Trembling at the thought that anyone might find it, I lit the lamp and, still naked, searched the room frantically. It wasn't anywhere to be found.

Kenneth or Angela must have taken it with them, for the little key was gone also from my bureau's secret drawer. Although my search was in vain, I felt I had to know for certain. Pulling on my dressing-gown, I tried the door leading to Angela's room. But it was locked. Crying with fear and exhaustion, I beat on it as loudly as I dared, but to no avail. I felt I had reached the end of my tether, and too tired to care anymore about what would or would not come on the morrow, I threw myself into my bed and slept until Miss Perkins woke me with some difficulty just before the last gong went for breakfast.

I have little recollection of how I passed the day.

Dear Mamma remarked that I seemed to be making scant progress in my endeavours to correct my absent-mindedness.

This brought me to myself with a snap and with all my might I tried to chase away the blurred, dreadful visions which the memory of the night's happenings cast before my eyes.

When I'd gone to see Mamma in the morning, she had remarked upon my pallor. At that moment I had thought of throwing myself at her feet, telling her what had happened to me, and imploring her forgiveness. I hesitated. I even bent my knees, readying to fall. But I couldn't. My shame was too great and I could not find the words with which to convey to her the horrors I had been forced to participate in. I tried to fall upon my knees, but I couldn't. Then I realised how firmly they have me in their power, at their mercy.

Instead, I lied to dear Mamma, saying that I had had a nightmare and slept fitfully, then left her, assuring her I felt fine but had a slight headache.

I used that pretended headache as an excuse to go to bed early, leaving Angela and Kenneth with Miss P. and Mamma in the music room. The brother and sister were singing duets and they sung well. They sung beautifully. That was another lie. And Mamma's delighted praise of their voices was more than I could bear.

I went several times during the day to my room to see if they had returned my diary. Or, I wondered, have they destroyed it? I hoped against hope that they had, abandoning their fiendish scheme as too dangerous. I had no opportunity to ask either of them, for they avoided being left alone with me. I could see they were enjoying my sufferings.

When I came up to bed, it was there on my desk, the key hidden in the drawer. My blood ran cold when I saw it, displayed in plain sight. Suppose Mamma or Miss Perkins had... but my cousins know that neither Mamma nor Miss P. is capable of such an indiscretion... and worst of all, they trust me!

If this document is ever found, at least someone will know what I have been through. That makes me want to write everything, everything, and write it fast and write it everywhere. Short of tearing out every page, they'll not be able to destroy this evidence. Every page must express the same thing, everything.

But, oh... I expect their immorality is such that...

Oh, I expect that nothing I write here could ever touch their hearts. Hearts are so hard to touch. "One must not he overly susceptible," everyone tells me. And so it is a useless appeal. A prayer no one but the devil can hear.

It had occurred to me during dinner that if I could lock the door between our rooms I might escape from them. For it would be risky, if not impossible, to come and go from my room by the corridor. I could even throw the key away into the bushes under my window. Dinner seemed interminable and I could hardly wait for it all to end. But alas! How could I have been so naive? the key of course has been removed and I knew only too well it was useless to hunt for it.

I am in a kind of daze, trying to convince myself it is all a dream. The very naturalness of their attitude during the daytime was truly stupefying. Angela's air of sweetness and modesty, Kenneth's polite calm all contribute to the confusion in my mind.

Kenneth and Angela have come upstairs now. I had left the double door leading into the hallway very slightly ajar so that in spite of the thick carpet I could hear them approach. I prefer to know what moment I will be in danger.

As soon as they passed, I shut the doors quietly. I took off my clothes and got into bed after writing this.

Later.

Yes, I'd got into bed and buried my head under the covers. Shaking with apprehension and pretending to sleep, I prayed they would leave me alone. The moments that passed seemed like hours until, as I knew in my inner heart it would be, the door between our rooms opened and they both entered. Kenneth was holding the lamp high above his head and without a word he advanced towards my bed and, pulling the blankets from me, told me to get up and remove my night-gown. I did so, trembling, and stood before them, naked and awaiting their instructions. Angela then led me to the armchair in front of my writing table and after attaching my ankles to each of the front legs, opened my diary, cleaned my pen, opened the inkhorn and told me to put my talents to work. "Immortalise your impressions of the day that has passed."

"I shall expect at least five pages," Kenneth put in.

They both laughed and left, shutting the door behind them.

A long time has passed since they left. The manacles are dragging cruelly on my ankles, for the utter immodesty of my position makes me instinctively try to draw my legs together. I am also tormented by the desire to satisfy a natural need. I dare not move. Yet I shall have to, dragging the armchair along with me until I reach my night table.

Later.

I am back in my armchair, with my ankles attached. It

is difficult for me to imagine that a short while ago I was deploring my situation. What can I say now, when a new feeling of guilt has added itself to my shame?

And the torment of writing this diary in which they say I have got to put down every last detail of what occurs, or else, as Angela tells as though in confidence, Kenneth will do something to me to make me have a child within the next month. She said that not only would I suffer the tortures of the damned, but I would bring open disgrace upon my family, and no doubt end my life shut up in a convent if I survived. Although I was beside myself with fear, I tried to threaten her in return with exposure. But she only laughed and said that no one would believe me. Such a thing has already happened out in India, she added, and only ended with the plaintiff in an asylum, where the family was glad to deposit such a monster.

I will not be allowed to go to bed until I have related what has transpired this evening, and although I feel it is practically beyond my strength, I know too that they will not relent. They are lying on the bed fondling one another in silence and watching me.

They must have heard me drag myself across the floor, for as soon as I reached the chamberpot and had succeeded in getting it under me, they both burst in, and jeering at the ridiculousness of my position, dragged it away from me before I had a chance to use it. Unable to control myself another instant, I felt the burning water run down my legs. Kenneth pressed his hand on my cunt, thus arresting this disgraceful exhibition of incontinence. "Courage," he said, "keep a grip on yourself, Victoria, my little cunt of cunts." Meanwhile Angela freed my legs from the cords binding them. Kenneth therewith lay down upon the floor with his head under me and taking away his hand, entreated me to 'let go'. "Fire, Victoria, right into my mouth."

I struggled to free myself, utterly horror-struck by his suggestion. But he pulled me down and taking my own hands away, pressed his lips against me and sucked with all his might. The steady stream ran out of me and into him for what seemed like minutes. I could feel the burn of his moustache on my tender skin. When I had finished he rolled his face around, drying it and kissing the inside of my thighs.

While this was going on, Angela, kneeling beside him, had encircled his prick with her hand, manipulating it in rapid jerks until it had swollen to its utmost size. Then, sitting astride him, she placed the palms of her hands on his chest and lifting her buttocks, she placed the smooth domed tip between her legs and very slowly it disappeared, just as the mysterious dummy tail had disappeared into her last night.

I was still kneeling above Kenneth, held down by the excruciatingly tight grip of his fingers around my waist. Angela's face almost touched mine, her blue eyes were aflame, with a strange fury she shook her loins in small sharp jerks, her white belly distended and then hollowed as she began to put what seemed to me to be a soft cunning rhythm into her movements, gradually increasing her speed until I could hear her buttocks slapping against Kenneth's thighs And then, all of a sudden, as though some magic hand had deprived her of all her previous strength, she fell forward, sobbing and kissing Kenneth's chest, uttering incoherent words in that peculiar language of theirs. She lay there panting, whilst Kenneth still holding me tight spoke softly to her; then, supporting herself on her hands and knees, she crawled forward, until she had freed herself from the ignominious, shrunken instrument which had fastened her to her brother.

"That's very pretty," Kenneth says "There is a certain flow in your phrases. But carry on."

When she had left him, Kenneth told me to clean him in the same way I had done the previous time, and while I was at work, Angela stood watching me with such intentness that, though I only glanced up at her once, I thought I could feel her gaze biting into my back as I used my tongue to furrow the matted sodden hair stuck to Kenneth's belly.

I was not through when he let go of my waist. "That's enough," he said and, with faltering steps, got up from the floor and went to the armchair Angela had drawn up for him in front of the bed. He sat there for a moment, his eyes closed, cursing, while Angela who seemed to know exactly what to do, covered his shaking body with his dressing-robe. Only his hanging prick showed, and she massaged his back until his prick rose up again, slowly. Opening his eyes, he came back to himself. His glance then fell upon me, for I was standing near him, my arms crossed over my breasts in an effort to conceal my nakedness as best I could.

Looking up inquiringly at his sister, with his hands he cupped the white globes of her already full breasts and said, smiling as though he had something intimate to tell her:

"Her piss is as sweet as wine, and, my darling, her little cunt has lips as tender as yours. This is a heaven-sent thing the Almighty Buggerfuck has given into our keeping."

On hearing him use the Lord's name in vain, a further wave of terror ran through me. Impulsively, I pulled towards me the Indian shawl Angela had used to cover the bed, and sought to drape myself as best I could. But no sooner did she see what I was about than Angela slapped my face, slapped me again and again until I thought I was going to collapse. "Do I have to tie your hands behind your back to teach you how to act in our presence?"

Blinded with tears I had not noticed the cat, which was pulling contentedly and sniffing at my legs. I now hated the poor creature. Apart from feeding it, I had stayed away from it all day. It reminded me of nothing but the hateful events of the previous night. Repulsed by the mere sight of Bluebell, I tried to thrust her away with my foot. But, undaunted, she returned and when she licked my leg I shuddered, unable to control myself.

"The cat," Angela murmured, looking at Kenneth with her eyes ablaze again. Kenneth glanced up at her, his face serious, his prick swelling until it almost touched his navel. And he nodded, baring his perfect teeth in a cruel smile.

"Better tie her hands behind her back after all," he advised. "Use one of the manacles, it might put her breasts to better advantage. They make rather a poor show as they are." He looked ruefully, contemptuously at the faint swellings on my chest, and, leaning forward, seized one of their small points and wrung it until I emitted a cry, which Angela's swift hand stifled instantly.

She then did as Kenneth had suggested, drawing up another armchair opposite his. She bade me sit down and place a leg on either arm. I did as I was told, I had no choice. Sitting as far back as I could, I tried to conceal myself; but, swearing under his breath, Kenneth dragged my buttocks forward until they rested on the edge of the seat, thus presenting to his gaze the entirety of my yawning body. But this did not suit him. With his hands he pulled me still further open, parting the folds of my inner flesh with his fingers, his palms resting against my thighs. He sat there contemplating me, silent. He was breathing fast and when he asked Angela for the cat, his voice was hoarse and hardly recognisable.

Some sort of strange pride had made me try and fight back my tears after Angela had slapped me, but this was too much and I began to cry again, terrified of what might happen next and suffering from the awkward position they held me in. For my back had no support, my weight resting on my shoulder-blades, my head bent forward until my chin touched my chest. After a while I could not help moving, my legs ever so little, attempting to find relief from that cramping posture. And this was enough to infuriate Kenneth. "Tie them so she can't budge," he told her: "and while you're about it, put a cushion behind her back."

Then, drawing his armchair nearer, he placed himself between my legs in such a way that I could feel his balls against my thighs, and the throbbing of the swollen veins in his prick pulsing against my open cunt. He remained quite still, breathing deeply, beads of sweat standing out on his forehead. Then, suddenly, he began to make water, holding me open with one hand now, and rubbing himself against me, while the vigorous jet gushed between my legs, causing me an intense sensation of burning that made me writhe and struggle in an effort to rid myself of his grasp. But my movements only made him pull me open with increased brutality until I felt that, if he did not put a stop to this, my soft, fragile skin would split at any moment.

Angela was standing behind him, the cat cradled in her arms, stroking its fur with a detached smile playing on her lips, as nonchalant as if she had been in some drawing-room listening to Mozart or Schubert being played on a piano. Her eyes were riveted on my face. When he was finished, she handed the animal to him without a word, and throwing off her dressing-gown, she placed one foot on the arm of his chair and, putting her hand between her legs, touched herself, pulling the brown lips apart so that I could plainly see the bright red of her slit and the way it was made. Even so, I failed to understand how that relatively small opening could accommodate the length and thickness of her brother's fearful prick. My stretched and swollen cunt itched until I felt I could stand it no longer, for Kenneth had not relaxed his grip, and I still remained spread as wide as his hands could force me apart. Tearing my eyes away from Angela's obscene exhibition, I looked down at Kenneth and saw that he had placed the cat between us and was idly passing his prick over its smooth fur. Bluebell did not attempt to get away. I supposed she must have been trained to obey her master. It was unbelievable: to think that only yesterday I had loved that kitten, and given it such a tender name, little knowing that it was nothing but the wretched instrument of abominable pleasures.

I did not know where to look. How slowly the time passed! How leisurely they were, the two of them! How long ago seemed their arrival in my father's house! How much had happened to me since then, and how different I was.

The sight of Kenneth's inflated rod reminded me of a picture I had once seen of a coiled adder, ready to strike: that thing of his terrified me no less than the snake had. I shut my eyes tight, praying that they would let me, for one brief instant at least, pull down the veil of modesty over their doings, and it was at this very instant I felt the rasping tongue begin to lick the burning cleft between my legs. I could also feel the gentle contact of soft fur against the inside of my thighs and I knew before I opened my eyes what was happening.

My whole being shook with revolt, I struggled frantically, battling to free myself. But I could not stir. My pleadings were as useless as if they had been unspoken, for my cousins feigned not to hear me, showing perfect unconcern for my pleas for mercy. And had they listened they would, I know now, have gagged me without a moment's hesitation rather than be disturbed by my outcries.

I closed my eyes again. At least they could not compel

me to view the hideous sights they were putting before me. I could expect no pity, and therefore resigned myself to bear, with as much indifference as I could muster whatever ignominious treatment they decided to submit me to. It was an attack. They were after something, I kept thinking, after something.

I consoled myself with the thought they would have to free me before morning. I could feel the cat's tongue, moving slowly over me, inserting itself between the delicate folds and opening them one by one, and then burying its nose in the middle groove, moving upwards, then coming back down again, guided no doubt by Kenneth's hand, and leaving no part of me untouched.

The sensation of burning little by little left me, and I began to feel a strange tingling in the small of my back, in my spine, a sensation such as I had never felt before, which gradually spread outwards, everywhere, reached my loins and my belly and seemed to centre at the very tip of the cat's tongue. I fought to open my eyes but I couldn't. I felt that my slit had become wet, yet I had no idea how this could have happened. The cat redoubled its lickings, never ceasing for one moment; the rasping sweep, the tiny proddings of its exploring tongue went on and on. This unbearable sensation grew stronger until I felt myself straining towards Bluebell instead of recoiling from her. I now wanted her to continue and it was I who tried to force myself open even further that I might feel that tongue even more, and then, soaked and sweating, I heard myself gasp and then moan in a delirium of mounting excitement. It was a feeling so delicious and at the same time so unendurable that the disgusting way it had been procured, the foul, dirty way left me indifferent. I heard Kenneth's laugh. I didn't care. I felt as though I was about to faint. But I wasn't worried. Then the room swam back into focus and with a rapidity almost beyond belief I was their victim once again.

I have been told I have done very well once again, that my prose is making great strides, that even if I fail as a whore I shall surely manage as a novelist. I have been told I can go to bed now on condition that before tomorrow evening I bring my diary up to date. But is it not up to date?

"Reread all you have written, Victoria. Perhaps you will have more to add. Perhaps not. At any rate, you have the right to indulge your pride, for your work merits pride."

They have not let me go out of kindness but because my state of exhaustion is such that they doubtless fear it be detected if I do not have sufficient rest.

sunday, the 8th of july

It is late afternoon and I have at last managed to escape to my room to resume my journal. I have to bring it up to date before this evening when Kenneth will demand to inspect it. Otherwise, he has threatened to expose me for 'the wanton slut' he says I have become after what took place last night. "You have no redress, you have not even got your innocence to appeal to, and so my recommendation to you is that you meditate upon your disgrace and draw the appropriate conclusions. Nothing will be more useful to you in this soul-searching than to put down on paper the feelings of remorse you have... if indeed you have them."

The monster! He is even willing to doubt my capacity to have feelings! He said that he had 'perfect confidence in me' and that it is not necessary, henceforth, that he keep my diary. "For your own safety, I advise you to hide it on top of the cupboard – or, devil take me, wherever you damned well please. But the thing is your own responsibility, Victoria. You are on your own. A grown-up girl. Splendid, isn't it?"

On top of the cupboard... it will be safe there at least until next year's spring cleaning. I tremble lest, through some negligence on my part, the thing be found... Oh, how I wish – provided of course no harm would come to any of my dear ones – that the whole house could burn down, destroying every trace of it. But I must hurry. I might be interrupted any minute. Perhaps this diary is a punishment from God who is forcing me, through the evil agency of these two demons, to realise the extent of my depraved wantonness.

From the moment I recovered from my bestial pleasure, Kenneth and his sister never once stopped tantalising me. Stressing the fact that of all crimes, to succumb to the antics of an animal in rut was certainly the most disgusting, they blew out the lamp, undid my bonds, and pushed me upon the bed. There they played with me in the dark as though I were a doll. I could feel their tongues and hands on me whilst they made me use mine to fondle whatever part of them they wished to have excited. The room was in complete darkness, for the heavy curtains had been drawn over the windows. I lost all count of those probing fingers, I ceased to be able to tell whose lips were responsible for the now cruel, now delicious titillations my body was subjected to. Closing my blind eyes, I surrendered myself to their hands and mouths, waiting for the moment when a wave of exquisite delight would sweep away what was left of my tattered consciousness. Forgetting for one moment the price I would have to pay when I returned to my senses, and the terrible remorse that would go with it, I lay back... and made the best of it.

Oh, to have to write of such things today!

Our Lord's Day. I drove to Church with Mamma, fearing as I entered the hallowed abode of GOD, that in His vengeance He would smite me dead for daring to come thus into His presence, covered with sins so black that the very thought of them makes my head reel and the blood rush in my veins.

Mr Gareth preached a very fine sermon. It went straight as an arrow to my heart. It was taken from the 1st chapter of St. Matthew, 21st verse:

And she shall bring forth a son,
And thou shalt call His name Jesus:
For He shall save His people from their sins.

I listened with tears in my eyes, for I knew that I was past redemption. And to add to my distress, dear Mamma, taking my grief for a sign of great piety, congratulated me on leaving the Church, but added an affectionate warning against a too great show of sensibility in public places. And although I had no desire to see her, it was with a feeling of intense relief I rushed forward to greet Ursula. Trying to hide my confusion, she nevertheless remarked on my crimson face and chided me in a loud and peremptory voice until, in my exasperation and despair, I own I could truly have killed her there on the spot if I had had the means to do so. The thought that I WOULD

HAVE TO BE POLITE TO HER ALL DAY LONG (for Mamma never fails to invite her and Mr Gareth every Sunday for lunch and sometimes even for supper) was almost too much for me to contend with. She had on an ugly foulard dress with a large coloured handkerchief under a large muslin collar. And to add to this, a frightful little pink bonnet. Her curls were as stiff as a chimney-sweep's broom straws. She always puts her curling pins in wrong.

When Kenneth came up to her, she literally devoured him with her eyes. But after a polite bow, he turned away, interrupting her in the middle of a sentence. Mamma beckoned to us and we went to join her and the vicar. Then we left in the barouche. The vicar and Ursula followed in their carriage. I could tell she was furious not to accompany us.

On the way to Church we had passed a gypsy encampment. We had not had time to stop, but on the way back Mamma sent the footman to enquire into the story of those poor wanderers. He came back telling us that a poor woman and her baby were sick, very weak and miserable, and that they mainly wanted fuel and nourishment. Mamma ordered a pack of coal and broth to be sent, and also two blankets, and Miss Perkins sent old flannel undergarments and a little worsted knitted jacket for the poor baby. I was allowed to send half-a-crown from my money-box. I cannot say how happy I am that these poor creatures are assisted, for they are such a nice group of gypsies, so quiet, so affectionate to each other, so discreet, not at all importuning or forward, and so grateful. I am sure, as dear Mamma remarked, that the kindness they have experienced at our hands will have a good and lasting effect upon them.

What I have been dreading has happened. Mamma has just come into my room. She has seen me here, writing. I did not dare shut my book. I got up, my hands trembling, and felt my face go red when she asked how I was getting on, remarking on the great number of pages I seemed to have written already. She came around and stood beside me, leaning over the desk and saying that I must take greater care with my handwriting. By the grace of God, I was writing about those gypsies. But I was in agony lest, for some reason or other it occurred to her to turn the page. She laughed at my visible despair, saying that of course she would not read it but that, at my age, one needn't feel apologetic for one's style. "It's a very private affair," she said, "and as time passes things work themselves out. Come down for supper soon. We shall be at table in half an hour."

My tormentors are out of the way. They left me as soon as lunch was over, and are spending the afternoon with Lady C——— who was Aunt Margaret's school-friend. They will drive back after supper. I walked down to the lake with Ursula and Miss P. while the vicar sat on the lawn with Mamma, reading aloud to her and asking her opinion and advice on the new sermons he is preparing. Such a relief to have dear Miss P. with me! She kept the conversation going with a great stream of anecdotes about her Devonshire childhood, and although, gracious knows, I have heard them all many times before, I never tire of listening to her voice. Ursula was at great pains to hide her disappointment and, very rudely, hardly opened her mouth, leaving with her father soon after tea. Mr Gareth had to call on poor Mrs Leyton. They say she is quite ill.

Later.

The heat was so stifling we sat in the garden after supper, waiting for the others. But it is now half past ten and, as they have not turned up, I have been sent to bed. Though very tired, I must await their return so as to give them my diary. If only I could flee from my thoughts. This afternoon at one moment I had almost forgotten. Everything seemed, for that moment, as it had been before... I can hear their carriage on the drive...

The iron strip on the wheels scratches and tears on the gravel.

monday

It is ten o'clock and I can hear them all talking on the lawn. I have been sent to bed early because of the dark rings under my eyes. I have tried to put on an air of gaiety but they still show. Mamma has given instructions that I should have an egg-flip every morning at 11:00, and that I should ride Sunbeam before breakfast every day without fail. For when she asked about that, I admitted I had not been out on him since my cousins' arrival. My dear Miss P. was the one who suggested it. Plenty of exercise and good food would put me right in no time.

Kenneth immediately offered to accompany me on my outings and Angela, of course, was another willing chaperone. In this way I shall never be free of them. I am like a fly caught in a spider's web, a helpless and voiceless victim of their every whim.

Dear Mamma not only showers affection upon them but is actually lavish with her praise for Angela, for her grace, her modesty, her accomplishments. For Angela has started to do a miniature portrait of Mamma and the likeness is quite astonishing. Mamma is delighted and says that as soon as it is finished she will send to London to have a locket made for it. Angela seems to know just what to do to please her, pretending shamelessly to show the keenest interest in Mamma's interminable pious dialogues with Mr Gareth and her discourses on art delivered to Miss Perkins.

Last night she came up almost at once, expressing her satisfaction with my prompt obedience; then she took my diary away and left the room, telling me to go to bed.

She seemed completely oblivious of the torture in which I had passed the day. Oh, she is truly without any vestige of human sentiment unless it is that of dire hypocrisy and the filthiest kind of adoration for her brother! How can such a pure and lovely flower hide in its bosom a serpent of such wickedness!

I tried to sleep, but couldn't, being gripped by a fearful trembling which had laid hold of me when I heard them come upstairs, laughing and joking, bidding each other sweet dreams and peaceful sleep, only to meet again as soon as the house was quiet.

Angela had left the door between our rooms open. I could hear her leafing through the pages in my journal, stifling the bursts of laughter that rocked her; her mirth only redoubled when Kenneth joined her and the two of them entertained each other reading aloud what I had written.

"My God, what a fool that creature is!" Kenneth exclaimed. "A pretty fool and ready enough to be–" "Now?" Angela asked, interrupting him. "And why not now?" he asked in turn.

With that I heard him cross the room, and his tall figure appeared framed in the doorway. He was breathing, his nostrils were dilated in a way I had come to recognise and dread. Angela followed him, and putting her arms around his waist, pleaded with him in words I could not, as usual, understand. She then knelt on the floor, opened his trousers and buried her face between his legs, wheedling and cajoling and talking to him. He seemed ready to lose patience, for he tried to push her aside, but she clung to him like a leech, holding in her mouth the very stem of his being, baring her teeth whenever he sought to spin away from her. Her evil skill was such that he soon gave up resisting her. Surrendering completely to her will, he allowed her to bring him to the point where the intensity of his desire would demand her immediate and absolute surrender. Angela must have known just when this moment would come, for she suddenly left him. Lifting her skirts and tearing off her underclothing, she placed her hands on the chimney-piece, bending forward so that her white buttocks stood framed in a halo of billowing petticoats. All that had taken place within the space of an instant. In one stride Kenneth joined her. Staring at the globes that smiled pleadingly at him, he pulled them open, buried himself between them with one great shove. Then placing his hands on her shoulders, he bent her forward, forcing her head through the space between her extended arms. His trousers had slid down to his ankles, revealing his long legs, now straight, now flexed, as he moved his belly, as he searched inside her, pursuing the source of his wicked satisfaction.

He called out to me with great urgency to come to his aid. He ordered me to kneel behind him and he fitted my fingers like a ring around the base of his prick. His balls beat against my nose and he ordered me to lick them and more especially the hard thin ridge I could feel running down the middle of his prick's underside. My head obediently followed the movements of his body. This seemed to give him great pleasure for he called out to me, naming me his 'little vicious prick-kisser', 'his dirty-cunted little virgin', and other dreadful things I did not understand.

I had twisted around and, squatting beneath them, I could see Kenneth's hand holding open the deep slit of Angela's cunt. With his fingers he tickled a tiny pointed mound of flesh, placed just beneath its opening, at the very entrance of the parted lips. This was the first time I could see the place into which he liked to bury his prick, and this terrified me. For it looked like a small red mouth, strained and distended, laughing and yawning, sucking a rod of such dimensions that at any moment it was apt to split. And yet it fearlessly met each of Kenneth's terrible jabs, greedily swallowing the huge thing to the hilt, letting it go and then moving forward hungrily to meet the next push. With my free hand I furtively searched to see whether I had a similar crevice in my own cunt. I couldn't find one.

Kenneth must have started making water inside Angela, for a hot salted spray fell on my face and body, and in the moment that followed they reached the place they wanted to get to, breathlessly clinging to one another.

Supporting Angela, Kenneth led her out of the room. They went as if they had forgotten my presence. Kenneth pulled the door to behind them.

I think they must be asleep. There's no sound in Angela's room.

Yet I didn't dare go back to bed without writing down all the events. They might come back to see my diary.

I am weak, so weak, so weary. I will creep into bed. I pray they've forgotten me.

Later.

Despite my fatigue I couldn't get to sleep.

For no sooner would I shut my eyes than the vision of Angela's small red mouth, hidden between her legs and hairy, would appear before me with such vividness that my searching fingers would go fumbling between my own legs, bringing no answer to the question. Getting up as quietly as I could, I lit my lamp. I took my hand-mirror and, placing myself in front of my dressing table, tilting the mirror and lying down on my back with my legs spread apart, I was determined to find what I was looking for. But I feared to look into the glass. Shame overcame my curiosity and I fell back upon my pillow, exhausted. The abrupt thought that Kenneth or Angela might come into my room at any moment and find me in this posture... that thought electrified me. Placing the lamp so that the mirror was well lit, I peered down between my legs at my unknown self... Unknown. And yet I knew now that it was from within this small crevice that there came to me those blinding sensations, those sensations which had hurled me beyond the edge of any conceivable morality into a world of indescribable damning delight.

The light of the lamp flickered gently on the smooth shiny and almost transparent surface revealed before my eyes. Between the double set of parted lips I recognised now that minute protuberance to which Kenneth, when he had done the drawing in my journal, had given that strange name I couldn't keep straight. Below it was another opening, the one, as Kenneth had said, which was just large enough to fit the head of a pin into. And below this, or rather behind it, was a pale grey puckered ring, the sight of which made me blush and take away the mirror.

I lay with my legs pressed together. I comforted myself with the thought that such as I was I risked nothing of what Angela had to endure from Kenneth's rod. The sheer disproportion was such as to make it senseless for him to try to drive into a place he could never hope to force.

That discovery reassured me.

I don't know what Kenneth will think when he reads this tomorrow.

I shall go to sleep now. Or try.

tuesday

Miss Perkins woke me early, appearing with a hot cup of tea in her hand and a cheery smile on her face. "Come, lazy bones," she said, "up with you," and she helped me get dressed. For indeed I was still so sleepy I could hardly stand. I endeavoured to look and do my best to forestall questions to which my weary mind felt unable to give the appropriate answers in the appropriate string of lies.

I could hear Sunbeam stamping outside. Joseph's harsh voice was exhorting him in a combined roar and a whisper to hold still.

Not a sound could be heard coming from Angela's room, and I wondered whether they had decided not to come after all...

The night before, after Ursula's departure, I had tried to suggest timidly to Mamma that perhaps it might be better if we had the groom accompany us, but she had only laughed and dismissed the notion for a childish whim, asking, me if I took myself for the Queen. "Do you fancy Kenneth is not man enough to look after the both of you?"

Upon hearing that I could say nothing at all. As I have already pointed out, Mamma seems with each passing day to become more fond of Angela, and she did not allow the occasion to go by without repeating her high opinion of Angela's delicate manners and uncommon modesty, bearing and temper, saying that she could wish for nothing better than that I should grow up to be as sensible and yet as full of sensibility as my dear cousin.

I enquired of Miss Perkins to learn their whereabouts. She told me that they had been up and abroad for some time and had gone to fetch their horses at the stables, where I was to join them directly I was ready. She remonstrated with me, saying that, "For heaven's sake, Victoria, it is not proper, do you think, to keep people waiting." I dragged through my toilette as best I could, my limbs numb with fatigue, while dear Miss P. did my hair for me.

When I came down I saw the pair of them riding towards the house, smiling and bidding me a hearty good morning. They both rode beautifully. Angela looked nothing short of superb, her fair complexion enhanced by the black material of her riding habit, her lips slightly parted in expectation, a fine sporting light in her eyes... We rode off toward the lake, Kenneth taking the lead, and Angela following after me. I had thought of escaping from them, warned by I know not what premonition. My plan had been to drop behind and then veer off towards Henderson's farm at a canter and, once there, under the pretext of drinking some warm fresh milk, remain in the company of Mrs Henderson until it was time to go back for breakfast. But how could I have been so simple! I was their prisoner. For even when we got to the lake, where the path widens, they never left their respective positions. I thought I could feel Angela's keen eyes transpierce the nape of my neck like two blazing sapphires. The sun was warm. But I shuddered.

We soon quit the lake shore, and riding in silence, we followed Kenneth into Grawborough Woods. Kenneth appeared to know where he was going. He had been out riding once with Uncle John and Papa and must have explored the terrain, for he never once lost his bearings. A little later he broke into a canter. We did too and soon come to a narrow path where, without hesitating, he turned to his left. From there on the branches became so low that we had to bend our heads to avoid losing our hats. I had started to shake, and for the first time in my life I heard my teeth chatter. A Painful sensation of sudden weight filled my stomach and dizzied me and my mouth went dry. We went on until it was practically impossible to push any further; then Kenneth signalled with his hand and we stopped. Dismounting, he helped Angela down gathering the three horses' reins in a bunch, he tied them to a tree; and only afterwards did he lift me down from my saddle.

We had not exchanged a word since leaving the house.

Still in silence, we walked along the path until we came to a small glade carpeted with moss and surrounded by a dense thicket The density of its leaves prevented the morning sun from penetrating it, darkness, save for small patches of light here and there, where the moss showed a brilliant, wild green against the almost black earth underneath.

Kenneth had not let go of my hand. My eyes were filled with tears of apprehension, for I knew now from their deliberateness and their silence that they were putting into execution a well thought-out plan, a scheme whereof, no doubt about it, I was to be the victim.

As far as I could judge, we were in the dead heart of the Wood. If I called out for help no one would hear me. There was of course Hayward, our old gamekeeper, who might have been in the neighbourhood passing on his rounds. But he was old and had for years just carried out the motions of attending to his duty. I was certain he was nowhere around.

I looked at them. I thought I knew what their intention was and yet, after what I had seen in the mirror, I knew it was impossible.

All this raced through my head during the few seconds it took us to reach the glade, Kenneth released my hand and in so doing twirled me around like a top until I nearly lost my balance... and grabbed at a nearby tree to keep from falling. Meanwhile, Angela stood watching me, complete indifference written over her face, absently lashing at the brush and an occasional tree with her riding crop, a faraway look in her eyes.

"We've got to hurry," Kenneth said. Angela nodded and without uttering a word stepped up to me. I thought at first she meant to whip me and covered my face with my arms. I was sobbing uncontrollably now, beyond words miserable and wondering how I was ever going to escape them and how I had ever managed to deliver myself into their hands from the very first moment of their arrival.

"Hurry," repeated Kenneth in a flat voice, "I don't think I can wait forever, no, by God, I don't think so."

I could see the outline of his prick stretched to its fullest length under the fine-woven cloth of his riding breeches. Noticing the direction my gaze had taken, he smiled a fiendish smile and, undoing his buttons, pulled his thing into view with a grunt. He worked its loose sheath up and down, gently, firmly, so that the swollen head was sometimes hidden and sometimes uncovered, the small dark hole gaping and oozing a white froth.

"By God," he muttered again, looking at me with narrow raging eyes.

Struck dumb by this repulsive exhibition, I had failed to notice that Angela had undone all the hooks of my riding habit and was pulling my clothes off, folding them carefully so that they would not be wrinkled. When she had finished, I stood naked before them, wearing only ·my short boots and stockings.

Kenneth had removed his trousers and with his heavy tool grasped in his hand he advanced to where I stood, petrified. He rubbed its scalding length against my breasts, tugging at their points with his fingers, stammering and saying things to himself, his face red, his hair tumbling over his eyes in long disorderly strands.

"I believe I'm going to bitch you, Vickie," he said, "and I believe you're going to feel it and I believe I'm going to too." His laugh made me shiver.

With two sharp slaps of the palm of his hand on my chest he sent me tottering back. I fell upon the moss, my legs sprawled out. Before I could get up, Angela, with the speed of a tigress, was upon me, holding me open for her ignominious brother to do with me what he wished.

I wanted to scream, but as in a nightmare not a sound passed my lips.

With the monstrous ugly object still in his hand, he knelt down between my legs. Peering at me, squinting, he exclaimed again that it was bloody small it was, shaking his rod in front of me and saying, "Look, what do you think? Wouldn't a matchstick do better than this? What about it, Victoria?" He was delighted at the thought of the suffering he was about to inflict upon me.

No good struggling to get away from Angela. I tried, but she dug her nails into my skin, causing me to whimper in pain. As always silent, she turned towards me, her blue flint-hard eyes flashing and her expression one of serene interest. There was no pity in her face, no sign whatsoever of human decency.

She had not taken off her clothes, and her long habit spread out on the moss around her. Her hat was tilted at a jaunty angle, and it gave her an air of strange, ludicrous respectability that contrasted just as queerly with my involuntarily wanton posture and Kenneth's obscene licentiousness.

He was still fondling himself in front of my open legs. He seemed to have reached a paroxysm of excitement and became unable to control the rhythmical movement of his hand on his prick. But suddenly he aimed it down towards the tiny entrance and started to press against it with all his might. I could feel its flaming butt trying to bore into me. He twisted and squirmed, his toes chopped away patches of moss; I fought desperately, caring not for Angela's nails, dodging my buttocks from side to side to elude his brutal penetration.

I was about to give up the hopeless fight when Kenneth, cursing and shouting, let forth a long jet of thick white stuff which inundated my cunt and the inside of my thighs. When that jet stopped, there was nothing left in his wet hand but a small wrinkled object, harmless and pitiful.

His fury seemed to know no bounds. Shaking it violently, he tried to revive his prick, the while hurling insults at me and blaming me for this disaster, as he called it.

He then appealed to Angela who, letting go of my legs, took up her riding crop and started to thrash his bare buttocks with all her might. He gritted his teeth, shut his eyes tight, moaned with pain, and still shaking his prick, rolled around on the ground, simultaneously avoiding and seeking the lash. I lay there transfixed, not daring to move lest I drew their attention. Angela kept at it until Kenneth seemed about to faint. But it had been for no purpose. His hand still clutched the dejected, silly piece of spiritless flesh which, only a short while ago, had threatened to impale me.

Leaving him in a huddled heap on the ground Angela picked up her sweeping skirts and told me in a cutting voice to get dressed. When I was ready, Kenneth opened his eyes and looked at Angela with a begging, beseeching expression. She brushed past him, announcing that she and I were leaving and that if he had any intention of reaching the house at the same time we did, he had best hurry.

She seemed in a state of violent but nevertheless controlled rage. Helping me onto my horse, We rode off slowly in the direction of the house, leaving Kenneth behind to follow as best he could.

When we got to the lake, she dismounted and, dipping her handkerchief in the cool water, washed my tear-stained face. Then, in silence, we resumed our way until, hearing Kenneth's horse in the distance behind us, she broke into a canter and we reached home with Kenneth galloping after us, pale and looking as though he might collapse.

And once again I had the opportunity to observe their remarkable genius for dissimulation.

Breakfast was ready. Mamma does not often come down for it, but this time she did, intending to join us around the table. I went white with shame and dread when I saw her emerge into the terrace, certain that regardless of Angela's ministrations some trace could be seen upon my face of the horror of what, by some miracle, I had so far escaped. But as soon as I had kissed her and said good morning, Angela's sweet vivaciousness captured her attention and Mamma was treated to a detailed account of our early morning promenade. Angela described the beauty of certain walks and pathways in the park, the glory of the lake just after dawn, the rich colours of the moss. Kenneth, who seemed to have collected himself, joined in the conversation. It became animated and I, with nothing to say, thinking only of saying and showing nothing, but aching to scream out the truth for which I knew I would not be able to find words... I bent over my steak and potatoes while they tossed their heads and chattered and dew shone on the lawn and birds twittered happily. I ate in silence, the silence that befitted my tender years, and I listened respectfully to the conversation of my elders.

Angela devoted most of the afternoon to painting Mamma's portrait. Mamma rested on her chaise-longue. I wondered whether she was trying to avoid leaving us together,

I wanted to think so. Kenneth spent the afternoon in the library, reading. I found him there when I went to fetch Miss Perkins the copy of *Paradise Lost* which the vicar had forgotten on one of his recent visits and which we intended to return to him when we went for our walk.

Kenneth was lying on the leather divan in front of the fireplace. He was peering absently at the pages of John Stuart Mill's treatise *On Liberty*. He couldn't have been able to read much, for the room was almost in darkness: the blinds had been drawn because of the heat and I did not notice him until he had grabbed the edge of my skirt as I passed. He tried to draw me down on top of him. Fighting with him noiselessly, fearful that Miss P. might come in the midst of it, I managed to fasten my teeth in his hand and bite him until, writhing with pain, he let go.

That strange boy stared at me in the obscure light. "It's rubbish, this Mill," he said, grinning.

I was shaking all over when I left him and went upstairs to my room to try to compose myself I could hear Miss P. calling and searching for me throughout the house.

Kenneth came down to dinner with his hand bandaged. He apologised for having broken a vase in his room. I noticed Angela watching him, amused. He sulked through his meal, so obviously in a bad temper that Mamma asked him what in the world could be ailing him. "Victoria," she said, "you must be deferential towards your guests. Endeavour to distract them."

We played draughts after dinner and everyone retired early.

It is late now as I finish. I can hear no sound at all in Angela's room. A while ago, although their voices were subdued, they seemed to be quarrelling.

They have not come to get my diary. I will go to bed now. Perhaps they have forgotten me.

wednesday

Kenneth has ignored me all day, except in Mamma's presence. He and Angela have obviously not made up their quarrel, for even though they are coolly polite to each other, I – who, alas! know them only too well – can tell that there is a strain between them.

Could it be possible that, after all, Angela wishes to spare me? Can she have taken my side?

Later.

I had been in bed for some time when Angela came into my room, telling me to get up and follow her. I tried weakly to plead with her. Pulling me rudely from under the bedclothes, she peeled off my night-gown and pushed me into the other room where Kenneth was sitting in an armchair, naked. Placing me on the bed opposite him, she ordered me to open myself, and to remain that way. Then seating herself near us, she spoke to Kenneth in this foreign tongue they use with each other. While she spoke she watched, amused, the manifestations of his foul interest in my posture, which did not fail to arouse him. Kenneth's tone was one of supplication whenever he answered her airy prattle. She gestured towards me once or twice, as though detailing some aspect or other of my body. I could see that Kenneth was beside himself with lust and yearning, and yet he did not touch himself. But his eyes never left me, greedy and at the same sorrowful eyes that feasted upon the sight of my indecency.

The long object vibrated on his belly, like some eyeless, hideous reptile rearing itself to strike at a bird.

The palms of my moist hands left two dark patches on the silk cover when I moved them, striving to change my position without being detected.

Kenneth was now talking to his sister, in a low,

unhappy whisper. It soon grew hoarse and I knew his rage was mounting. I thought that I would not be able to escape him much longer. But to my surprise and indescribable relief, Angela ordered me to get up and go back to my room.

I dared not shut the door behind me even though I had been dismissed. Badly shaken I crept into my bed, overcome with thanks for having been saved.

Very soon afterwards, before I could fall asleep, strange noises came from Angela's room. Prompted by I do not know what curiosity, I stole to the door. Kenneth, a handkerchief in his mouth to muffle any sound, lay naked across the bed, his two thumbs tied together and secured to the bedpost by a length of sash-cord. Angela, with the riding-crop I had already seen her use on him in the forest, was beating his buttocks with all her strength. Faint with terror, I tiptoed back to my bed where I buried my head under my pillow so that I could not hear the slashing of the whip falling on his skin. But I dared not go to sleep. I had this to write in my diary.

thursday

I saw neither Kenneth nor Angela last night. If they did come back into my room, they did not wake me.

And now the saddest and at the same time the most wonderful thing has happened!

Mrs Thornton, the vicar's housekeeper, has a little boy who has just come down with the measles, poor child! and Mamma has offered to have Ursula stay with us until he is better and to avoid any possibility that Ursula contract the same sickness. I have had it – I was a baby then – and Kenneth and Angela have too. Although they tried to lie to Mamma, saying that, to the best of their recollection, they'd never had measles (but, after all, in India they'd perhaps given it some other name), Mamma reassured them, saying she had written to Aunt Margaret who had informed her that, yes, the darlings had indeed had, each of them, a bad bout of measles several years ago. "Bless my soul," said Kenneth, when he saw his mother's letter in Mamma's hand. Nor was Angela any more disconcerted. And so. anyhow, it has been arranged. Ursula is to come and remain with us until Mrs Thornton is out of her predicament. And best of all, Ursula is to share my room!

I think that Angela suspected that it was I who suggested this arrangement to Mamma, who after arguing that there was ample room for Ursula to have a separate accommodation, finally gave into my pleadings. "Well, it shall only be for a week or two, and I simply hope Ursula doesn't object." I showed the relief and joy I felt as soon as I had extracted Mamma's consent; and Mamma related our conversation to Kenneth and Angela, saying that one would think I was starved for companionship,

Angela of course pretended to be delighted, saying how charitable and thoughtful Mamma was and how nice it would be to have another young lady staying with us to share the holidays.

With the help of Miss Perkins and Martin to do the heavy carrying, I have arranged my room, Putting in two small beds with a chest of drawers between them. We found two white bedspreads to match and it's such a large room that the extra furniture hardly makes any noticeable change.

It's nearly tea-time and my dear Ursula is due any minute now.

Oh, I really do love her for coming to my rescue at such a moment as this and for saving me from their clutches. What would I have done without Ursula? How I regret having written such unkind things about her!

Later.

Ursula is in bed and nearly asleep. We have installed all her things, including a set of quite lovely silver-backed brushes that belonged to her dear departed mother, and which make my plain ivory ones look quite shoddy and drab by comparison. I have noticed that Ursula has a certain tendency towards ostentation.

Kenneth and Angela paid almost no attention to either of us the whole evening. Mamma suggested a few duets. They complied, singing together wonderfully and with such great warmth of sentiment that, for a moment, I completely forgot their underlying and true nature...

I could see that Ursula was quite piqued by the way they snubbed us (especially Kenneth) and I do think she would have shown off had not Mamma been there. Ursula, I am afraid, is brazen.

I sang *Maman dites-moi* in French, Ursula accompanying me. She played either too fast or too slow – as usual. I could see that Angela was pained, but Mamma did not seem to object at all, and complimented us on the progress we have achieved since the last time she heard us. I forgot to mention that Mr Gareth was also present, and as soon as he had gone we all went up to bed.

I let everyone pass on the staircase, then proceeded up, Kenneth behind me holding the tall lamp. When we had passed the first floor leaving Mamma and Miss Perkins at their doors,

Kenneth took advantage of the fact that no one could see him and put his hand under my skirt, opening the slit of my panties and touching me as high up as he could reach. I let out a muffled cry of surprise, which made the others turn and ask what could be the trouble. I said I thought I had seen a mouse. "A mouse indeed!" said Kenneth. He looked quite composed, the very picture of innocence.

Angela came in to say good night to us. To my utter horror, she told me in front of Ursula to continue my diary without fail. Although her tone of voice was as sweet as could be, I knew she meant to convey a threat. As soon as she was gone, Ursula set in pestering me. "Show me your diary, Victoria, please do, please!" and she kept on asking me over and over again. Luckily, I had decided to wear the key around my neck on a string, for she snatched the book from my desk and started dancing about the room with it, teasing me and saying how easy it would be to break such a fragile clasp if anyone really wanted to. I was more dead than alive with fright, and fought with her, scratching her hand until it bled. Then, with a cry of pain, she surrendered the diary to me.

Then I had to comfort her and say I was sorry. In exchange for my cameo brooch – she had always coveted it – I made her swear on her head that she would never try and read what I had written. "It's personal," I told her. I am ashamed to say that in spite of this solemn oath I do not feel I can trust her. But I doubt she'd dare break the lock. I must be careful always to close it and lock it before I put it in its hiding place.

How, I wonder, could Angela ever have been so imprudent as to mention my journal?... That creature fears neither God nor man. She is never at a loss for a new way to torture me. But surely, surely they would never dare do anything with Ursula here.

friday

I think my head is going to explode! I think I shall go out of my mind! Is it possible that I should be surrounded by nothing but monsters? that everyone is evil? that Ursula, Ursula of all people! that Ursula, whom I have known since we were very little girls together, should have behaved herself in the disgraceful way she did today in the bathroom?

I had had my bath. I was washing my hair and drying it while Auburn was bringing up fresh hot water for Ursula. It was my intention to leave as soon as the tub was ready. That was what I intended. Well, Ursula came in and offered to help me untangle my hair – naturally it was snarled. I was grateful for her assistance. With long hair it is hard to manage alone. Miss Perkins, who usually helps me, had gone to the village to see Mrs Thornton's little boy; Mamma asked her to take him some sweets on her behalf. When Ursula had finished, I thanked her and was about to depart and leave the bathroom to her. Then, to my surprise, she asked me to stay and keep her company. Stay and keep her company!

I exclaimed that it was not, in my humble opinion, modest to remain while another person performed her toilette, but she made fun of me, saying that, after all, we were intimate friends, weren't we? and that it was of no great importance especially as 'old Perkins' was out of the way! Before I could answer she snapped the bolt on the door and was stripping off her clothes. Before you could say Jack Robinson she was quite naked, sticking out her tongue and jeering at my embarrassment. I thought she had suddenly gone mad. Indeed, I was so disconcerted that I didn't know what to do or say. I tried to take it as a joke, and to avoid eyeing her nudity, But, despite my efforts and myself, I could not help noticing how she was made, appraising her... For under the triangular mat of tight fair curls, the lips of her cunt hung down between her legs, slack, like two long cockscombs, their heavy red rims opening out fanwise so that I could see the inner lips. And strangest of all, instead of the tiny crest both Angela and I possessed, there was a large protuberance of smooth pink flesh almost the size of a nut! I put my hand to my mouth to stifle a cry of surprise. I could see she was watching me closely, curiously. Before I could say a word, she licked the tip of her finger and then started to rub that protuberance gently. At last a stream of piss began to run down her legs. Her fingers were gripped round the knob of flesh which she twisted and pulled until it became an angry, inflamed red and looked as though any moment it might start to bleed. She started to pant in loud gasps, opening and shutting her legs with a smacking sound, and then a thin cry of satisfaction broke from her lips. She let go of herself and leaned against the bathtub to recover her balance. Scared and speechless, I stared at her.

She was soon herself again. With a natural air, she asked me whether I ever did the same thing adding, when I shook my head in denial, that it was high time I begin, for it was one of the world's most pleasurable pastimes, "Short of a man, Victoria, one can't do better. And besides, men are dangerous."

I asked her if she had ever had anything to do with a man. Laughing, she sprang into the bath and told me that the only one she had ever had was the old gardener at the vicarage, "If you could call that one a man. His tool was so flabby it took me ages to whip him into shape. He's not much good – wasn't then and probably hasn't got better since. He wouldn't interest you," she concluded insolently.

She lay floating in the water, pondering, her long pointed tongue stuck out and she amused herself trying to touch the end of her nose with it. Her pear-shaped breasts, buoyed up by the water, seemed far too large for her frail, almost skinny torso.

I deliberately turned my back on her and stood in front of the mirror, brushing my hair without knowing really what I was doing, and my brain in a whirl. Questions rushed to my lips, but I didn't dare ask them. She, Ursula, knew what it was like to be with a man. She seemed unterrified of men. I had a vision of Hayward, the old vicarage gardener, toothless and bent and unwashed, and I wondered how she could have brought herself to do what she had done with so repulsive a creature.

"I'll tell you," she said, interrupting my thoughts, "if you want to know the truth, it's Kenneth I'm after. And I think I can get him too."

"Do you?" I said. The words that came from my mouth startled me: I had spoken harshly.

"Yes, I do. I'm certain. I'm also certain I can teach him a thing or two. He looks as though butter wouldn't melt in his mouth, but, do you know what, Victoria? I think it's a facade. I think it's a front he puts up. He might not be so sorry to learn, either, and I want you to help me get that pious goose Angela out of the way."

I felt my face grow a flaming red and my knees nearly buckle under me. Ursula was watching me from between narrowed eyes. "So," she said, "you too. You've got a tender feeling for him, do you? Is that it? You're too young, Victoria, and I don't advise you to try and get in my way." There was a threatening edge in her voice.

"You don't understand," I began.

"Oh, I understand," she replied at once.

Realising I could go no further, I let her mock at me to her heart's content. She accused me of puppy love and said that if Mamma ever got an inkling of my sentiments, "Then it would be goodbye little Victoria!"

I could not listen to another word. I left the bathroom and went to my own room to get dressed.

I was in such a state I had forgotten to lock the door and was just going to slip into my chemise when Ursula made me jump by walking in without knocking. I was struggling with a ribbon that had caught in my hair and had to ask her to help me undo it. I had my back to her, and was doing my best to hide my nakedness by pressing against the bed. As soon as she had freed me, she whisked my chemise back over my head and told me to turn around so that she could see how I was made, adding that I would have the honour of being the first naked girl she had ever clapped eyes on. I knew it was useless to argue if I wanted to retrieve my garment, and so I turned around and faced her. She emitted an exclamation upon catching sight of the soft bald mound and the tightly closed lips of slit.

"Show me!" she said in a strangled voice, "show me properly!" and without further ado she pushed me back onto the bed, pulled my legs open, and peered down at me with avid curiosity.

Then handing me back my chemise with a slow gesture, she asked me if I had ever seen another naked woman. I lied, saying I hadn't. She looked puzzled. I prayed she had not noticed the tremor in my voice, for I was thinking of Angela and thinking that Ursula was made differently from both Angela and myself.

We got dressed, each of us immersed in her own thoughts, and went down to breakfast.

Kenneth and Angela had not yet returned from their ride. And this reminds me that I have become so callous that I have not even mentioned that my precious Sunbeam has developed a limp. I must go down to the stables and see how he is. Although I adore him, I cannot help wishing that he will not recover in too great a hurry. For Mamma will not permit me to ride any other horse, until I am older at least.

Later.

Joseph has come to say that Sunbeam will be fit to ride tomorrow. Ursula is to mount Thunder.

She is doing her level best to attract Kenneth's attention. I can tell that he is amused even though he pretends to pay the strict minimum of attention to her. Angela is by no means deceived by her antics. She has just suggested that we go for a walk together and leave Kenneth and Ursula to play a game of croquet *en tête à tête*.

saturday

I hardly slept a wink last night. This morning I looked pallid and worn and my head is still throbbing, more from mental than from physical anguish. I told Miss P. when she came up to wake us for our ride that I had a bad toothache. So Ursula has gone off alone with them, and I have permission to stay in bed for breakfast. Miss P. has looked into my mouth. Of course she can't see anything. How could one see a toothache? But all the same, she decided that the best remedy would be a hot poultice which she proceeded to have concocted out of a mixture of bread and milk. Having applied it with the help of a silk kerchief tied around my head, she has left me with instructions to rest and keep the poultice on until it has lost all its heat. It burns me dreadfully, but any discomfort is better than risking myself with the others, for I believe that Ursula is not one whit better than my cousins and, worse still, she is WILLING AND EAGER to fall in with any plan they might suggest. Yesterday I walked with Angela towards the lake. We went in the direction of the part that edges the forest. As soon as we were out of earshot, she relapsed into her usual silence, speaking to me only once, and sharply, when I stumbled against the root of a tree and turned my ankle. We went on almost as far as the narrow deep end where Papa keeps his skiffs for duck shooting. They are moored to heavy boulders placed at intervals along the shore. I could see that Angela was looking for a suitable place to stop, and very soon she found one and sat down, her back resting against the trunk of a tree close to the water. We were well sheltered here, for the trees and undergrowth come right down to the water's edge, casting their dark shade upon the boats which were bumping softly together, rocked by tiny waves and the gentle breeze.

      Angela told me to come and sit down beside her.

Lifting her skirts, she took from her underpocket the dummy tail I had seen her employ that first night. She brought her knees up and, opening her legs, she looked down at herself. I could see she had no pantlets on. Her moist red flesh lay open, its colour accentuated by the blackness of the curly hair around it and the whiteness of her petticoats. She lay back watching me with her eyes half closed, the hard instrument dangling loosely from her fingers like some monstrous obscene nose. She lay back in an attitude of expectant abandon, her buttocks stirring slightly up and down, the deep hole opening and shutting spasmodically, while she inserted one finger of her other hand between the grey pleated lips of her other secret hole.

A thin shaft of light fell on her, and the moist flesh and hair gleamed in the sudden glow. Its warmth seemed to rouse her from her daydream. Taking hold of my head, she put it between her legs and held it there, rubbing herself against my face, pushing my nose into her yawning hole until, suffocating, my mouth was forced open. She guided my head where she wished to feel my tongue, making me move faster or slower, ordering me to nibble the pointed crest Kenneth loved so to fondle. As had happened before, a gush of hot liquid seemed to ooze from everywhere at once. It soaked my face. I protested in terror, saying that my dress would be stained if she did not let me go. Instantly, she got up and, taking hold of the plaything she had dropped on the grass, she lifted up my dress and fastened the belt around my hips. She told me to bear my back against one of the boulders. Then, bending my head backwards and down and drawing my feet in until I was arched to the very utmost, the horrible object jutted straight out from my belly, looming huge and rigid, swaying with every movement, hideous in its lifelessness. It did not seem possible that I could hold this position for long. Its very unnaturalness made every limb in my body hurt, I was strained beyond anything imaginable. But before I could straighten up Angela was sitting astride me, pinning me down with her knees in the same way she would have ridden a horse. Taking hold of the instrument, she lifted herself and slowly pushed it in until it completely disappeared and her buttocks rested on the pair of pallid artificial balls. She remained for a moment without stirring, then slowly she began to revolve like a top, using her feet to support her, her legs passing in front of my face with every turn. She must have done this two dozen times. Gradually her speed increased until, satisfied at last, she fell forward between my legs, the object, still inside her, faintly stained near the base with her blood, My back felt as if it had been broken. Caring not for the consequences, I lifted her buttocks up, using what strength I had left, and, with a sucking noise, it popped out of her. She groaned and grabbed wildly, blindly for it, trying to replace it in its sheath, but the stinging of her torn flesh was making her shake and cry with pain. Climbing off me, she told me to get up and get ready to return. But I was unable to move. My body was one terrible bruise. Placing her hands under my arms, she hauled me to my feet, but such was the pain in my back I was unable to stand and I fell in a crumpled heap to the ground at her feet. She freed me from my grotesque disguise, pulling my dress down over my soaking undergarments. I think that for perhaps the first time in her life she was frightened. For when she enjoined me to get up, her voice, though urgent, held a quaver. And when, seeing me lie still, she resorted to threats, they proved useless. I told her to do what she pleased, to do the worst, I could not walk home until I had rested. So she knelt beside me. Skilfully, she massaged my limbs. Loosening my corset, she rubbed the small of my back until the pain eased and at last I was able to stagger to my feet. It took her no more than a few seconds to rearrange my toilette. She combed my hair and, putting her arm around my waist, she supported me until I had sufficient strength to walk alone. By the time we reached the lawn, pale but composed, she was the very image of subdued innocence.

  I had just enough strength left to fall into an armchair on the lawn and, there, I pretended to be engrossed in the croquet game Kenneth and Ursula were playing.

  The poultice is cold now, and very uncomfortable. But is it not right that I should suffer for my lies? And the same tormenting question always lingers at the back of my mind: how long shall I be able to escape from Kenneth?

  I cannot remain here all day. I shall have to tell dear trusting Miss P. that my toothache is better. Otherwise Mamma will send for Dr. Hunt and the whole thing will be exposed. How could dear, God-fearing Mamma ever imagine to what depths of turpitude I have sunk!

If only I could catch some contagious horrible disease which would quarantine me from them. I have about lost all my faith in God's protection and I am not so sure anymore that evil is always punished. And now what am I saying! I am resorting to blasphemy! Oh! I shall be punished for writing this.

In a queer sort of way, this diary has become my only real friend in spite of the fact that the things I am forced to write down are so sad, so wretched. For, beyond them, I can think of little else. However great my sufferings were yesterday, my body was not defiled. A meagre consolation... but it does give me some comfort all the same.

Kenneth is now pretending to appreciate Ursula's ridiculous advances and her ceaseless chatter. I say pretending because I noticed him wink at Angela several times while Ursula was not looking, and Angela answered him with a smile and a negative shake of her head. I have no idea what they are up to. But something is brewing.

When we went to bed last night, Ursula whispered on and on about Kenneth, talking of his beauty and of his great intelligence and fine discrimination. She repeated that she was determined 'to get him' and that a boy of his age and with his looks, even with no experience whatever, would be something worth having. "What do you think of that?" she asked in the darkness. I didn't reply. If she only knew. But I can say nothing... Monstrous as the thought is, I must admit that I have half a hope that her obvious wantonness will divert some of their attention from me.

They seem to he biding their time. At least, since Ursula's arrival they have behaved with greater prudence, and in the evening, apart from the nightly check on my journal, they retire to their rooms and the door remains locked.

A sudden horrible thought has just occurred to me. No doubt that Ursula, by her forward attitude, has made plain her intentions regarding him, In that case, they will have nothing to fear from her. Then what are they WAITING for? I have no faith at all in Ursula. She is a slave of her desires. They only have to put the idea in her head and she will join them, increasing the number of my tormentors to three.

And yet when I think of the vicar I wonder how such a staunch supporter of virtue and goodness, such a highly proper and one might say almost rigid man in his virtuousness, I wonder how Mr Gareth could have given birth to such a brazen, unprincipled, immoral daughter? The very idea of the old gardener makes me shrink with horror. But I now know that this thing they call pleasure can lead one to sink to the very depths of degradation. I don't know why this train of thought has reminded me of Bluebell. I have managed to rid myself of her continual presence by complaining that she has awakened me in the night.. I've had her basket put down in the sewing room. Mamma observed to me the other day that I seem to have totally lost my interest in the delightful little animal. "Always a first burst of enthusiasm with you Victoria! Too much enthusiasm at the outset inevitably leads to disappointments later. And that is why I have always recommended restraint to you." I could only blush and stammer when, after telling me that I must learn to be more constant in my affections, she scolded me for my excessive timidity, especially where she was concerned, saying that she was at the same time my mentor, my friend, a loving mother and my hoped-for confidante.

Oh, I am so mixed up.

Later.

I am supposed to be doing my French lesson. But somehow Polyeucte fails to hold my attention. I can think of little else than the two others... or must I say, from now on, the three others?

I was still in bed when Ursula came up to the room to change after breakfast. As soon as she came in, and although she said nothing, I could see that she was in a towering rage. Tearing off her clothes, opening and shutting the drawers with a great clatter and bang, it seemed to me as if she wanted to vent her rage on something, couldn't find the right object, and was simply lashing out in all directions.

Kenneth says he adores my exact analyses. "And you have such a superior insight into your own self! Rare, my little cunt, rare indeed! It is not given to everyone to have a lucid intelligence of mind and spirit and flesh... and flesh. I repeat. Don't neglect the flesh, Victoria. You have that tendency. Continue."

He told me to write those sentences and I did.

I was about to ask her what could be the matter when she threw herself on the bed and broke into a violent fit of sobbing. I went and attempted to console her. I asked her what ailed her, but she pushed me away with her fists, telling me to go away and leave her be.

She was in such a state that I thought the best thing was to do as she told me. Without waiting for Miss Perkins to come and take off the poultice, I withdrew into the bathroom. What can have happened?

I must go down to dinner now. I shall be alone with dear Miss Perkins, that model of sanity, that one pillar of certitude and unfailing guide to my inexperienced self. The rest of the party is going over to Lady Hawkes' for dinner and a musical evening. I am to remain here because Mamma believes the night air cannot but bring on my toothache again. I asked her whether I might not be excused from riding tomorrow morning;, saying that I was infinitely better but dreaded those stabbing pains caused by sudden jolts, and that I could not expose myself to the saddle without risking the most dreadful aches.

"The most dreadful aches? Dear, dear. Then don't ride tomorrow morning."

Later.

We have spent the most wonderful evening together, just the two of us. Several times I wanted to bury my head in dear Miss Perkins' lap and tell her everything. But I simply couldn't bring myself to do it. For the thought of losing her tender affection and esteem seemed even a worse fate than my present one.

I forgot to mention that this morning; we had our first letter from Papa. He gave us all the news. He says that Rome is quite fraught with interest.

sunday

We all went to Church as usual. The vicar preached a very long and in my humble opinion a very dull sermon. He and Mamma had prepared it together. The text was taken from the 1st chapter of Isaiah:

Wash you, make you clean.

I could not keep my mind from straying. I dared not look at Ursula. She seemed perfectly at ease and was listening devotedly as if she had entirely forgotten the scene that took place in my room and hour before.

As soon as I heard that the others had come back from their ride I went down to breakfast. I saw immediately that something had taken place. Several of the hooks on Angela's riding habit had come undone, her blue eyes, bright as new-forged steel, showed me that she was in high spirits. And alas! I have come to know the kind of pastimes that give her this look of exhilaration. They talked and joked with each other, sometimes speaking in Hindustani (I now know what their language is called. They always speak it when they don't wish to be understood by outsiders. Their nanny taught it to them when they were children).

Ursula was nowhere to be found. I was just about to ask where she had disappeared to, when she came in, and after bidding me a curt good morning, took her place at the table in silence. It was plain that she had been crying, and that she had done what she could to hide her tear-stains. But not with much success, for her face was blotchy. Seeing that we were alone, she made no attempt to provide an explanation, but simply sat there, hardly eating, sullenly watching my two cousins who went on with their conversation as if she were not there. Each peal of laughter seemed to run through Ursula like a knife. She seemed to know that she was the object of their derision, or their mirth, and it soon became apparent to me that at any minute she would dissolve into tears anew.

I am glad to say that I have not become so inhuman as not to sympathise with her. Rising, I suggested we go and get ready for Church. Mamma, I said, would not forgive us if we were late.

We went up together, and even before I had time to close the door, she had thrown herself upon the bed, her head buried in the pillow, trying to smother her sobs. She was muttering Angela's name, and Kenneth's too, and connecting them to imprecations of the most dreadful sort. She said that she wished she were dead. And, what was still more terrible, that, before she died, she wished she could kill the two of them.

Not knowing quite what to do or say, I sprinkled some eau de Cologne on a handkerchief and bathed her face, doing my best to calm her and praying that Miss P. would not come in or, if she did, that I would have sufficient presence of mind to dream up some plausible story to account for all this. I spend so much of my time labouring to contrive lies!

Anyhow, I did not ask Ursula what the matter was, for I knew only too well that it was something I did not wish to hear.

When her sobs subsided, her grief turned into anger, an anger of such intensity that she positively scared me. Grabbing hold of my shoulders, she shook me and poured forth an account of what had happened during the past two days. Never once letting go of me, speaking at great speed and her nails digging into my flesh, her cheeks aflame, she related the shameless story of her woe.

As I had suspected, Angela and Kenneth had taken her to the glade in the forest. I gathered from what Ursula told me that she had been all too willing to accompany them! It seems that she had had occasion to boast to Angela about the gardener, and that Angela had taken a great interest in that episode. Asking her all sorts of precise questions and demanding every detail she could possibly give, Angela had behaved like a friend; at least Ursula thought, she told me, that this would create a bond of friendship between them by proving to Angela how much she trusted her And Ursula had also wanted to impress Angela that, despite her plainness and age, she knew something about life. In exchange, Angela – consummate liar that she is! – had told her that Kenneth was more than taken with her and that she would willingly play the role of an accomplice, ready as she was to do anything in her power for their happiness. She then suggested that they repair, on that morning ride, to the deserted glade they had noticed in the wood. Ursula went on to say that she had not realised until the last minute that Angela meant to go with them. She had expressed surprise then, upon getting to the clearing, Angela had dismounted too and asked Kenneth to give the word when he wanted her to leave them alone. And Kenneth had laughed gaily and said that she, Angela, was his very life and soul and that he could not and would not be parted from her.

Ursula says that Kenneth is completely under his sister's domination and does everything she says. Her words cut short by sobs, Ursula continued by telling me that, without giving her any explanation at all, Angela had ordered her to strip, and that Kenneth, having exposed himself, she did as she was told, for she was out of her mind with desire for him. With Angela's help she was soon naked too, and thinking of nothing but Kenneth's male nudity displayed before her eyes, she had gone towards him hardly conscious of what she was about.

It was then that they had burst into uncontrollable laughter, poking fun at her for the way she was made, saying they had never seen anything so ridiculous and ungraceful in all their lives. They pushed her down on the moss and examined her with no more feeling for her humiliation than if she had been a fish or a frog they'd caught. They poked here and tweaked there, they pulled her long lips, calling her cock-a-doodle-doo and saying that, truly, she wasn't fit for much better than to be beaten. And this they then proceeded to do, using small branches of gorse they plucked from nearby bushes, taking turns, one of them doing the flogging whilst the other, behind her, held her feet in the air and held her steady by sometimes planting a foot on her chest.

Opening her dress, Ursula showed me the bruises between her breasts where their heels had dug into her.

Then, she continued, they had gone off together, further into the forest, leaving her there to look after herself. She said she lay there, listening, and she knew what they were doing only five or ten yards away... and she said they'd made as much noise as possible, on purpose, using filthy language and commenting on what they were doing. Unable to stand it any longer, Ursula had started to get dressed, but before she was ready they had returned and, at that moment, their attitude changed completely from one of utter vicious brutality to another of gentleness and tender compassion. They consoled her, and explained to her that this was simply a test they put all their 'friends' through before deciding whether they would have anything further to do with them. Saying that she had shown remarkable courage and tolerance, and that on the morrow everything would be different, they asked her to pledge herself to secrecy.

But, notwithstanding all their assurances, things had been pretty much the same today. She had been cruelly beaten and this time they had misbehaved in front of her, saying that, ugly as she was, she ought to be grateful to them for allowing her to witness something very beautiful indeed. She should count her blessings in this vale of sorrows, Kenneth had told her, and Angela had invited her to get what satisfaction she could from their display.

At this point in her narrative Ursula became almost hysterical, saying that no matter what she could not live without Kenneth, that she wanted him inside her, she wanted his meat, and she said other obscenities I would never have thought it possible to hear come from a lady's mouth.

I could listen to no more and told her that if she did not get a grip on herself we would surely be late for Church. With greatest difficulty, I managed somehow to pacify her and aid her to get ready in time. The poor creature was incapable of doing anything at all for herself, trembling and whimpering, alternately abusing me and thanking me for my thoughtfulness. My actions were prompted by terror as much as by sympathy. I feared that dear Mamma would not fail to notice her state. In her present frame of mind, I feared Ursula would throw all caution to the winds and take her revenge by exposing my cousins and hence myself, heedless of the certain consequences exposure would have for herself. At the same time I wondered if Kenneth and Angela had spoken to her about me. I too started to tremble but I reassured myself with the conviction that, if she had known, she very surely would have told me so.

As the time to leave approached she seemed to make a tremendous effort to collect herself We went down together, talking quietly of this and that. Dear Mamma, being late herself, paid very little attention to us. We all bundled into the carriage and left at a brisk trot. Mamma has never in her life been late to Church.

This afternoon the heat is so great that it has been impossible to stay out on the lawn. Angela suggested we do as they do in India and take an afternoon nap. Mamma was reluctant to grant her permission, saying that she was not one to encourage idleness in the young. Angela (who as usual was determined to get her way but, as usual, clever enough to get it easily) pointed out sweetly that both she and Kenneth had taken afternoon naps all their lives, and so far without ill effect. The weather today, she continued, might truly be compared with what one encounters in the Far East. Mr Gareth, of course would hear nothing of it. "Stuff and nonsense. There's a world of difference," and he went away with poor Ursula whom he says he has missed all week. They went away, that is to say, for a long ramble.

We will all meet again for supper and afterwards for evening prayers. Miss Perkins has gone down to see Mrs Thornton. Her little boy is still running a very high fever. It is so sad for everyone, Mamma is going to pay a round of calls and drop her off at the village on her way. I asked Mamma if I could accompany her, but she said I must stay and play host to my cousins during her absence. Angela immediately said that she wished to show me a game of checkers she had brought back from India. She said that it was an extraordinary set and that she would he grateful to me if I would help her unpack them.

Perhaps it being Sunday the Good Lord will protect me. For Mamma and Miss Perkins have been gone for some time and although I can hear faint sounds coming from their room,

my cousins, so far, have not come near me.
　　I must endeavour to accomplish my French lesson.

monday

I have no tears left to shed. For now, horror and shame and bewilderment combine to make my predicament seem beyond the limits of human endurance. And that I should be forced to write down in detail these disgraceful episodes makes my plight all the more abominable. The pen is slipping from my moist fingers making it that much more difficult to write at all. My head is spinning, I doubt whether I can see or think clearly. And now, now it is too late for me ever to slip through their fingers, for THE WORST HAS HAPPENED, and I am bound to them forever by the total nature of my degradation. And, worst of all, I am condemned to live with Ursula at my side, witness of all that has come to pass, and who, depraved creature that she is, ENVIES ME and WISHES SHE WERE IN MY PLACE! Venting her hatred and jealousy on me, caring not what I have to undergo, she jeers at my sorrow and torments me as much as she dares, to the boundless delight of the others.

  She is sitting on her bed watching me like some evil female demon. I am still dressed in a long pink corset belonging to Angela, and I have black stockings on. The top of the corset leaves my breasts bare, and Angela has laced it so tight I can barely breathe. The whalebones are cutting into my flesh, for I have no chemise on underneath to protect me against the rough lining. And the choking heat (it is awful, even at this hour late in the night) adds to the discomfort of this veritable suit of armour. The wide lace ruffle around the lower hem is soaked and bloodstained, for Kenneth, with Angela's help, has torn me open for his pleasure!

  I had had time to write in my diary at some length before Angela came in, silently, like a jungle cat, and asked me IF I KNEW WHAT WAS EXPECTED OF ME. She told me, before a strangled word could come out of my mouth, that Kenneth was READY and that I had better come straight along without making any fuss. The very evenness of her voice contained a terrible quality of menace, and as though dazed by a shock I had been expecting for a long time, and which had come at last, I bent my head and, like a lamb, followed her into the room where Kenneth lay naked, his tool in his hand and waiting for me.

Because of the weather, the shutters, the windows and the curtains were all closed, leaving the room in pitch darkness, in velvet-like blackness. Near the bed glowed a faint light. No sooner was I in the rooms than the door was closed and locked behind me. Angela started to remove my clothes at once. Kenneth, his distended horror squirming up to his navel, tried to grab me as I passed the bed, saying he could not wait for me to get undressed and that as long as he could get at what he wanted, the rest was of no importance. Angela paid no heed to him. She acted as though she knew best. Freeing me from his grasp, she stripped me bare and, taking the pink corset out of her painted chest, she laced me into it, pulling the cords until my respiration was almost blocked by the pressure. Turning me around to survey the effect, she said that the outfit was lugubriously 'proper' and catching up a pair of scissors, she cut out two round holes in front. My small breasts jutted through them, pressed outwards by the constriction of the shell in which she had me encased. Whenever I made a movement, the jagged ends of the whalebones sawed into my flesh. The bottom of the corset was short, it left my buttocks exposed. Truly, she had made me look the very essence of immodesty. Shortening the suspenders, she handed me a pair of lacy black stockings and told me to put them on.

Meanwhile, Kenneth was cursing her under his breath, pleading with her too, saying that her only excuse for delaying everything was that she had no idea of his sufferings. She went over to him, kissed him on the mouth, stroked his chest, and told him to have a little patience. Grabbing hold of her hand, he tried to make her caress him, lifting up his balls and pushing them upwards so that his prick seemed to lengthen, quivering and stretching, seeking her fingers. Shaking her head disapprovingly, she opened her tight-bodiced dressing-gown and gave him her breast to suck. He caught the brownish tip between his lips and pulled on it greedily, grunting and writhing with delight. His hands went up to his belly, but she caught hold of them and held them to his chest, gesturing to me to make all haste, for I had been standing there watching, the stockings in my hand, unconscious of the passing time and of what was required of me. As in a dream, I did as she told me and went submissively towards the bed. I was now beyond feeling fear. The bewitching obscenity of my reflection in the mirror seemed to be foreign: it was not I, but someone else I saw. It could not be me. I made a conscious effort to breathe.

Kenneth had closed his eyes. He was still pulling at Angela's breast drawn down near to him. He had buried his hand between her legs. He seemed a little more calm. Drawing away from him, she murmured a few words in his ear, pushing him gently towards the further side of the bed. With a sigh, he let go of her breast. The end was drawn out and marked by the sharp bite of his teeth. Angela seemed not to feel any pain.

Taking a pillow, she placed it on the edge of the bed and instructed me to place my back against it. Then she lifted my feet up and caused me to fall back, my head lower than my body and level with Kenneth's face. He had turned around on his side and was watching his sister's every movement. His hands went wandering over my breasts, playing with the points until they rose hard and sharp. Then cupping one of them with both hands, he took the end between his lips and fondled it with the tip of his tongue. At the same moment my legs were spread wide open and I could feel Angela's burning soft mouth searching my gaping cunt. I do not know what came over me, but within a matter of seconds the only too well known and shameful sensation of pleasure swarmed over me, coming and going in ripples that ran from my buttocks to the very tips of my breasts, from my open slit to the nape of my neck, from one mouth to the other, I knew not which, I did not care, straining my body with all my might towards both of them from fear that it would stop. Then I knew I was going to scream. Kenneth must have known it too, for he put his hand over my mouth. Only a muffled sound was able to escape my lips before I collapsed and, rolling over the bed, released by both of them, sobbing with delight and distress, my body remained shaken by waves of lascivious and disgraceful joy. I tried to hide my face in my hands, not daring to look at either of them, but before I could recover possession of myself, Kenneth had picked me up in his arms and had carried me around the bed, placing me again on the pillow. Angela took his place. She knelt down, her white thighs and black slit formed a menacing dome over my head. She pulled up my trembling legs, opening me and offering me to her beloved brother. Kenneth was gasping as he stood above me, his prick in his shaking hand. He passed its hot smooth tip over the fragile wet wound which lay exposed to him. Exploring it carefully, he went on until he seemed satisfied that he had found the place he was looking for, and then with slow deliberation he began to push downwards, gently at first so that I felt no pain. Nevertheless, I shrunk away from him in an agony of apprehension of what was coming. Then, with an abrupt thrust, he split me open with the end of his prick. He removed it instantly, bending down and licking me until the pain subsided. My head was now firmly gripped in the vice formed by Angela's strong knees. She seemed irritated by something Kenneth had done. Looking up from between my legs, he smiled at her and said in an apologetic whisper: "But I don't wish to hurry. She's narrow, do you see, narrow as the eye of a needle." Angela let go of my legs and went to towards her dressing table on which she kept the key to her chest. She opened it and drew out the dummy tail which, after taking off her dressing-gown, she strapped into place, fitting it around her waist and securing it with a strap that ran between her legs. She tugged on the wide hands until it was just where it belonged, stoutly anchored. She had on nothing else but her stockings and brocaded high-heeled slippers. Her round breasts bounced as she walked towards us with her habitual air of calm deliberateness. In a sudden flash I understood what she had in mind. Recoiling in terror from the soothing comfort of Kenneth's lips, I pleaded with him to protect me from her. Getting up, he stood for a moment irresolute... in a reverie... and then holding me open with his fingers, the palm of his hand driving like a weight down upon my belly, nailing me there so that I could not escape him, he put his dagger into my slit and, again with a downward thrust, he forced it into me; it wrenched and tore its fiery way in until, although only half its length had disappeared – and try as he would he could go no further – its tip was arrested by a wall inside me. I could feel it throbbing and pounding and pressing in vain, swelling and stretching the small smooth tunnel it had discovered.

I think I must have fainted. I remember nothing of the minutes which followed. When I became conscious again of my surroundings, Kenneth had left me. With the rubber tail buckled round his loins and covering his own shrivelled tool, he was kneeling buggering Angela. She too was kneeling, or rather she was on all fours. Her hands were clawing the carpet, her shaking buttocks were impaled by that hideous instrument. She seemed demented.

Not knowing whether I could trust my legs to carry me, I jerked myself erect and fled from the room, feeling as though I were about to collapse again. My torn body and my swimming head... I reached my bed. Not an hour had passed.

I must have fallen off into a sleep of exhaustion and despair. I woke up late and just had time to throw on my clothes when I heard Miss P. knock at the door, telling me that supper was being served on the lawn. I had not had enough time to take off that hateful corset. After struggling with the laces, I found I was quite unable to undo the tight knots without someone's assistance. I gave up, fearful of being late, and went down just in time for my arrival to pass unremarked.

Everyone was discussing the heat wave. Angela told us how in India there was but one way to survive. That was to take as many cold sponge-baths as one possibly could. And, in India, the water was more often tepid than not, and even, so it would seem, boiling! Truly, our colonists seem to have suffered acute discomfortment. But of course it is a wonderful thing they are doing, bringing the benefits of our civilisation to those unfortunate and benighted countries.

Kenneth and Angela came down soon after I did, walking towards us, hand in hand, the very picture of grace and tender affection. Mamma was moved to remark again how devoted they seemed to one another, adding that they had never been separated since they were born, and she wondered whether the pleasures of a debut in London would be any compensation for an enforced parting when Kenneth went up to the university in the autumn.

We were all sitting under the big cedar tree. Mr Gareth and Miss Perkins were next to each other, talking with great animation 'en aparté' about the forthcoming Church bazaar and paying little heed to Ursula who, alone, remained silent and sullen, making little effort to conceal her chagrin. I prayed no one would notice for I felt that, upon the slightest provocation she would break down completely and lose all control of her tongue. The very thought made my scalp tingle. To increase my uneasiness, I imagined myself fainting away on the spot and being undressed by my dear Miss Perkins who would then find me garbed in the disgusting cut-away corset Angela had put me in. The very idea made me dizzy and feeble, and I blessed Mamma for changing the course of my thoughts by sending me to fetch the Bible from her room. The vicar was to read it before we had supper. Angela came in after me and asked me on the stairs what I had done with the corset. I replied that I had not had a moment to take it off – that I'd tried and been unable to. She laughed and asked me if I had taken a fancy to it.

We had supper on the lawn. I could scarcely eat, even though I was starved. I had but one idea in my head: to retire early and rid myself of that awful corset before Ursula came up to bed. Strangled with anxiety, I asked Mamma, as soon as the meal was over, to grant me leave to go to bed, saying that the heat had been so exhausting that I felt utterly done up. But, with great firmness, she requested me to stay in their company, saying that it was cooler out of doors and that after an afternoon's rest I could hardly be very tired. Lingering in bed, she added, was, in her mind, an exceptionally bad habit, giving encouragement to the worst of vices: laziness. The vicar, to be sure, agreed very heartily with her, and launched into a discourse upon the subject. I felt quite sure he was repeating one of the sermons I had heard him deliver at some point in the past. But Mamma and Miss Perkins listened with keen interest whilst Angela and Kenneth were giggling behind their hands and keeping an eye on Ursula who seemed quickly to be reaching the final limits of exasperation. As for me, his words droned steadily through one of my ears and out the other, for I was preoccupied with something else. How, I wondered, would I he able to get undressed without Ursula's prying eyes discovering what I had on? Perhaps I could manage to get it off after I'd put my night-gown on. But even then, how could I dispose of the thing? What explanation could I give her if she were to catch sight of it? None. And no doubt not content to contemplate my own distress, she would hate me for deceiving her. Disposed as she was towards Kenneth, she would do everything possible to destroy me, and there was a great deal she could do. I was by now on the verge of tears. I fought them back as best I could, thankful for the dim evening light which made our faces blurred, indistinct shapes against the darkening blue sky.

Angela and Kenneth seemed to have not a care in the whole wide world.

They were conscious of my predicament, I knew that. I remembered Angela's laugh on the staircase. Did they want Ursula to find out? Were they completely sure of themselves? Did they feel they could do anything at all with impunity? Clearly, they had lived in a well of vice ever since their earliest years, and under the very eyes of their doting parents they had succeeded, cunningly, in escaping discovery. But Ursula was dangerous. She was not well. She was losing her balance, it seemed to me, and she was capable of doing things without a thought to their consequences. I wondered whether the other two were aware of that. And now I felt willing to go to any length to prevent their vile actions from being revealed. For I was as deeply implicated in all this as they were, and by what imaginable means, by what proof could I demonstrate that I was their victim and not their willing accomplice? Had I not a tongue in my head? Then, everyone would naturally wonder, why hadn't I used it? Why had I not spoken out? Strings of questions whirled around in my head... tailless questions, without answers... I wiped my damp hands on my handkerchief and tried to think of other things. I thought... I tried to stop thinking and listen to the vicar.

When he shut the Good Book, Mamma rose, giving the

signal for departure. My first impulse was to dash upstairs. But of course it was impossible for me not to wait until we were in the hall collecting our lamps and bidding each other goodnight.

I had at last hit upon a plan: I would go into the bathroom and remove it, dress again, and hiding it under my dress, I would wait for a moment when Ursula's back was turned in order to throw the corset into a drawer.

As soon as we were upstairs, I retired, as I had planned; undressing as quickly as I could I endeavoured once again to untie the laces at the back. Throughout it all I struggled to remain calm. I couldn't properly reach the knots – I saw in the mirror that Angela had tied, not bows, but knots – and I realised this would take hours. Frantic, I searched about for a pair of scissors. There weren't any. In tears, I dressed again and went back to my room. I would either have to keep the hateful thing on – and by now the flesh of my breasts was raw, bitten into by the protruding, sharp whalebones – or keep it on under my night-gown until morning... For I dared not go back and forth from my room to the bathroom, fearful that my repeated comings and goings would attract Miss Perkins' attention. I knew that, in my shattered condition, I would break down under questioning.

Ursula, when I came into the room, noticed my unhappy look at once. Before she had a chance to question me, I said that, like a clumsy thing, I'd stubbed my toe and that the pain had been quite enough to bring tears to my eyes.

She offered me no sympathy. She sat sullenly on the edge of her bed, immersed in thought, her large watery eyes fixed on the opposite wall. I spoke to her again, wishing to get in her good graces. I asked if I could help unhook her dress at the back. She turned slowly towards me, then, probably awakened by the sound of my voice, but not having heard what I said, and as though continuing to express out loud one of her own secret thoughts, she asked me whether I had ever had anything to do with Kenneth.

I sat, or rather dropped, down upon my bed. Knowing I had gone pale as death, I replied in a whisper – which was all the voice I could muster – that I didn't understand. "What do you mean, dear Ursula?"

"Have you been in bed with him?" she asked in a flat voice.

"In bed?"

"Have you let him put it in you?"

I opened my mouth in denial. Not a sound came from my throat.

She was watching me carefully and must have read the truth in my countenance. Springing up from her bed, she reached me in one leap and started to pull my hair, dragging me backwards, holding her face close to mine. With a look of hatred that made my blood freeze:

"So you have! You have, you little innocent bitch! Have you then! Have you?!"

I had put my hand in front of my mouth to avoid screaming in terror, I was gnawing my knuckles. For, far from letting go of my hair, she pulled it harder and harder with every word:

"I'm going to kill you!" she said, beating my head against the bed. "Kill you, do you hear? Kill you!..."

And for the first time I was relieved to see Angela walk into my room.

Without a word, she came towards us.

Grabbing hold of Ursula, she slapped her twice across the face and flung her onto her bed. She lay there, stunned and whimpering. This seemed to infuriate Angela for, taking Ursula by the shoulders, she grated in a low and terrible voice that wasn't a woman's voice at all:

"If you cry, if you make any noise at all, I am going to slap you senseless. Do you understand what I am saying to you? Senseless... then perhaps we shall have a little peace in this house. It would be a good thing if you were to remember that you are here on sufferance, and that we tolerate with difficulty anyone or anything that acts as an hindrance upon our pleasure." She had said all that very slowly.

Kenneth had followed her in and when Angela was finished, he nodded in token of approval, and smiled at me benignly, quite as though nothing untoward had occurred.

"Well, then, what are we going to do with her?" he enquired of his sister. "She is such a drab thing I find even her tears dull. But we had better take her with us, don't you. fancy? Who knows, there might be some purpose we could put her to..." His voice trailed off, expressing his indecision or bored indifference to Ursula's fate. And as usual relying upon Angela to arrange matters to please him, he undid his trousers buttons and, having brought out his prick, lay down on my bed and bade me suck him until his device had attained the proportions my delicious cunt unquestionably deserved.

In the meantime, Angela had undone my dress and was peeling off my clothes, keeping an eye trained on Ursula as she did so. Ursula let out a gasp when she saw me standing in my strange attire, otherwise naked, and in front of them all.

I dared not look at her and wished that at this very moment GOD in HIS mercy would strike me dead. For I was damned. And Hell could not be worse than this.

Smiling strangely, she thrust me towards Kenneth, saying she would take Ursula with her into her own room, and that we had best join them and see to it that the doors were locked. Taking our dressing-gowns, she left, ordering Ursula to follow her.

Kenneth leaned over and, taking me by the waist as though I weighed no more than a doll, he lifted me up and placed me astride him, my face touching the tip of his prick, and my slit directly over his mouth. Gently, with his fingers, he opened the swollen lips and inserted his own into the breach he had dug that very afternoon, the while stroking my breasts and lifting his buttocks upwards, his angry swollen instrument searching my mouth.

I felt practically no pain now. Rather, a faint tingling which his tongue, on my sensitive skin, aggravated until again, as this morning, I became inundated by a feeling of blissful contentment and without knowing what I was doing, I seized his prick between my lips and, holding its base in my hand, thrust it into my mouth as far as it would go, sucking it gratefully, oblivious to any feeling of shame, until at last, unable to contain myself any longer, I let go of it and buried my face between his legs, stifling my cries of ecstasy in the soft fur on his thighs.

Some moments passed. I don't know how long it was.

Although I had not fainted, there was a passage of time of which I remember nothing. While I lay there inert, I could feel Kenneth's hard prick trembling as it lay imprisoned between my breasts. My legs had gripped his waist, and with a moistened finger he was gently stroking the cleft between my buttocks.

As soon as I moved he lifted me up and, laying me down again on the bed, he said that it was his turn now. He must have seen the look of fear in my eyes, for he laughed and said I would learn to enjoy it in time. And without further ado, without any apparent misgivings, he spread me wide and drove slowly into me, moving backwards and forwards, widening me gradually until again I felt that soft beating tip at the innermost bottom of my being, He remained thus until a warm stream gushed out into me, filling me with a wonderful sense of well-being which caused me to lift my legs and place them upon his shoulders. I moved my buttocks upwards so that, if possible, I could feel him better, I could work his prick deeper. And with a simultaneous grasp, our mouths met, hung together, and we rolled over upon the bed, clinging to one another in the throes of sinful delight.

At that moment, I neither felt shame nor knew any fear. I felt happy. It is only now, as I look back on what has happened and realise what in the space of a few brief days I have become, that I am overwhelmed with horror at my own lust. Oh! there can no longer by any doubt of it! I TOO AM A MONSTER! For can I truthfully say that I am any better than they? or any different? Willing as I am to do whatever will procure me that sweet and terrible feeling of incomparable fulfilment, a feeling of which I never tire, of which I have begun to think all the time?...

I rested my head on Kenneth's chest and reclined thus, in a kind of coma, and I think that I would have fallen asleep if I'd not been roused by his laugh. He lay there shaking, and, wondering what on earth could possibly be the cause of his merriment, I raised my head and saw Ursula standing near us. She was wearing the strangest apparel.

Quite naked, her hair dishevelled, she wore, tightly strapped around her waist, a large dummy tail... on the end there was a painted head of a clergyman. Of monstrous proportions, the instrument had not, like the other one, those other attributes. It was continued by a wide band of thick padded leather which went around to the back and covered her slit and buttocks. I mean to say, it went round, underneath her legs, and back up the other side and there it was fastened by a little padlock. Her cunt was completely covered.

Angela pushed her towards us so that we could have a better view of this monstrosity.

Then I had a terrible shock. The painting on the tip was a miniature portrait of Mr Gareth, the vicar. The likeness was startling. There was his severe expression, his long nose, his thin lips, his eyes raised up towards the skies as though in prayer. It was a shocking and grotesque caricature of Ursula's dear father. For some reason I cannot understand, Kenneth's uncontrollable laughter was infectious. It gained me, and I laughed, for the situation was ludicrous as well as impious. Angela watched us, she smiled, clearly delighted at the success she was having. I thought of the hours she must have spent at work on this fiendish picture.

As for Ursula, silent tears coursed down her face as she fondled the rigid, indifferent dummy, spitting on its head to give it a semblance of life, her eyes averted from the terrible face staring up at her.

Her long, pear-shaped breasts, with their almost white tips, swayed with every movement she made. Lifting one hand, she tried to stroke them. But Angela, standing behind her with a small whip in her hand, cut at Ursula's arm, causing it to fall back down again, and she went back to that hopeless caressing of the numb and lifeless and frigid object which jutted bulkily from her belly. With a cry of frustration, she leapt forward, trying to catch it between her lips. Unable, however, to reach it, she went back to her rhythmical, senseless task.

This appalling scene amused Angela no end. Coming towards the bed, she took off her dressing-gown and seated herself cross-legged beside Kenneth. Her slit was well open. She took his hand and placed it in her nakedness, saying that, it seemed to her, this was surely the best way to enjoy the spectacle. Kenneth's dexterity brought forth sighs from her. This seemed to increase Ursula's agony. Her tears redoubled and she tried in vain to insert a finger between the leather pad and her yearning flesh. As usual, Angela had left nothing to chance. Try as she might, Ursula could get nowhere, the band adhered tightly, isolating her from all human contact.

Kenneth's hand moved more quickly now. An unbroken stream was running from Angela's cunt and soaking the counterpane. She was arched backwards, her hard breasts pointing at the ceiling, their tips puckered and rigid. Bending forward, I took the point of one in my mouth and pulled it hard, nibbling it as I had seen Kenneth do. I caused her to sigh louder, while I felt Kenneth place in my hand his own source of pleasure, full of new vigour. Opening my slit, I allowed him to render me the same service he was rendering his sister. We soon reached a state of frenzy where our hands were no longer sufficient. Angela motioned to us to give her more room. She lay on her back and placed me astride her so that we were face to face, our gaping slits touching each other. Bending forward, I could see, between my legs, Kenneth's tool lancing into Angela, disappearing and coming out again, until it pointed upwards and I knew it was my turn. He thrust with such enthusiasm that he truly bore me aloft, supplementing my lack of depth by his own hand which I could feel like a knotted ring superimposed over my cunt. Then, freeing himself with a rapid jolt, he passed and rubbed its slimy length over me, from front to back until, when the signs of my mounting excitement made me cry out to him, he went back to Angela's drooling hole, into which he buried himself utterly.

He went on thus from one to another, from Angela to myself, until finally I ceased to know which of us was which, and at the same moment we found the same exquisite, rapturous relief whilst Kenneth, lodging his prick between my hairless mound and Angela's dark-furred one, pressed me down on him, clamped me down as the creamy liquid rushed from him, endlessly soaking Angela's body, Kenneth's own body, and my body too.

From the moment I had felt Kenneth's hand on me, I had forgotten about Ursula. When, in that state of half-slumber which seems to follow pleasure, I remembered her with a pang of anguish, I could not see her. I wondered whether she had gone back into Angela's room. The doors were all locked – hence, I knew, she had not escaped. Then a truly terrible sight met my eyes. I clutched Angela and Kenneth, shook them until they came back to themselves. I made them look.

Although I could not see, from where I lay, anything of Ursula, I was able to see the long dummy tail swaying as if suspended in mid-air. It hung just above the edge of the bed, seemingly attached to nothing. We got up and coming round to where she was, we found her. She was arched backwards, her feet were bent inwards, her hands were touching the floor. She formed an almost complete circle, an O. I have seen acrobats at the circus do things like that. Ursula did not attempt to straighten herself when she saw us, but remained where she was, muttering Kenneth's name, sticking out her long pointed tongue, straining towards some inaccessible object. I emitted a cry of terror which Angela checked with her hand. Looking at Ursula, Angela was rather entertained than perturbed, and she told me to be still. I asked her what the matter was with Ursula whose utterly rigid body appalled me. Then Kenneth kicked Ursula. She didn't budge.

"Hysterics," was all Angela said. There was a silence. "That's all," she added, "just hysterics," and her eyes were gleaming. She snatched Kenneth's prick and told him to piss if he could. He complied almost at once, and she guided a spray of urine over Ursula's electrified, taut body. Using his prick much the way she would a garden hose, she directed the hot salty jet over Ursula, sparing neither her face nor her open, unblinking eyes. Then she fetched a small bottle of oil from her room and spread some on Ursula's lowering, monstrous, ugly unreal prick. When she was done, she got astride Ursula, mindless of her own weight. With slow movements she eased herself down over that hideous tail, swallowing every inch of it into her. Then, bending forward, she pulled her buttocks apart. Kenneth understood. He came up behind her and to my stupefaction, in spite of the narrowness of the little grey hole, he inserted himself with the greatest ease. Tuning his movements to hers, he was soon in the throes of delight. I felt a pang of jealousy.

Angela, as though riding some animal out of a

nightmare, slapped Ursula's flopping, sorrowful breasts, pulled at them as though they were reins, mocked and jeered her with ever increasing coarseness as her own pleasure increased. Ursula still seemed insensible to Angela's poundings. Recollecting what I had had to endure near the boathouse, I was spellbound to see the poor girl's incredible endurance. As I have said, she did not even seem to feel the weight which she supported in full, for Angela's feet were lifted from the ground, she was digging into Ursula's ribs with her knees. It was just as though she were on horseback. And when, at last, she fell forward, with Kenneth on top of her, the added burden still didn't change things: Ursula remained like a bridge, still apparently insensible, and but for the fact that she was whimpering, she might just as well have been made of stone. Kenneth then disengaged himself. Angela moved slowly forward, paying no attention whatever to the breasts she was crushing, simply endeavouring to free herself of the freakish tool. After some effort, it came out of her with a revolting sucking sound and shot back up again into its provocative position; the sap of Angela's pleasure dripped down the dummy tail's length and puddled on Ursula's belly.

Sliding down over Ursula's chest and deliberately brushing her wet fur over Ursula's face, Angela moved off a distance and watched her, a look of bored disgust written over her lovely face.

She came nearer then, took careful aim, and kicked her twice. To no avail. She then went to my washstand and, picking up the pitcher of cold water, emptied its contents on Ursula.

The effect was instantaneous. As though touched by fire, Ursula's frame quivered and collapsed on the sodden carpet. She was shaken by violent but almost inaudible sobs.

Paying no more attention to her than if she were as much a dummy as the loathsome object she wore, Angela handed me the key to my door and departed with her brother, leaving me to cope with Ursula as best I could. Although I was almost beside myself with fright at the realisation of what faced me, I dared not appeal to Angela, for, the game over, she now had that look of vicious cruelty on her face and I knew it was useless to make any demands upon her sympathy. Truly, to this day I have never seen her exhibit the least sign of humanity to anyone except her brother, and even Kenneth has been beaten when he has displeased her. I remember that day in the forest... and again the other night... Of course, I do not know how she treats him when they are alone. But when we are all together, she is practically silent, thinking of nothing but her pleasure and of his, ignoring me and caring not for my sufferings, for my desires, for my fears. When the door shut behind them I felt both awe and hatred for those two. I know that Kenneth, had he not been under her evil influence, would not have left me to take care of Ursula alone.

Catching sight of myself in the mirror, I fetched my scissors from my sewing box and freed myself from the soiled pink corset. My body was streaked with long purple welts where the whalebones had borne against my skin, and cut it. The globes of my breast were haloed with tiny painful nicks.

I felt dirty and clammy. Rubbing my sore flesh, I went over to the washstand to refresh myself. But then I remembered that my pitcher was empty. I didn't have the courage to go out into the hallway to the bathroom to fetch more water. Ursula was still lying on the floor, a quaking mass of misery. Quickly, I got into my night-clothes and, bending down, struggled to lift her onto her bed. But she clawed at me savagely, caught me once with her nails, and I dared not go near her again.

Knocking softly at Angela's door, and hearing no response, I turned the knob and went in. She was asleep and alone. Shaking her till she woke, I asked her what I was to do. But she rolled over away from me after having opened her eyes, and told me with finality to let her alone.

The counterpane on my bed was rumpled and stained. I understood now why Angela always threw a large thick Indian coverlet over her bed. She kept the coverlet folded away in her painted chest, for just such occasions.

I have been toiling to set things to rights. I have had to work quickly. The point is that everything must be dry by morning. Creeping back again into Angela's room, I took her pitcher and with the corner of my towel set about removing all traces of what has happened. While I worked I tried to invent some story I could tell in the morning if Miss Perkins, when she came in, was to notice spots or stains.

It is daybreak now.

And still I am writing, sitting here. I have filled in pages and pages but I doubt whether anyone could ever read them. I dare not go to bed, despite my tremendous fatigue. I go on writing mainly to keep from falling asleep. Ursula is still lying on the floor. She is sleeping now, I think. I have tried to lift her. But she weighs too much. I am praying that perhaps a little later on, after she has rested, I will be able to persuade her to climb back into bed. I have managed to clothe her in her night-gown without awakening her. She still seems to feel almost nothing. Her pallor is truly shocking to see.

Kenneth! Oh, Kenneth, why did you do it?

Why have you left me?

tuesday, the 10th of july

Ursula is in bed with a fever. I managed to wake her up at six o'clock, at least to get her upon her feet and into bed. Then, beside myself with fatigue, after at last locking our door, I fell in to a nightmare-filled slumber from which Miss Perkins awoke me an hour later.

Although I was half-asleep, the events of last night flashed through my brain in an instant. I caught sight of my crumpled and utterly ruined bedspread which, even after all my efforts, still bore marks of the disorder... I had to think quickly, either that or we would have been found out. And truly the Devil must have stood at my side, helping me, for, without blushing and before Miss P. could ask me any questions, I advised her that poor Ursula had been indisposed during the night, poisoned no doubt by something she had eaten, and that I had done my best to look after her and repair the damage without disturbing her rest.

After complimenting me for my thoughtfulness, she scolded me all the same for not having gone in search of her, saying that my conduct could easily be interpreted as a slight on her devotion. She said that Ursula, if she had indeed been ill, ought to have been treated, given some medicine, and so on... Our conversation took place in whispers, for Ursula was still asleep, and I begged Miss P. not to wake her, explaining that we had not got to sleep until morning and that I too would be grateful for a little rest.

"Then I'll leave you until ten o'clock," she said, and went off to instruct Joseph to unsaddle our horses.

The minute she was gone, I jumped out of bed and shook Ursula until she was wide awake. Repeating to her the story I had just told Miss P., and telling her to substantiate it if she wanted to save us from disaster, she listened to me without appearing to grasp what I meant. Her hands were burning. Begging me to bring her a glass of water, she then asked me to repeat what I had just told her. I did, and she listened meekly, applauding my presence of mind, and, saying that, indeed, she did feel sick, that she seemed to have a headache, the very worst headache.

I patted her pillow for her, smoothed out her bedclothes and besought her to try and go back to sleep again until ten o'clock. I was anxious lest she wish to talk about last night's events. But she seemed exhausted and, shutting her eyes, fell asleep almost immediately. I too retired to my bed with the hope of getting some much needed rest. Although my eyes were burning with weariness, no sooner did I close them than the memory of what had happened rose up before me. I realised I would have to make an effort to conjure up the remorse I would naturally have been feeling. This made me understand the depth of perversion down to which I had sunk and with what bewildering speed I had learned how to lie to my dearest and nearest. The thought of Kenneth, instead of inspiring me with horror and aversion, gave me a voluptuous shock in the pit of my stomach. I yearned for him and placed my hand on my wet slit.

I soon found the exact spot in which my pleasure was born and moving my fingers deftly, I discovered that I could control my delight, stopping just before the crest of the wave broke (I can find no other image to express it), then letting it surge up again; and I kept doing this until, my fingers no longer obeying my mind, and my head full of Kenneth, I rolled over onto my belly, squeezing my legs tight together and burying my face in my pillow so that Ursula would not be disturbed by the sound of my sighs. Thus I fell asleep.

Miss Perkins came back at exactly ten. We both woke up. She brought my breakfast on a tray and a cup of camomile tea for Ursula. Miss P. sat down on the edge of Ursula's bed and made her drink the tea and asked her for details of her trouble. I dreaded lest Ursula fail to remember what I had told her earlier in the morning. At first she did not seem to understand what Miss P. was alluding to. I looked pleadingly at Ursula, praying silently, but with what fervour! that she would not betray us. Ursula seemed to undergo a moment of hesitation. I was paralysed with fear, I wondered if her justifiable feeling of vindictiveness would make her tear off the mask and through all caution to the winds. There was a pause during which I could feel beads of perspiration running down my forehead. My hands trembling so that the cup I was drinking from chattered on the saucer and, with great difficulty, I managed to put cup and saucer down on the tray.

It was dear Miss Perkins' innocence that saved us. Taking Ursula's speechlessness for an indication of excessive fatigue and embarrassment, she herself repeated the story I had told her, saying that, after all, there was nothing to he ashamed of, was there? And she interpreted Ursula's continued silence for corroboration. By then I had managed to regain possession of myself, and was able to chat with her. The tender solicitude I showed for Ursula was, of course, based more on fear than on tenderness; I announced however that I would gladly keep her company until she got entirely well. To be truthful, I dared not leave her alone. I was ready to invent any plausible excuse for staying with her. At first, Miss Perkins seemed opposed to my suggestion. She mentioned the boating party that had been planned for this afternoon, and said that she knew how much I enjoyed being on the lake. Her counter-proposal was that I go with the others and that she keep Ursula company. We had quite an argument – my voice became a trifle shrill – before she would give in, concluding:

"Your mother will not doubt be pleased to observe that, to you, friendship is of greater consequence than pleasure." She complimented Ursula for having inspired such devotion, then gathered up the breakfast things and left, telling me to get washed and dressed and that later on she would have lunch sent up on a tray.

Prattling unceasingly, she had failed to notice the extent of Ursula's indisposition or the depth of her silence. Or if she did notice them, she continued to fancy that they were perfectly normal in one who had spent an unpleasant night. When she had shut the door behind her, I heaved a sigh of relief, forgetting for a moment that the relief was only temporary.

Everything depended upon Ursula's mood and my

ability to pacify and placate her. She was watching me now with a look of unconcealed hatred twisting her mouth and bordering her eyes. I felt like a mouse trapped by a cat. I did not doubt then but that she intended to expose us and have her revenge. We truly deserved it. At the thought of what would happen, I was overcome with a sensation of nausea which sent me flying to the bathroom, my handkerchief pressed over my mouth.

When I returned, she was smiling cruelly, knowingly, her eyes pinned to my face. I knew I had to talk to her, but I had no idea what to say... and the only words I could find were those by which I would implore her to spare us and I knew it was useless to utter them, for she was waiting for nothing else. I wondered what Kenneth and Angela were doing, and bitterly resented having been abandoned by them. Surely, I thought, they must be aware of our dangerous position? It was danger they had created and had left me to cope with in whatever way I chose. I told myself that I had to go and find them...

At that very moment there was a knock at the door. Angela came in. She looked radiant, happy and rested after her morning ride, oblivious of my troubles.

She greeted Ursula with a warm good morning. Sitting down on the edge of her bed, she took Ursula's hand and asked her if she were feeling better. Her impudence was breathtaking. She had put on her best drawing room manner of saccharine sweetness which she usually reserved for Mamma and Miss P. I wondered what her motives were, why she had decided to treat us to this unconvincing act. Ursula, after the first moment of astonishment, seemed – as I had expected – unimpressed. Interrupting her in the middle of a sentence, she said in a hollow voice that the game was up, and that as soon as she could come downstairs she intended to expose us for what we were, in front of her own father and Mamma. She let fly a horrible volley of insults, hissing in Angela's untroubled, smiling face. I began to fear she might become hysterical again.

And then I realised that Angela's calm indifference itself contained a threat. What threat?

Ursula's scalding voice finally trailed off, and as her rage abated, she too no doubt noticed the incongruity of

Angela's phlegmatic unconcern for her insults and, what was still stranger, for her repeated promises to expose us. Those promises were enough to make my flesh creep; but Angela remained serene. In fact, there was a moment when I thought Angela was on the verge of laughter... as though she were amused by the dreadful words that were coming from Ursula's lips. Perhaps, I thought, perhaps Angela has lost her mind...

But I did not have long to wait... For soon Ursula, leaning back to catch her breath, stopped talking and in silence waited to hear what Angela would have to say. There was triumph on Ursula's face: she surely expected Angela would begin to crave pardon and would surrender the thing she, Ursula, in her turn craved for: Kenneth. And then – this, I thought, was her plan – and then, after having humiliated Angela and made all sorts of difficulties, she would at last consent to hold her tongue. I could read all this on her face. There was a short interval between the moment she brought her insults to an end and the moment Angela stepped forward and knocked her head sideways with a whistling, tearing slap.

That slap seemed to echo through the room and through my very bones. I would not have been more stunned had I been struck by lightning. Ursula, the first moment of astonishment passed, was overcome with rage. Flinging off her bedclothes, she sprang from bed with the intention of grappling with Angela and clawing her face. Ursula was as pale as a sheet save for the mark left by Angela's hand on her cheek, and she was beyond herself with fury. Angela didn't move.

Taking Ursula's wrist in her hands, she dragged them down to her sides with as much ease as if she were dealing with a rag doll. Holding her there, she commanded her to be quiet, for Ursula had started to speak again, saying she was going to scream if Angela did not release her instantly. And I too was about to intervene, to beg Angela to let too. Then Angela did let go and, with the speed of lightning, flicked her hand and crashed it against Ursula's other cheek.

She had struck with all her might and Ursula dropped back on the bed, felled. Before she could recover. Angela was on her, pinning her down and telling her in a quiet voice that she had best listen to what she had to tell her, if she, Ursula, wanted to save herself.

Ursula laughed derisively, with unspeakable bitterness, saying that she was not scared by Angela's brutality and that no matter what she did, short of killing her, her mind was made up... she would spill it all, everything, the very first time the family was assembled in one place...

"All," Angela said, smiling sweetly, "all? Then we can mention the gardener, can't we?"

But Ursula had obviously thought of this too, for she answered at once:

"You haven't got any proof. He's an old man and he's been with the family for years and years and he's known in the village for his decency and his piety and he would deny everything. No one would believe it. Especially after what I am going to say about the three of you." She smiled at Angela. "I've got you all in a corner, and the sooner you realise it, the better for you."

So Angela's gambit had failed. What Ursula said was true. No one would believe this when confronted by the horrors Ursula would surely relate.

Unconscious of myself, I stood there, wringing my hands, the familiar hollow sensation of fear big in the pit of my stomach. Knowing that the truth was now going to be let out, I also knew that, if I were interrogated, I should not be able to conceal my confusion.

These thoughts flashed through my mind pell-mell. Dropping down on my knees, I was about to implore Ursula's pity, when Angela, in a voice as dead and as heavy as lead, spoke again. The words of distress I was about to pronounce withered in my mouth as I listened to her.

"My dear, dear Ursula. I am not in the least worried by the old man, or about him. It's you. You are aware that you are pregnant aren't you?"

Ursula turned grey. Her pale eyes, wide open, stared at the carpet. "What?" she murmured.

"Pregnant, my dear."

Her eyes travelled slowly towards Angela's face, moving slowly, but her head moved even more slowly. She looked at Angela askance, her mouth gaping. I felt as though

I were going to swoon, and caught hold of the bedpost. Iclung to it, waiting for the room to come back into focus.

Although I could hear Angela speaking, I could make no sense of the words she was uttering. Her tone was a new one of matter-of-fact half-gay, half-sober informativeness, whilst Ursula, white as death, looked at her spellbound, small groans coming from her throat and her head shaking in bewildered denial of the ghastly facts Ursula was putting on display for her consideration. The horrible old man, Angela was saying, was old enough to be her grandfather, but all the same... how could Ursula have been such a fool?

"But how do you know?"

Ursula's voice had become high-pitched with cowering terror.

Angela spared her no detail of what the consequences would be like. Ursula's denials became less frequent, less urgent as she listened and little by little became convinced that Angela was telling the truth. For, in answer to her question, How did she know? Angela smiled indulgently and said that she had seen every one of the usual signs of it with her own two eyes, and that her feigned innocence and ingenuousness were either masterpieces of self-deception or, if genuine, of stupidity. And to prove her point, she invited Ursula to stand up and find out for herself what she, Angela, meant. And when Ursula had done so, standing in front of Angela and shaking from head to toe. Angela lifted up her night-gown and, revealing her round white belly, pressed on it with her fingers, saying she could feel it there. Taking Ursula's hand and holding it under her own, she said that Ursula could feel it herself, if she cared to bother. Ursula remained thus, all modesty banished, holding up her night-gown With her chin, poking and prodding her white flesh until, with a moan of horrified conviction, she sank down on the bed, sobbing and pleading with Angela to forgive her for her behaviour, saying that she had only meant it as a joke, and that she did not know what was to become of her.

Angela was now all sweetness again. "Calm yourself, my dear. If you keep still and do as you are told, I think everything will work out to your satisfaction and ours and that you will be saved from dishonour. However, I will require total submission from you."

Overcome with gratitude and relief, Ursula promised to do everything Angela wished, kissing her hand and repeating that she was truly her saviour and her friend. Her aggressiveness had been replaced by the most abject servility. With difficulty dissimulating her disgust, Angela rose, saying she must go now, and putting her arm around my limp waist, she all but carried me into her room, kicking the door to behind her with a tap of her heel. She sat me down on the bed and, lying down beside me, buried her face in the pillow, as best she could stifling an uncontrollable fit of laughter. Tears of mirth streamed from her eyes. She hunted for her handkerchief. And I watched it all, stunned by what I had heard, unable to unravel my confused thoughts in which Ursula, the old gardener and Angela's revelation and present flight of laughter danced a crazy turmoil round in my head. It wasn't logical, any of it, and I understood nothing.

At last Angela's outburst subsided – she sat up on the bed, dabbing her eyes. She saw my expression of bewildered despair and, shaking me by the shoulders, told me not to be such a little goose. Assuring me that there was nothing the matter with Ursula except her incredible stupidity of which she had had to take advantage in order to extort her consent to keep still, Angela described how splendid it would be now, for Ursula would do just exactly what was asked of her.

"She's a perfect victim, don't you see. From now on she will give us the fullest satisfaction, for she's completely in our hands and her very life depends, she thinks, on our goodwill and forbearance."

If she realised the monstrousness of what she was saying, she didn't show it. Giggling as though she had played some schoolgirl's prank on poor Ursula, she rejected my efforts to make her see the cruelty of it all. She was full of scorn for my attitude. "Ursula? Ursula's nothing to me. She's not even pretty. She ought to be flattered that Kenneth and I are willing to have anything at all to do with her."

Then, seeing that she could not convince me, her manner changed and a tone of warning crept into her voice. She made me swear to keep the secret. "If you reveal the trick, you'll regret it. She'll tell then. And it will be only that much more terrible for you. And you'll also have to count upon us. We'd not take that from you sitting down, you know..." She did not specify what they might do, but I knew her only too well to realise that this was no vain threat.

I wanted desperately to be alone and to try and sort things out in my own mind. I said, however, that I would stay with Ursula – I had said so to Miss Perkins earlier – even though the idea of going back into that room and being alone with her terrified me. I had no choice, though, for Angela bade me leave her, saying that she had things to do and that Ursula surely had need of company and good cheer.

When I returned to my room, Ursula was lying on her bed, her night-gown still pulled up. She was scrutinising her belly. On her face was an expression of mingled wonder and horror. Upon seeing me, she blushed a deep red and hurriedly pulled the covers up. To give herself a countenance, she asked me to hand her her hairbrush. I pretended not to have noticed anything, and dressed myself, taking as long as I possibly could over my toilette, dreading the moment when I would no longer have anything to keep me busy and would have to face her agony in silence.

And when she did start talking, questions poured from me. I had not known until then from where babies come, nor what took place, and when she had explained everything to me, I realised the implications of Angela's veiled threat over what she would do if I were to betray her confidence. My own fear almost obliterated the pity I felt for Ursula's dreadful state of distraction and helplessness.

It's late afternoon now, and Ursula is sleeping. I am still writing in my diary with the hope that, if I put everything down, I may be able to have a clearer view of things.

Mamma should be coming up any minute now to see Ursula. I must hide this journal, for I am sure that, if ever she sets eyes on the cover, or if ever she asks me anything about it, my face will betray me.

wednesday

In spite of my state of fatigue, Kenneth came into my room last night and did with me what he pleased, paying no more attention to Ursula than if she had not been in the room. My terror was such – now that I know of the possible consequences of pleasure – that I could not lie still, even though Kenneth swore under his breath and pinched me brutally. Stammering and crying, I explained that it wasn't because of him, it wasn't for any reason but that I didn't want to be pregnant. When he heard that he laughed, saying that I was still too young to find myself in Ursula's situation, and that he advised me to forget any lies Angela might have told me to the contrary. But this did not reassure me, for I know his own capacity for telling untruths. Had I not, but a few hours before, had more than adequate proof of it? But I dared not say anything, especially with Ursula there. For all his coaxing, though, Kenneth could do nothing, even though he said he was determined not to spoil me and that I had but to leave matters to him. Every time he would put his prick to my cunt's opening, it would shut of its own accord, and finally even against my own will. For he was losing his temper again and I was beginning to be more afraid of it than of the possible outcome of his pleasure.

The same thing repeated itself several times. Putting his tool in my mouth, he said he was going to punish me, and he pissed with all his might, ordering me to swallow every drop. And as I did so, his temper worsened. He said then that if I played the little fool and held back for so much as an instant, I would suffer for it. Placing me once more upon my back, he pulled at my slit, prying it apart with his fingers until the end of his prick was placed at the opening. But the moment he let go with his fingers, it snapped shut again, constricted by the same force that was making my entire being shrink with icy fear. Cursing now, and calling to Angela, he turned me over, and passing his wetted finger over the slit in my buttocks, he inserted it into the other hole, then took out his finger and, bending down, titillated that hole with the tip of his tongue until, to my horror and shame, I felt it open. Suddenly realising what he was about to do, I fought wildly to free myself, scratching his body with my fingernails, hoping that if I caused him pain he would let go. I then heard Angela's cool voice.

She ordered Ursula to get up and hold me down. Ursula, of course, obeyed immediately. She pulled my arms away and stretched them out in front of me, causing my head and chest to fall forward on the bed. Held thus, I couldn't move. My back was arched and my buttocks were exposed to Kenneth's enquiring tongue.

I don't know just when he substituted the smooth end of his prick for his tongue. But I suddenly felt it penetrate me gradually, my hole closing around its warm hard length in a tight grasp as little by little he eased his way further in until at last his balls were resting upon my opened cunt.

Circling my waist with his spread hands, he began to move. The pain I felt made me cry out to him to stop. He did stop, and remained thus, his prick throbbing inside me. And then I felt a soft moist mouth cover my slit and a strong tongue drive into my cunt, until now it opened wide too, seeking its wanton pleasure from Angela's wicked dexterity. I knew it must be her, for Ursula, beads of perspiration pouring down her face, was still pinning me down with all her force, made stronger by the hatred that animated her. The grip of her hand had become like iron. I could hear her convulsive breathing as she watched us, tightening her fingers from time to time until I thought my bones would be crushed.

In spite of the pain, I felt that the moment was near when, for all the horror of my situation, I would be unable to prevent myself from yielding to the now well known feeling of rapture. Gradually, it was enveloping me and making me stir my buttocks as Kenneth explored them. I could hear myself panting, sighing, sobbing and imploring him all at the same time, I could hear myself telling him I was willing to undergo anything they wished if only they would allow me to satisfy my lust. And when Angela's lips left me, I begged her to come back and continue. I was beyond myself with excitement, my dripping, craving hole was searching her mouth, but instead, I felt another tail penetrate me. Colder and stiffer than Kenneth's, it slid into me and began to move, synchronising its action to his. Finally, enraged and not caring what happened, I let them hammer into me at their will; then, swooning with pain and delight, I sank into a delicious oblivion.

When I came to myself again, I saw Kenneth's tall figure standing between Angela's wide-flung legs. They had piled up pillows so that her slit was level with his prick. His hands on his hips, his arms akimbo, he furrowed her slowly, idly, hardly moving his body, his prick so deeply inserted that all I could see were the superimposed triangles of fair and dark fur grinding against each other. With every jolt, Angela emitted a guttural cry, biting her arm with such force that traces of blood appeared on her fair skin. Her face was something terrifying to behold. Although her eyes were wide open, nothing could be seen of them but the whites.

Kenneth was studying her face and body, seemingly taking great care to time his movements so as to delay as long as possible the moment of her release. After a while she pleaded him to move more quickly, saying she could not contain herself any longer. But, instead of doing as she had asked, Kenneth began to withdraw himself. I watched, fascinated, as his long rod emerged unhastily, like a thick rope. And as he backed away, Angela repeated her injunctions that he should not leave her now. But Kenneth retreated until his prick was altogether in sight. I let out a gasp of choked surprise.

For fitted around its rim, was a stiff circular brush of coarse black horsehair which stood out around the tip as stout as wire.

Hardly knowing what I was doing, I reached out my hand and touched it. Each bristle seemed as sharp as a tiny steel needle. Kenneth, his eyes never once leaving Angela's face, pushed my hand away and, placing his collared prick's end against the mouth of Angela's hole, he went back into her, each black bristle turning out as he did so and making an incongruous black ridge around the pink slot before vanishing completely, followed by the thick stem that supported them. After a second of immobility, Kenneth started moving in and out of her in long sweeping strokes. I could almost feel the spikes lacerating her soft inner tunnel as, with increasing speed, they rubbed up and down its length.

Instead of feeling pain, Angela only begged Kenneth to go at it with greater ferocity. She placed her legs on his shoulders so that he could probe her to the last inch of his possibilities, so that the instrument of torture could reach the last depth of her cunt. She now seemed to be suspended from his shoulders, only her neck and head touching the bed. She clawed wildly at the shawl beneath her, and as she was approaching the moment of ultimate fulfilment, I saw that her transport had reached such a pitch that, indifferent to the consequences, she was readying to scream. I clapped my hand to her mouth in order to stop her cries, allowing her to bite me cruelly while she wriggled like a snake, her body racked and contorted with ceaseless spasms of mingled agony and delectation, avoiding and then seeking Kenneth's terrible thrusts until all of a sudden she became rigid and, as though stricken to death, fell back upon the bed. Life returned to her body in undulating waves, all of which started from her soaking loins, whilst Kenneth's spurting and grotesquely ornamented prick sought the warm haven of her gaping mouth and I swallowed long draughts of the tepid, grass-flavoured milk that gushed out of her cunt and down my throat.

During all this time I had not devoted a thought to Ursula. It seems so hard to believe that, in this short time, I have become so depraved that I could not care about her being there. I only remembered her after Kenneth had left me. Even then I didn't care that she had been witness to these disgraceful scenes in which, finally, I had taken a willing part.

I still held Kenneth's shrivelled end in my mouth, my lips locked around its base, when, pushing me away from him, he darted towards Ursula's bed, calling out to Angela to come to her senses.

I was so placed that for quite some time I had had my

back turned towards her and had not been able to see what she was doing. Now turning around, I saw her sprawled out on the bed, her thick cotton night-gown rucked up in a bunch under her chin, her legs wide apart and between their long, pendant thick lips, she held what could be seen of one of Angela's little whips, the sturdier end of which she was using as if it were a man, prodding herself violently in what seemed a sterile attempt to obtain relief from the furious desire burning inside her.

Her cheeks were a flaming red. Although she was pronouncing his name, she hardly seemed to notice Kenneth watching her with an air of bemused curiosity. Meanwhile, the thin plaited leather stick moved rhythmically in and out, its smallness contrasting strangely with the breadth of the gap that hungered for it and which it was searching in vain.

Angela stretched herself and yawned.

She got up in a leisurely fashion and went over to look at Ursula. Seeing what all the excitement was about, she started to laugh. Without further ado, she caught the slender lash-end of the whip, gave a tug, and pulled the instrument from its sheath. Holding its slimy length away from her, and a look of disgust on her face, she left the room, announcing that she was going to bed.

This painful scene seemed to arouse Kenneth, for his prick was rising again. Holding it in his hand, just out of Ursula's straining reach, he waved it in front of her in the most offensive manner while the wretched girl, her hand rummaging in her slit, her eyes riveted to the object of her desire, sought by her own means to obtain a semblance of relief. But her efforts were wasted. She lay there panting, her lips parched. Her cunt yawned, angry and wet, a yearning chasm; and Kenneth held himself just out of range.

There was a look of madness in her eyes when Kenneth, tiring of this game, decided to leave us. I begged him not to leave me alone with her, for I was indeed almost out of my mind with fright. Looking down at himself significantly, he said that I would suit his purposes, and in spite of my great fatigue, I followed him, letting him do with me what he wished, learning by my docility to feel no pain even if I felt no pleasure.

I fell asleep before he was through with me.

thursday

I had quite forgotten about the picnic Mamma planned for today. The vicar had been invited and he joined us early in the morning and we set out at half-past-ten. The sun was already very hot. We drove to Stanton Forest in the barouche.

We found an agreeable shady spot not too far from the road and we settled ourselves under the trees. Miss Perkins and I unpacked the hampers of sandwiches and other things, and set out the food on a large white tablecloth on the ground, decorating it with moss until it really looked very festive and charming and earned me the compliments of both Mr Gareth and Mamma.

After our meal was over and the vicar had said grace, Mamma suggested that we children go for a walk, reminding me that if I kept a sharp look-out I would surely find some interesting plants or flowers to press in my diary. I blushed and thanked God for the half-light of the tall trees which permitted my confusion to pass unnoticed. Ursula, who had scarcely touched her food, asked to be allowed to stay behind, saying that she felt rather weak, what for the heat of the day. Her permission was granted; she remained with the three grown-up, while the three of us went off obediently.

Angela announced gaily that she would help me find some attractive shrubs for my journal, and talking about this until our voices were out of the range of their hearing, Angela started to imitate dear Mamma, parodying her voice in the most shocking of disrespect.

Kenneth, baring his prick, placed it in my keeping, and thus we walked along. He seemed quite unconcerned by the indecency of our attitude, and talked in the most natural way with Angela until, at the edge of the path, we came upon a nest of grass snakes, curling and twisting in a tangled, loathsome knot. I let go of Kenneth with a shriek of alarm, staggering several steps backward in an attempt to flee. But Kenneth took hold of my wrist and told me not to be babyish. Dragging me back to where the hideous heap of snakes was, he crouched down beside his sister who, with fascinated interest, was scrutinising the writhing, slimy mass at her feet. To my utter horror, Angela advanced a white finger and probed and fondled those reptiles. Then she even picked one of them up, twisted it about her arm, not one bit troubled by the contact of its cold, viscous skin.

I felt gooseflesh prickling all over me and fought against a mounting sensation of nausea. Kenneth, his prick still dangling through the gap in his trousers, trimmed a small stick with his penknife and began to play with the snakes, lifting up several at a time and letting them slide back into the seething nest. They amused themselves thus for quite some time, silent and absorbed, while I watched, nearly overcome by disgust.

Then Angela put an affectionate hand on Kenneth's arm. "Dear Kenneth!" she exclaimed, her eyes full of merriment and dancing, "dear Kenneth, just imagine!" In her voice was a strange note of exultation that made me look down at her. She was smiling, her eyes were glittering as she drew out her handkerchief and, selecting one of the snakes, put it on the square of white linen, tying the ends together so that the creature could not escape. Then, lifting her skirt, she put it in her under-pocket and carefully smoothing down the folds in her dress, she got up and said that she felt that the time had come for us to rejoin the party.

Kenneth had watched her all this time without saying a word. His brow was puckered as though her intentions were not at all clear to him. But then he must have reached some sort of conclusion, for he started to laugh softly. Getting to his feet, he went towards Angela and crushing her against him, he kissed her passionately on the mouth until she thrust him away, breathless, saying that we ought to get home as soon as we could induce those fools to move. She took the lead, seemingly thoughtless of the nasty thing she had under her skirts. Kenneth made me hold his prick again, and did not let me release it until we were well within earshot of the party. I stumbled along behind them, dizzy with apprehension of I knew not what, picking nervously and at random any small plant that grew along the way.

When we rejoined the others we found Mamma and the vicar and Miss Perkins engaged in a lively conversation – they never seem to tire of talking about problems and principles and forthcoming Church bazaars. Ursula, making no visible attempt to participate in the conversation, stiffened when she saw us approach and kept a keen eye on us, doubtless wondering what we had been up to.

She looked quite ill and I was astonished that no one had noticed this. From time to time, as though following her own inner thoughts, she unconsciously wrung her hands as though pleading with someone, in some mute and hopeless dialogue. I began again to fear that at any moment she might break down and no doubt Angela had noticed the same danger, for, putting her arm affectionately around Ursula's waist, she helped her up and the two walked away under the trees, where I saw them talking together for a while. When they returned Ursula had changed completely, now appearing quite gay, smiling at Angela and looking at her with an expression of positive adoration on her pale face. I could understand none of this, but instead of feeling comforted, I shuddered as I wondered what new piece of devilish mischief Kenneth's darling sister had been dreaming up.

Rising, dear Mamma said it was time to return if we were to get home in time for tea. After picking everything up, and burying the leftovers, it was a very gay party that rolled up to the house.

We played games that evening and went upstairs at a rather late hour. Dear Miss Perkins seemed reluctant to let the vicar go, although it is frankly beyond me what she can find of interest in him. He is so dreadfully dull and so severe that he puts the damper on any fun one could have, and I shouldn't be surprised if he – who is so upright and stern and so godly – found our dear Miss P. a trifle 'fast', as they say.

While wishing Mamma good night, Ursula, to my surprise, asked Mamma if we could have the horses to go riding tomorrow morning.

"Why, of course, my dear Ursula," Mamma replied.

And Ursula thanked her with such exaggerated profusion that I grew concerned again.

"I am so delighted to hear that you are well again. I shall have word sent to Joseph at the stables to have the mounts saddled and ready for half past seven."

I was so tired I could hardly find the energy to undress. When Kenneth came into my room, a feeble, useless "No!" escaped from my lips. I think he realised that truly I was too worn out to be of any use to him and I dare say he found his pleasure only in the fact that Ursula, her body trembling like a leaf, was obliged to sit and watch us.

As for myself, indifferent to the scandal, I waged a losing battle against sleep and only woke up when he slapped me. Soon after, I returned into an exhausted slumber.

friday

It was with the greatest difficulty I woke up this morning. Every bone in my poor body was aching. I could hardly remember what happened with Kenneth late last night, nor how I had ever managed to wake up and conclude the day's happenings by writing them down. I have learned, I do think, to write in my sleep. Some evil spirit guides my hand and aids my hand across the page.

The very thought of going forth for the morning ride made me hurt. Miss Perkins helped us get dressed. In this way I was spared any *tête-à-tête* with Ursula. Pale and drawn though she was, she kept up the conversation, probably so as to divert dear Miss Perkins' attention from my listlessness. For, to tell the truth, I don't know how I am going to go on much longer. I have no strength left in my body. And my mind is so depressed, I am so despondent...

Kenneth had used and abused me. I felt I had no more resistance left. The strain has been too much. It is not my fault... and yet, of course, it is, and my fault alone. Whilst hating Kenneth, the very notion of his (I cannot write the word) makes my heart beat more quickly, and my blood tingle there in the very place where my shame is seated. I know that I should loathe both of them. Yet even so, the memory of Angela's lips, blush though I do at the thought, sends a delicious thrill down my spine, obliterating all sincere sentiments of guilt.

It is only when I am temporarily out of their clutches that I realise I am in their clutches. It is only when I am, for the time being, away from them that I realise what they are turning me into: A MONSTER, like themselves.

When we came down, Angela and Kenneth were already astride their horses and waiting for us. They both seemed in excellent high spirits and talked a great deal as we rode off, Angela turning now and again to give Ursula a smile of secret understanding. I had no idea what was between them. And although Ursula smiled back fawningly and preened herself under Angela's advances, I could not help noticing that look of fleeting dread that raced across her face when she thought she was not being observed.

My mind full of questions and forebodings, I hardly noticed the moment when, having reached the woods, we were nearing the fatal place I knew so well. And I was seized by an irresistible impulse to wheel my horse about and gallop back to the house. Bringing up the rear as I was, the plan was feasible. I was already gathering in the reins in preparation for spinning Sunbeam about, when Angela, her fiendish mind having, apparently, divined my thoughts, ordered me to ride out in front of her. Her voice was harsh. Meekly, I did as I was told.

Having dismounted, I fumbled with my horse, pretending to be unable to attach him properly, and when Kenneth came back to give me a hand, I asked him in an agonised whisper what was in store for me. He laughed, patted my cheek, and said I had nothing to fear. Angela, he said, was going to rid Ursula of the fruit of her sin, for this purpose using an old method she had learned from her nanny in India. I almost cried out, saying that I knew they were lying about the poor girl's condition, abusing her naiveté to torture her for their own evil pleasure. But a selfish fear for my own safety stilled the words rising in my breast, and I said nothing.

By the time I had recovered my wits, Angela had undressed her victim and was taking out from beneath her skirt a ball of flat, ribbon-like cord. She directed Ursula to lie down between two small saplings. Still chattering in a gay and soothing manner, Angela tied her outstretched arms to one tree and her legs to the other, explaining that it was of the highest importance that she remain immobile. Trembling and as pale as death, Ursula complied without a word of protest.

Kenneth's eyes followed his sister's every movement. Almost absent-mindedly, he was holding his prick in his hand until, as though seized by a sudden frenzy, he tore off his clothes and, begging Angela to do the same, got her to leave Ursula. The cousins rolled over on the moss in a savage embrace. It seemed for a while as though nothing were going to appease their hunger for each other. Breathlessly and with unbelievable brutality, they sought pleasure in each other's body, shifting from one position to another, exploring every shameful crevice, and this with such rapidity and such fury that one could have thought that they were people condemned to death and had but this moment left to them in this world, a moment they wished to exploit in order to satisfy their every mortal yearning. Their bodies, like two flounders, made a slapping noise as they collided wildly, both of them soaked with perspiration and piss. The strange sound of this battle echoed through the forest stillness, from time to time punctuated by a sudden rustling of the breeze or the faint strangled gasps that came from Ursula's mouth as she, shaking in every limb, tried in vain to rid herself of her bonds.

And then, as suddenly as they had gone for each other, like a pair of mad dogs, they parted, as if by common consent, and they drew off a distance, smiling and panting. I saw to my surprise that, fierce though the battle had been, Kenneth at least had lost none of his potency during it.

Coming back to where I stood (for I do not think I had stirred a muscle throughout that time), Kenneth looked meaningfully at his still charged weapon and I obediently took it in my hand. He bent over me and undressed me, making me change his prick from hand to hand while he slipped off my sleeves. Using my chemise, he wiped his brow and his armpits, then rubbed his lean supple body until his skin glowed and with a sigh of satisfaction he threw away the crumpled rag and pressed himself against me. My face was buried in the fur of his chest, and I stayed thus, with my eyes closed tight, until I heard Angela call out that everything was ready.

At the same moment I heard a scream come from Ursula. It rent the air and went through every nerve in my taut body, causing me to jump away from Kenneth and in spite of myself to rush towards Ursula. Then my brain registered what I was looking at. I stopped dead in my tracks, like a hunted animal that knows there is no way to escape. My flesh crawling with horror, I stood still and watched.

Angela, still quite naked, her body stained with streaks

of brown and muddy green, stood before Ursula holding the snake in her hand. Ursula's legs were widely opened, held in place by the tapes. (I realise now that she had thought it all out in advance. To carry out her scheme, a considerable length of tape was necessary, and she had plainly left nothing to chance.)

Ursula, thus quartered, her eyes starting out of her head with fear and revulsion, struggled to free herself, and, of course, couldn't. Angela, the greenish reptile wriggling between her fingers, was asking Ursula if she were ready, saying that, after all, these screams were unnecessary, that all this was for Ursula's own benefit, and that good-breeding required her to at least put up a show of gratitude.

Ursula was speaking – but no sound came from her lips. Bending down beside her, Angela, a smile playing over her face, pulled Ursula's cunt open, widening the opening with her fingers, and then slowly shoved the twisting pointed tail of the snake into the orifice.

I shut my eyes, grasping the air for support. I thought the earth was giving way underneath me.

I heard Ursula say: "Gag me, gag me quickly or I'll scream!" and then I heard no more until, after what seemed an interminable silence, Kenneth began to speak.

"Bless my soul," he said, I believe the dear girl has fainted, damn me if she hasn't."

I heard him walk forward over the springy moss, calling out to me to come along. When I opened my eyes I was standing over Ursula, looking down with curiosity at her white body and ashen face. Her gaping cunt contained a wriggling snake. The snake was emerging from it. It emerged finally all the way, slid over her body, then down upon the moss, and vanished into the forest.

"Jolly good, don't you think, eh? Think I might as well jam her now. She'll not even know the difference."

He knelt down and pushed his way into her lifeless body. "Quite a joke, I'd say. And this time she's going to have a pretty little bastard right enough, I'll see to that!"

Angela, greatly amused by this new game, diverted herself with the tapes, which she pulled and released, jerking Ursula's legs into the air and letting them fall back down again.

This pleased Kenneth enormously. The impact on his prick, he said, was delightful and "by George, I'm too worked up to bugger her." Lifting her buttocks into the air, he breathed deeply, gasping each time he filled his lungs, and while his body was shaken by long spasms of ignoble satisfaction, he released himself in Ursula's very depths.

After he left her she lay there swaying by the tapes, still in a profound swoon. For one dreadful moment I thought they had killed her. Her head had fallen back as though her neck were broken. Her closed eyes, her pinched nostrils, her curled, half-shut fingers looked exactly what I imagined death to be.

It was getting late. Angela began to dress hastily. She told me to hurry. But I lacked her skill in arranging appearances and doing up innumerable hooks in no time. So she was ready long before I was. She then lent me her impatient assistance.

Ursula had still not regained consciousness. I saw Angela fling a glance at her from time to time. A worried expression began to come over her face. As soon as Kenneth was ready, Angela told him to slap Ursula until she came to her senses. He did so, with no result. Angela said nothing. Undoing the tapes and winding them into a neat ball, she then proceeded to dress Ursula, before she did so wiping away, with care and thoroughness, every last trace of what Kenneth had done. Then, helped by Kenneth, Angela supported Ursula in a sitting position, did up her hair tidily, then let her rest again on the earth. Now Angela took her turn at trying to revive the girl. She slapped her face, then her hands and forearms, talking to her all the while, pinching her cheeks. All in vain.

My heart sank, a feeling of dread encompassed me, sank down over me. What would happen if they failed to bring the poor creature around? What would they ever be able to tell Mamma? What were we going to do now?

It was now very late. Kenneth took a glance at his watch, then glanced meaningfully at Angela.

"The bitch won't stir," Angela muttered under her breath. "Help me pick her up." They carried her onto the pathway and set her down once again. "Well," said Angela, "you two had better go back to the house alone. Tell Miss Perkins that Ursula has had a fall and must be suffering from a concussion. Tell her we haven't been able to get a sign of life out of her." And she then went on to compose every detail of the story and made us repeat it until we had got it by heart and could answer questions without faltering. I could tell that Kenneth was growing anxious about the time. But Angela said that she didn't 'give a damn'. "Even if they were to come now," she said, "it wouldn't make any difference. We're safe so long as we know what to say... safe for the moment. But when she regains consciousness, well... we'll have to think about our problems one by one. Are you certain you have the story of the accident straight?" Though she appeared to be perfectly calm, there was a certain urgency in her instructions to us, and it confirmed my impression of mounting danger.

And this terrible anxiety must have shown on my face, for Angela admonished me, saying that everything would be all right provided we kept our wits about us and I did not lose my silly head. She reminded me of what would happen if I broke down. "In such an event, Vickie sweet, you're through, remember that. I'll not lift a finger to help you." If the worst happened, we would all resort to flat and unalterable denial of everything – at the same time, be it understood, putting on a great display of modest incomprehension of the questions that might be put to us.

She said she would stay with Ursula in case she came to during our absence. She would then be able to tell us what frame of mind and mood she was in.

We rode back to the house as quickly as we were able; Kenneth sprang to the ground and rushed up to Miss Perkins who, already in a great state of agitation, was standing on the terrace talking to Joseph whom she had summoned to go off with Henry the stable-boy in search of us. My pallor was such that, upon catching sight of me, she surmised, before Kenneth could speak, that there had been some misadventure. I struggled down from Sunbeam and fell into Miss P.'s arms, sobbing uncontrollably, as if my heart would break. Meanwhile, she listened to Kenneth's account of what had happened, then sent him, with John and Henry, to fetch Ursula.

Leading me into the breakfast room, she made me drink a strong cup of tea before questioning me. And being the incorrigible chatterbox that she is, she herself supplied both questions and answers. I had only to contribute an occasional nod. The strong tea and my relief – it did me good to cry – enabled me to gain a little control of myself before Ursula's return. But, despite Miss Perkins' urgings, I could not swallow a bite of toast. We went out on the terrace together to watch for the others' return.

We were soon joined by Mamma. Miss Perkins recounted what had happened. Mamma was in a terrible state. She sent Violette running to the vicarage with the news and to ask Mr Gareth to come as soon as he could. Miss Perkins was now going through her version of the accident for the second time, whilst I, crying for reasons best known to myself and which they interpreted as shock, did my best to keep my head clear and my thoughts in order. I think that for one brief instant I was even wicked enough to hope that Ursula was dead.

And when I saw the group arrive, Joseph and Kenneth bearing the stretcher and Henry and John leading the horses, I thought for one sickening instant that my wish had been granted.

Ursula was still dead-white and as inert as she had been when we'd left her. Mamma had her transported to my room, where we laid her out on her bed and waited for Dr Hunt to come. He had been summoned at the same time Violette had gone after Mr Gareth. Miss Perkins brought smelling salts and vinegar, made compresses, and applied them to Ursula's forehead. And Mamma sent Kenneth to fetch a small tumbler of spirits which she poured with difficulty between Ursula's tight-drawn lips.

After a while some faint trace of colour came back into her cheeks and she opened her eyes. She looked wildly around her. The moment I dreaded had come. But I could not budge, paralysed with fear of what was sure to follow.

Kenneth had gone out of the room. Ursula's eyes roved from one face to another, and when they alighted on Angela, who was watching her intently, her body began to shake violently and she started to shriek, pulling up her clothes and putting herself in an indecent posture. "The snake!" she screamed, "the snake! I have the snake in my belly! It's a child, a man's child! A shrivelled old man's child! I did it, I did it, I did it! I hate her, I'll have it, give it to me, give me Kenneth's thing to put inside me!..."

I saw Angela blush a deep red and fly from the room.

Mamma and Miss Perkins listened, aghast, spellbound. The string of incoherent obscenities worsened and went on and on. They suddenly remembered my presence and bundled me out of the room. Soon afterwards, Miss Perkins followed me, her face flushed purple with shame. For a minute she was almost speechless with embarrassment until, brushing aside the thought that I might have understood something of what Ursula had said, she declared that the poor girl was very sick and plainly delirious, and that the best thing I could do would be to go down quietly and stay in the library and offer a prayer to the Good Lord for her recovery.

I did what she told me to do, seeking refuge in the darkened room where once – years ago, it seemed – Kenneth had tried to misbehave with me. There was the leather sofa. There was his book about liberty.

So many thoughts dashed through my mind that, finding it unendurable to be alone with them, I went out and hid myself in the shrubbery along the drive. I saw Dr. Hunt arrive. Ursula's father came a few instants later.

I stayed there until I heard Miss Perkins calling for me. The bell had not yet rung for lunch and I had no idea what time it was.

Miss Perkins told me that the doctor had diagnosed a grave case of concussion, and had ordered as much quiet as possible That was why I had heard no bell rung.

It was a very quiet meal we had. Mamma looked ill. Angela and Kenneth appeared quite suitably downcast. Miss Perkins, dear Miss P., put up a brave but unsuccessful front of small talk.

I spent the afternoon wandering around the grounds, endeavouring to chase away the thought of the awful moment when, no doubt about it, dear Mamma would speak to me about Ursula. How I envied Angela's diabolical power to lie and even to blush at will!

When I came back Ursula had been moved to the spare

room which gives out on the north side. The room next to Miss Perkins'. A nurse is to come from London tomorrow.

Violette told me that Mamma, the vicar and Dr. Hunt had spent nearly two hours shut up in Mamma's boudoir, but that she could not hear what they were saying because they were whispering all the time... She said she had tried to go 'and have a peep' at Ursula, but Ursula's door was locked and Miss Perkins caught her and stopped her and asked her what she meant by this, trying to come in without being asked? Miss Perkins had said it was all very 'bizarre'. And Violette had replied that she was worried, she was, and that Watson had heard some awful screams and words he thought no nice young lady ought to be saying or could even possibly know of. It was all so silly, Violette and Miss P., arguing about it. I tried to hide my own distress by dabbing at my eyes with my handkerchief and Violette, good-hearted girl that she is, told me not to worry, she'd seen worse than this and she wasn't so old, these 'English people and their riding'. And Miss P. said hush.

Not knowing what else to do, I went up to my room. That's how I got here. I am still here writing all this down in my diary. I can't explain why I'm doing it... or why I do anything. Perhaps I find some strange kind of solace in being able to put everything down in black and white so that, at least, it exists on paper. For I'm not sure it exists in my mind. And, too, my diary already contains so many horrors, that it cannot hurt to add a few more that I am writing of my own free will instead of being constrained.

Anyway, I don't care anymore. I haven't any friends. My diary is something at least.

Later.

Angela has just been in to see me, asking me if Mamma has questioned me about Ursula's accident or about anything else. She seemed very cocksure, absolutely unperturbed and left soon afterward, telling me to pull myself together. "It's not over. There'll be a denouement."

I have just seen her (from the window) go off across the lawn for a walk with Kenneth. They look as though they haven't a care in the world!

Miss Perkins has just come up to say that Mamma is

waiting for me in her boudoir. This is the end.

Late at night.

I think I'm saved!

Yes, dear Mamma received me in her boudoir. She was lying on her chaise-longue. I know that I looked pale and shaken and my mind was in such a state of turmoil that I wondered how I should ever be able to face up to the ordeal that I was certain was awaiting me.

Mamma instructed me to sit down on a chair opposite her. After a short silence, during which I felt sure the pounding of my heart was shaking the whole room, she began to talk, choosing her words with care.

She told me that Ursula was very sick. Dr. Hunt had said that the accident had deranged her mind and produced a very serious form of delirium. She said that the poor girl was temporarily out of her mind – that could not be doubted. "For, as you will surely agree, Victoria, what she said was pure nonsense, stuff and nonsense concocted out of whole cloth."

She was looking steadily at me while she spoke. But at this point she averted her eyes and a deep colour spread through her face and down upon her neck.

I pretended not to notice, pulling at my damp handkerchief. Seeing she expected an answer, I said: "Yes, Mamma," in a low voice.

It was an answer that meant nothing. However, it was all she wished to hear and sighed with relief. Then she resumed:

"Ursula is leaving tomorrow, as soon as the nurse arrives. She will be taken to London where she can be properly looked after. I hope you will remember Ursula in you prayers, for the Devil in his wickedness cares not whom he strikes down. You are not to see her," she went on, "between now and the time she leaves. There is no reason why you should – I forbid you to do anything that might cause her harm. No visits at all – Dr. Hunt has ordered that, no visits even from her dearest friends until she is better. Please stay out of the north wing. Any noise will be harmful."

I answered as I had before.

Satisfied as to my submission and my apparent lack of

curiosity, she then enquired about the accident. I repeated precisely what Angela had told me to say, ending my story in an explosion of sobs for having to look dear Mamma straight in the face and tell her such a long lie. And all the time she heard me out in perfect faith. I felt as if my heart would break.

She called me to her and, after consoling me, suggested that we two kneel down right away and say a prayer for Ursula.

While we were still on our knees, Miss P. knocked at the door and came in before Mamma had time to answer. She seemed to be in a terrible state – Mamma, I mean, and Mamma went straight out of the room.

Maybe Ursula has started to scream again.

I think that was what brought Miss Perkins in while we were praying.

The vicar came back this evening, but did not stay to supper. I met him on the staircase. He looked so distraught he did not seem to recognise me, but rushed out of the house as if pursued by the Devil himself.

Miss P. did not come down. Mamma told us she was devoting herself to caring for Ursula.

Angela and Kenneth, as I expected, seemed quite their natural selves. They maintained a conversation of sufficient sobriety to suit the circumstances. That certainly met with Mamma's approval, for she later thanked them for being so helpful to her in her affliction.

I was glad to be granted permission to go to bed early... Oh, how I wish I were like them! But I am, in a way...

Still, though, I am the victim of guilty feelings. If only I weren't!

Angela has just been in, as I finished writing. Kenneth was not with her. She explained his absence by saying that we ought to be prudent for a while. "See whether you can't control yourself, Victoria. By the way, your mother is in a shocking state. It's worse than I'd realised or than perhaps you do. She tried to question me about Ursula. It was all so easy. I just pretended to be an idiot. And, I tell you, I thought the old fool was going to perish from embarrassment!" With that Angela started to laugh. Tears rolled down her cheeks.

I don't know whether it was from relief, or because my

nerves are quite shattered, but to my utter horror I found myself laughing too. Some of my tears have dropped on the page.

monday, the 23rd

My darling Kenneth has been up to London and has brought me back another diary, identical to the one Mamma gave me. We found the name of the shop before he left. There is a little label inside. And Kenneth duplicated it.

We have agreed it would be a splendid idea if I were to fill in a good bit of it just in case Mamma should ask to see it one of these days. It's a very tedious piece of work, but I've gone thirty pages, and they're all so dull, so dull!

Ursula has been gone for ten days now. Mamma has asked us not to mention her, saying that the subject causes her much chagrin that she would prefer not to be reminded... The vicar has gone too. He will stay in London for a while, so as to be near Ursula. A young man is coming to replace him during the interim. But we haven't seen him as yet.

It's drawing towards the end of July. Then there will be August, most of September and... Angela has promised to show me tonight just for what purpose she wears the corset with the pointed tips over her breasts...

linda's strange vacation

chapter one

Linda arrived at her uncle's villa. A splendid sun paved a golden pathway to the white stucco mansion gleaming like a clean sheet under a soft blue sky. The young girl's eyes sparkled in the yellow day that poured its transparent veil of gold over the rocks, the joyful pines and the dappled sea. One week of vacation, one long relaxful week, had just begun.

"Here we are." Lola waved. She met the youngster at the station in her small sports car.

Linda had not met the blonde woman before, and she was not at all surprised. Her uncle Arthur changed his mistresses often, and this did not go without notice in the family. Despite their

attempt at hiding their shock at his behaviour, it managed to blurt out at the most unexpected moments. The family was composed of uncles and aunts. Their parents were dead, but an inheritance saw them through the more troubling aspects of their material existence. Even Linda was fortunate in being protected by a small annuity which not only gave her a college education, which she was now undergoing in a girl's school near London, but also offered her independence and a certain ease of mind. She had been receiving the consoling sum of some £125 since the age of ten. It was enough to permit her to expand her wings and yawn without a true worry in the world. If she needed more, there was always uncle Arthur and the others.

"Oh, I like this auto." These were her first words opening the conversation which had to begin at one time or another. She smiled at Lola in an effort to win the woman's friendship.

Lola was the first to climb out of the late model two-seater. She moved with alacrity and pride. She was only wearing a pair of shorts, cut extremely high and showing a lovely pair of bronzed legs, long and shapely. A mere blouse which had been negligently buttoned could not hide her luscious solid breasts, almost popping out of her opened sporty chemise.

Instinctively Linda compared her own 'quality' with that of her companion, whom she estimated to be about twenty-five years old. She had been complimented on her beauty many times, although there were those horrible low whistles she loathed in the streets of London. After all, they were compliments in a way. Feeling appreciated by all, the significant and the insignificant, was a source of well-being and assurance for the young girl. Naively and a little fearful, she wondered whether she would not appear too thin in contrast to her uncle's favourite, especially when she put on a bathing suit. The idea was quickly dropped as Lola signalled her to follow. Valise in hand, she stumbled after Lola toward the house.

"You'll like it here. You'll see." The young woman opened the door and continued to praise the merits of the locale. "There isn't a house around for miles. The beach on rocks are so deserted that you can go in bathing completely nude."

Linda's eyes slipped to the floor on the last hanging words of the sentence. She felt that Lola had brought them out as a jibe, but then she pinched herself for groping with her hypersensitive imagination.

She smiled back timidly. Her eyes caught the steel glance of the handsome woman. Linda was able to visualize Lola's superb body perfectly modelling the deserted beach with its bronze-golden tint.

Her mental picture was diluted when a boy rushed out of the house without a word or gesture. He was clothed in scanty bathing trunks and a towel thrown over his left shoulder. His aspect was young, perhaps he was fifteen or so, and his body had a feline grace that was exhibited in his slightest movement.

Lola called to him and asked him to come back for a moment.

"Here is your cousin Robert, Linda. Come here, Robert,

and say hello to your cousin."

Linda had only seen Robert once in her life. She was about nine at the time and he was five or six. Their infantile capers did not register in their memories. Robert was the only child of one of Linda's sisters, a half-sister on the part of her mother who had been married and divorced four or five times. Uncle Arthur was a brother of her mother, and, in a way, a chip of the old block.

She barely remembered the young lad.

"Hi there," Robert said approaching his newly discovered cousin. Linda noticed that the boy had a peculiar ironic smile which curled his lower lip. His eyes switched from her to Lola and then he looked her up and down as though he were measuring her for a beauty contest.

"Did you have a good trip?"

It was hard to know just how to take him, so Linda responded as politely as she could. There was no sense making enemies over a simple question, however tainted it may have seemed.

"Oh, yes, thank you. This is a magnificent place. I think I shall like it here."

"You'll see that it is even better than you might imagine." He literally twitched with irony and his smile broadened.

"Why don't you come for a swim?" he proposed affably.

Lola interjected with her right as an adult seeing things in their proper proportion.

"No, wait awhile. Linda has only just arrived. We'll see you later. Is Arthur in the library?"

"Gee, I don't know. The last time I was in there I didn't see him."

Lola took Linda's hand and led her away from the chipper, ironic puppy. Robert had a tendency to be a little heavy in his humour and Lola walked out or turned her back when she sensed he was on the verge of playing the wise-guy.

"Come along," Lola said with a wholesome winning smile. "I'll show you your room."

Once alone, Linda arranged her belongings neatly, and every now and then she looked out of the half-opened window.

Linda's Strange Vacation

The view was magnificent. There was a scent in the air that she rediscovered. It had been three years since she inhaled that marvellous perfume of the sea and pines combined. The woods buzzed with the sound of a million happy insects.

She laid her swimming suit out on the armchair by the window. It was a small two-piece affair, brightly coloured. From her suitcase she took her toilet articles and placed them on the glass ledge in front of the mirror.

Linda thought of the quaint villa and of the few rooms she had seen. It was curious to see the first-floor lined with bedrooms and she immediately thought of the Walpole Inn she had stayed at during Christmas time. She still hadn't seen the library, the kitchen or the maid's room.

Suddenly someone knocked on the door, and opened it without waiting for a response. It was Lola.

"Are you ready?" she asked. The bronzed-skin women was wearing a green beach-robe which was slightly wrapped at the waist by a simple cord. Linda saw Lola's splendid muscular legs and noticed that she was wearing a tiny bikini that barely hid her pubic hair. The upper part resembled a thin mask and failed to conceal the round ample breasts. The points of her nipples stood brazenly firm in the small pockets of the meagre bra.

"I'll be ready in a jiffy," Linda reassured Lola.

. "Good. Don't rush, we have time." As she smoked, Lola stretched out on the bed and brought out a pack of cigarettes from her robe pocket as well as a gold-plated lighter. She lit her cigarette and inhaled deeply.

"Oh, excuse me. You don't smoke, do you?" Lola had forgotten that she was with an adolescent adult.

"No, I don't smoke. Well, that is, I smoke in college once in a blue moon. You know how it is?"

Linda began to get undressed slowly. She was rather shy and not used to having another person in the same room when she stripped down. Even at school, where she had a private room, she locked the doors when she undressed.

It was true, however, that recently at school a sense of intimacy had grown between her and her mates, and she took more liberties than she had ever done before. Linda didn't want to give the impression of being a recluse. She decided to undress as though she had been doing it all her life in front of friends. Lola was a friend, or at least, she hoped she was going to be one.

All in all, Linda was intimidated. She might not have been, but the continual look that Lola gave her troubled her. The eyes of the lounging woman scrutinized her and they were filled with a glint of curiosity and mystery.

Just when Linda got down to her panties and bra, Lola leaned on her elbow and whispered.

"You're remarkably well-built for your age. You're just sixteen, aren't you?"

Linda, without answering back, turned her head away timidly. It was a gesture in the vague hope that not seeing, would mean not being seen. A stupid illusion of course. But those eyes haunted her and she didn't know quite what to make of them.

She deliberately turned her back to hide her sex as she slid off her undies. Little did she guess that Lola had a perfect view of her tufty triangle, that mass of curly hair that shielded her vulva, by taking advantage of the mirror over the dressing cabinet. Linda, feeling quite protected, slipped off her bra and revealed two remarkable young breasts. They were vibrant and alive with their two rose buttons standing cutely up in the warm summer air. The young girl reached for her bathing suit, still avoiding the glance of the intruder who she was sure was scoping her intently.

She had just placed her hand on her bathing suit when a hand touched her shoulder. It rolled down her back trembling and the touch electrified her.

"What's wrong, Lola?" she asked in a troubled shrill voice with her heart beating quickly.

"Nothing. Nothing at all." Lola's voice was low and hoarse.

She placed her arm around Linda's thin waist and brought her to the bed. The young girl was forced to give into the strange cajoling. Suddenly she found herself stretched on the bed besides the perfumed Lola.

The suddenness of this outrageous action, if that was

what she could call it (it may have been a playful act and she would be sorry to be so prudish), caught Linda by surprise and knocked the wind out of her.

She was flat on her lovely back gazing into the large warm eyes of the brown-skinned hostess. Lola's hand wandered over the quivering torso and her fingers played with the belly button and skimmed down to the fuzzy bush that Linda had deemed as sacred territory.

Seeing that the young lass was paralysed with apprehension and fear, Lola placed the same hand, that roving tinkling hand, on the girl's burning cheek. Linda was momentarily released from her sudden scare.

But Lola had not finished fumbling with the intricate and substantial sectors of the young girl's torso.

Her hand cupped a breast and her long painted fingernails tickled a nipple.

"We ought to be good friends, don't you think so?" she said softly in the same low voice that had begun the interlude.

She lowered her face toward Linda's. The girl remained petrified, but managed to close her eyes in escape. A pair of mature lips brushed the side of her mouth and then found the ample, dry, trembling heart-shaped mouth. A warm tongue, sleek and humid, tried to invade the adolescent's oral reaches. But Linda clenched her teeth, and Lola's impetuous tongue had to meet the obstacle of lovely white enamel.

But Linda could no longer resist the strange sensation that afflicted her all at once. Her mouth opened and her warm breath was met by a seeking tongue which explored the interior of her fresh-rose mouth. The hapless girl felt a hand crawl down her back and grip one of her buttocks. Long fingers encircled her vagina and frictioned the entrance. Linda sighed and the sound astonished her. It had been a long time since she had experienced this odd sensual flame rise in her body. She was troubled, afraid, but happy. It would be impossible for her to resist this voracious woman, who was taking possession of her as one captivates and tames a young animal.

It took her a couple of seconds to realize that she was alone on the bed. Lola had sprung up, brusquely interrupting her caresses. Linda felt neglected. Perhaps another time... but she was being silly and loathsome. Lola extended her arms and it was obvious that she had forgotten everything. She handed Linda her bikini.

"Come. Let's go. The sea is awaiting us." Walking side by side, Linda couldn't help thinking of what had just transpired a few seconds ago in her bedroom. The young girl had never had any sexual rapport. She was a virgin for man and woman. It was true that one night at college, a friend of hers playfully scrambled into her bed, and after some brief words interjected by guffaws and smiles and raw jokes, the friend began a series of caresses that went a little bit further than those of Lola's, but Linda had forgotten about it. Besides, her friend had not made any real impression on her and she tired easily of the slobbering kisses and inept handling of her lower body. Of course, she never was really sure whether that was just a tickling game in fun or the beginning of a rude adventure. Anyway, it had nothing to do with Lola. Lola was different, and horribly dominating, and at the same time terribly attractive.

A swift shiver stimulated Linda's slender backbone.

"It's over there where we usually bathe." Lola pointed to an obscure hidden cove. Linda felt her long handsome fingers once more on her shoulders, only this time they were not insisting, unfortunately.

The sea licked the red rocks with her white frothy tongue. The cove appeared deserted just as Lola described it. Linda was unable to resist the temptation of cooling her toes in the ocean. She threw down her large beach towel and ran to the brim of the water. Lola disrobed herself of her cumbersome apparel and followed the lithe, graceful girl.

Linda watched the well-rounded muscular body plunge into the surf. She admired Lola, whose marvellous body dripped with foam and cool sea. The woman came back to the water's edge and Linda saw how little she was covered by the scanty bikini. She appeared as a goddess coming from the sea with her long hair dripping and her svelte body outlined against the horizon. Oh, how she loved those buttocks, round and harmonious.

Instinctively Linda took Lola's hand.

"Let's take a dip together," Lola proposed.

Lola looked at her with the same fire that she had in the bedroom. A bizarre laughter crept over her lips and resounded in her superb chest as she brushed her long hair aside.

"You're still a virgin, isn't that so?" She didn't give Linda a chance to respond, but with one scoop of her hand she sprinkled the youngster with salt spray.

Linda was bewildered by the audacious question and she turned away to get a breath of air as another blast of sea water got her on the face and neck.

Finally she plunged in and the two swam together for a few yards. They gurgled and plopped around like two playful dolphins. They tickled each other and laughed and shouted like two happy children.

Lola had a powerful crawl stroke and she practically swam circles around little Linda. It was quite natural for Lola to be a good swimmer, Linda thought, for hadn't she the privilege of living by the sea eight months of the year? Linda showed her sportive best, and managed to do fairly well alongside the husky tanned siren.

They swam softly and evenly for about fifteen minutes. Lola noticed that Linda was tiring and she headed for shore. They reached another small inlet bordered by shrubs and deep-green pines. Lola waded ashore.

Linda staggered after her, completely out of breath, puffing happily.

"Say, you swim quickly."

"Not so badly." Lola responded modestly stretching her body from side to side to attain some warmth from the slightly cool air. The sun peeked out from a white passing cloud and appeared in the azure blue.

"How about some sun for awhile?"

Linda was already face down in the warm white sand. She watched her companion take off her bikini, shedding the two brief strips to reveal a torso completely browned with health-giving colour.

For a while, the adolescent couldn't take her eyes off the dark tanned nipples that extended at the end of Lola's ample breasts. Once her eyes did leave that fine proportion of bodily splendour, they roamed down to the triangle of hair that covered Lola's lower pelvis. It was light-brown and frizzled due to the sharp rays of the sun.

The tuft of hair gave her a marvellous animal quality. It demonstrated her vigour. Yes, the superb nest was her animal fur and it dripped with the last drops of the sea that melted on her warm, delicious torso.

The two women remained in the sun quietly. Not a word was spoken and they listened to the lapping sound of the surf.

Linda lay on her belly scanning the marvels of sun-worshipping Lola, who was stretched on her back in all her nude glory.

The young girl was surprised to see her own hand, as though guided by an unknown sorcerer, rubbing leisurely up against Lola's thigh.

Linda held her breath, but Lola didn't move. She wasn't sure if she was suffering from sunstroke or a rash impulse, but her hand kept moving along the thigh until it reached the borderline of Lola's pubic hair. She felt as though a wonderful current were passing through her fingers into the very veins of her body.

Boldly, Linda moved in on her friend who received her in her arms with a wide sensual smile. Suddenly the two women were startled by some voices coming from the brush.

Linda sprung to her feet, her face red with shame. Had someone seen them together? She was still inhibited by her bourgeois education. Lola merely looked around tranquilly while seated on her fabulous rear and two elbows.

"That's probably Robert and Alice. They really are like two overheated dogs the way they go at it." She seemed to visualize the young couple as an engaging smile formed around her mouth. "What are they doing back there?" Linda suspected what they may be doing, but she wanted to hear it from Lola's own lips.

"But, my dear, it's quite simple. Robert is just fornicating with our adorable maid. I must say that for a boy of his age he isn't lacking in certain qualities. As for that matter, Alice isn't either."

She giggled and smiled as she listened to the muffled voices with their effortless moans from behind the foliage.

Linda was dumbstruck and she couldn't find the courage to return to the outstretched position she had taken on the warm, form-fitting sand. Lola jerked her head up at once and concluded:

"Come along, we'll surprise them. The naughty children. For shame." She sprung to her legs with a teasing expression on her face.

She took Linda by the hand and practically dragged her by force to the wooded area. Linda followed like someone in a lethargic state, who vaguely has the sensation that something strange is going to happen.

At the brink of the pines, Lola pointed to a spot that was encircled by brush. She put her finger to her lips to signify that she wished the utmost silence. They both tip-toed forward cautiously, moving in on their objective.

All at once Lola threw herself to the ground as though she were performing a military manoeuvre. Linda imitated her, even though she was startled and rather fed up with the total aurora of secrecy.

Then through a clump of thinned-out bushes, she managed to see Robert and a winsome young girl in an odd position for two youngsters such as they. Lola was right. They were behaving in a most obscene fashion. Robert was straddling the girl as though she were a dog or something. Linda was surprised to see her on all fours. Robert was merciless in his push-pull, cork-snapping movements. The young maid emitted several cries. It was difficult for Linda to distinguish whether those cries were of pain or of pleasure.

Linda was transfixed to the spot. She was positively excited by these new erotic scenes. She said to herself that they were devastating, to say the least. With her right hand she brushed some drool away from her lips. Lola noticed her gesture and almost began to laugh.

"But he's putting it..." Lola covered her mouth to keep her voice under control.

"No, my pet. He isn't buggering her, as your boyfriends in London probably use the term, he's making love to her roman fashion. Of course, you don't know what that is?"

Lola gingerly stripped Linda of her bikini. Linda was perplexed. It was impossible for her to cry out for fear of disturbing the others. Oh, what a ridiculous situation she was in. But the adept hands of the undulating Lola brought about a new perspective to her limited horizons. When Linda turned to reproach her friend, she remarked that Lola's eyes were almost blood-shot. It had come about all of sudden as though she were stricken by some unknown condition – or passion.

Her hand went straight to Linda's pussy and the tips of her long supple fingers worked miracles in that lubricious region. Soon she had Linda panting and straining to keep from being found out by Robert and Alice. But anyway, they were humming their own tune, and it is a hundred to one that they would have heard.

Linda let herself be masturbated while looking onto the magnificent show in front of her. Good naturedly she thought of Lola. Poor Lola was being left out. So Linda, thoughtful and courteous, placed her trembling hand down on the curly blossom that thinned out at her companion's belly. The two women began to masturbate each other slowly, while watching a pair of minors screw with the rhythm of perfect professionals.

It wasn't long before Linda felt a wave of pleasure descend upon her. She sensed a multitude of warm prickly thrills invade her wet sex, which was carefully being explored by the diligent Lola.

She started to groan, but held back as best she could. Her teeth were sealed together. *Do unto others as you would have them do unto you.* The proverb took life and Linda gently fingered her impetuous companion.

Lola's thighs were divine. They were the thighs of a woman who was voluptuous and mighty. Linda did not feel disgusted by the act, which surprised her no end. Abstractly, if she had thought it over when alone, she would have berated herself a thousand times for being so low and uncouth, but this very real performance delighted her. She clutched at the thighs.

Lola licked the adolescent's belly all over, and then her big mouth hovered in the region of the breasts. The lips nipped at the left teat and then opened wide and engulfed the defenceless breast.

The husky woman sucked on one nipple and fingered the other. Then she switched over, and this excited Linda to the point where she thought, she thought... well she didn't think, she just drifted into a vague emulsion of sensations. She could not say where she was or why, or what she was doing. The young girl's eyes rolled in her head like two agates would in a pin-ball machine.

Her teats were being licked, sucked and massaged frenetically, while on the other side of the bush Robert and his little waif ignored the nearby presence of the passionate intruders.

The two teenagers were well on their way to reaching a paroxysm stemming from their rife and energetic gestures. They were coupled together like two little puppies who have just learned to screw and are highly delighted with their find.

To and fro they rocked, and Alice got wetter and wetter, and Robert, the active one, got hotter and bigger. It was just a matter of seconds now. Then the cataclysm erupted. Robert felt the veins in his stiff cock shake with panic. His loins swelled and the head of his penis dribbled its first throbs of white liquid. Alice felt heat in the region of her vagina. A heat that stirred a melting pot of wild sensations. She was building up to the explosion.

Robert inundated her pussy with spunk, and the soaking hole pressed back and forth, clenching and throbbing like an underground earthquake. Curly-headed Alice flopped to the ground, her head crashing in the sand under the weight of the fatigued lad. A thin thread of saliva poured from her mouth and trickled down her chin.

Linda puffed and gritted her teeth and let out an *ohhhhhh... ahhhhh...* that would have been heard by the others if they had not been so tired and *ohhing* and *ahhing* themselves in the last throes of orgasm. A viscous fluid flowed from Linda's hot, wet pussy. It trickled down her thigh unerringly to the sand, which thirstily absorbed the juice of her first real sexual climax.

Lola, the silent one, had come twice. Elegant, discreet and seeking pleasure at every turn, she held her joy for herself.

Perhaps she even longed for a third orgasm as her head buried itself between Linda's thighs. A tongue snaked out and lapped up the delicious nectar of the young girl, who was barely recovering her wits.

Linda watched Robert and Alice through her dream-weary eyes.

"Oh, Robert, my lovely boy." Alice's voice was shaky and she had difficulty getting her wind back.

And the little maid wasn't even looking at her handsome knight with his pink cock growing soft. He was flat on his back exhausted, and she was lying face down. But this awkward position didn't prevent her from toying with his limp dick.

"Now, what's the matter? Haven't you had enough? I'm going in the water."

"Oh, you're awful," Alice chided. "When you've had it and no longer want it, everyone else has to cede to his highness. It isn't fair."

"But that's not true, my little sweet. You can always get it *somewhere* in our household. Isn't there Lola or uncle to do you justice?" He struggled to a sitting position.

Linda turned toward Lola and her face showed a questioning perplexity. Lola simply smiled and stroked her hair.

"Your uncle? Why, I had him on top of me all night..." sighed Alice.

"And you didn't like it?" asked Robert.

"I'm not talking about that. But I prefer you, and I know whom you prefer. It's Lola. Just because she is more experienced and knows too much for her own good... And now your cousin Linda has arrived. You'll probably be after her, won't you?"

Linda listened attentively. She fidgeted behind the leafy plants, earnestly waiting for Robert's answer.

"Who, Linda? Come to think of it, I'd like to get to her before my uncle does. It would be funny, that." He laughed aloud. "Just think, and she's a virgin too."

"She's not bad," admitted Alice.

"Very nicely built, to tell the truth." Robert contemplated his future victim. That is, he saw her in his mind's

Linda's Strange Vacation

eye and hadn't the slightest idea that she was hearing every word, flat on her belly a few yards away.

Linda turned red. Only she could know how to take his remarks. Was it a pleasant compliment, or did she feel annoyed? Time was to judge – and witness an impending scene.

Lola and Linda snuck away as silently as they had arrived. Both were feeling the wear and tear of their little peek-a-boo session. Yet neither regretted it, by the happy smile that flushed on their faces.

◆

An hour later in her room, Linda began to think. She sat on the edge of her bed and nibbled her nails.

Lola knocked on the door and informed Linda that lunch was not a very common thing at the villa. When one got hungry, he or she might take the lunch where ever he or she desired. She told Linda that uncle Arthur usually ate lunch in the library, where he worked on his latest novel until midnight.

"Arthur is a real recluse. He hates to see people during the day," Lola confided to Linda. "He takes a morning swim very early and then he closes himself off from the rest of the world in his sanctuary. If he wants something," she added with a bewitching smile, "he just rings. I'll bring you your lunch right here in your room, if you wish?"

Linda nodded that it would be very kind of her to take such pains. Lola assured her that it would make her happy to be of service to such a pretty newcomer to the 'establishment'. She was out of the room in a jiffy.

The adolescent, once more alone, tried to gather the remnants of her thoughts regarding the near hallucinatory events of that morning.

What troubled her the most was what Robert had said, about seeing who would get her first, he or his uncle. He was perhaps only kidding...

Linda hadn't seen her uncle yet, but Lola told her he kept to himself during the daytime. She was sure her uncle, who hadn't seen her for years, would cut a more interesting figure than that whelping conceited pup, Robert. But then again, uncle Arthur had Lola. At least that's what Alice said... And yet Lola apparently didn't care about these strange, amorous deviations.

Linda was lost, utterly lost in her thoughts, which seemed to get more entangled as she strained her pretty head when somebody knocked on the door.

"Come in," she said cheerily, thinking it would be Lola. The young girl wore only a pyjama top and had nothing to fear since the intimate barriers with Lola had been broken down.

The door opened – and Robert entered. Linda jumped off her bed and instinctively grabbed her pyjama top and clutched it to her chest and stomach to conceal her semi-nudity.

"Well here you are miss... cold cuts, salad, fruit, milk, bread and butter and banana cream pie. Doesn't that look good?"

"I thought Lola was going to bring me my lunch."

"Oh, I'm sorry. Lola is busy for the moment. Uncle Arthur wanted to see her. I thought, well, maybe we could lunch together. That way, we could get to know each other better."

Linda was suspicious of her cousin. Something ironic and suggestive sparkled in his young face.

"You mean we should eat here?" Linda questioned Robert.

"Why not?" Robert affirmed the decision by shutting the door behind him.

He put the tray on the floor and sat besides Linda. The young girl didn't move. She now knew too well what might follow. No, dear sweet cousin Robert didn't come up to just have lunch with her! She had no time to really reflect if the idea pleased her or not. She was quivering with emotion and that was the one thing she was aware of, just that and no more.

"You know it's a shame that we haven't gotten together before. Our family is really just about as scattered as leaves in the wind." Robert was trying to make conversation. Even with his cynical attitude and his budding knowledge of certain amorous pursuits, precociously developed, Robert obviously had little imagination when it came to seducing a girl. He was too classic in his approach. This is what Linda felt as she waited for the attack.

She was amused in a way. An idea flashed through her head. There was no sense in sitting there numb and blustered by this whole nonsense. She might as well play a part and really have fun. After all, she knew what the score was. She got up from the bed and paraded toward the window. Her pyjama top just barely covered her dainty buttocks. Linda made sure that she wiggled her hips provocatively.

"Sometimes it isn't wise to meet so early. Young people are rarely interesting," Linda teased as she pulled the curtain to one side.

"You mean you prefer older men. Well, it's my opinion..."

She didn't give him a chance to finish.

"I only mean what I said," Linda retorted haughtily as she leaned her head close to the window pane, as though interested in something not too far away. "What do you say we have some lunch. I'm starved."

"Starved for what?" Robert said sardonically.

Linda turned around and was startled to see Robert lounging on her bed. The horrid fellow had taken off his bathing trunks and his cock was protruding in the air. His eyes never left the lower part of Linda's fine torso.

"I couldn't help it. It's your rear that did it, honestly," The boy confessed.

"Well you've got a nerve." She looked at him, half-angrily and half-amusedly. Linda noticed the size of the penis that stuck rigidly up between his legs.

"You're not going to tell me that this is the first time you've ever seen a man nude?" He was cocky, and extremely sure of himself. "Come here and have a closer look. No-one is going to bite you."

She didn't feel like being intimidated by a mere boy who was two years younger than she. She strode over to the bed, trying to lend grown-up poise to her young age.

Robert grabbed her by the hand and drew her to the bed.

"Take a good look at it. Not bad. Don't you like it?"

She did, but she wasn't going to say so. The whole

procedure was wicked and entirely out of order.

"You think you're smart, don't you? Well, you're not a man even if you think you are. And with that thing, that small pencil you're so proud of..."

Suddenly he gripped her by the waist and she found her head two inches away from his glaring glans.

"That's the way I like to see you. Fresh and cocky like me. I can't take little girls that cry and give in."

She began to kick and fuss. She tried to struggle loose, but the boy held a firm grip. Robert was strong for his age. He lifted weights and swam all summer, thus his strength was much greater than hers.

"You are a real brat." She pounded on his chest and scratched his thighs. They wrestled on the bed like two young kittens. Linda had no idea that her pyjama top had fallen open and her body was exposed to her youthful assailant.

He exhausted her to the point where she was feeling the struggle dissipate in her limbs. A new sensation crept through her. A new, sensual feeling took possession of the young girl and slowly she submitted to the know-how and ardent desire of the youth.

There was no use shaming. She let herself go and abandoned herself to the zealous young Robert.

He hastened to put his lips to her multiple splendours. He kissed her pussy, her musky armpits, and her pert breasts. Suddenly she threw her arms around her cousin, half in submission and half in desire. She looked at him curiously as his mouth moved toward hers.

"Oh, Robert. What am I supposed to do?"

"Don't be a shrew. Kiss me, first of all."

They arched over the bed quilt in a long embrace. Their tongues entwined like two seething serpents while four hands moved quickly, impetuously, over their locked bodies.

Linda felt her cousin's hardened cock and a burst of feverish enthusiasm went to her head. Robert moved away from her, and for a moment she thought perhaps she had insulted him somehow in her ecstatic state of mind and body.

"And now, you're going to kiss it. Aren't you?" He wasn't asking. He was commanding.

"Yes. I want to kiss it. And I want to have it in my mouth, it's so handsome..." The young girl lowered her head toward the object of her admiration, taking the member between her lips. She sipped on the head of Robert's rampant penis. An unescapable odour went to her head and she was drunk with delight for many minutes after.

"With your tongue." Robert breathed heavily; Linda began to lick his cock gently up and down the shaft. *It tastes like salt,* she thought, and then she placed a good part of its length it in her mouth. Robert moaned and put his hands on her head. Linda was sucking him steadily and her tongue was active, heightening his pleasure.

Instinctively Linda pivoted so her thighs were near her cousin's head. She awaited Robert's initiative. It wasn't long before the panting lad had plunged his tongue into Linda's quivering cunt. His tonguing was more diverse and stronger than Linda's. The combination of his sexual response and her growing appetite worked wonders, and the two writhed with violent caresses.

Linda thought she was going to go mad with excitement. She nibbled at Robert's testicles, which hung down like two ripe fruit. She felt a certain charge shoot through the boy's body. He jumped violently and stiffened a bit.

"STOP, stop, or I'll come!" he cried.

Linda was disconcerted, with her mouth opened, not daring to recommence her voluptuous act. She was embarrassed and annoyed by this brusque interruption. But already Robert was leaning down and caressing her hair.

"I want this to be on you. Or more precisely inside you. Now we're going to make love together. Haven't you ever done it before?"

"N... N... No, never," stammered Linda.

But Robert wasn't listening. With one hand he spread her legs apart and slipped his cock inside her wet crack. He hadn't gone far when Linda's eyes bulged widely. But Robert pressed forward brutally. He had every intention of ripping home.

The young girl cried shrilly. She felt as though she were being knifed in two. A tear rolled down her cheek.

"Don't cry," murmured Robert... "Now you're no longer a virgin. Look, see. You're a grown-up now."

Linda felt a trickle run down her thighs. She feebly looked down at her shapely leg and saw a streak of blood flow irregularly along her soft skin.

"It hurts. Oh, what pain I feel." She was in tears out of suffering, out of shame and out of the sight of blood.

The boy withdrew his penis almost completely.

But it was only to dig it in farther. Linda let out a suffocating cry, but strangely enough the pain had dissolved and a sudden pleasure was enthralling her very being. A soft wave of sweet delight spread through her belly and fired her vulva. Robert meanwhile moved like a piston, well greased by the mixture of liquids that were pouring out of the depucelated virgin.

With each movement, Linda sighed her acquiesence to the handsome Robert. Welcoming every stroke, she felt her pleasure augmenting and she gripped Robert with all her strength as if she were afraid that the mounting joy would cease.

"Faster, faster Robert." She begged him to pulverize her bruised pussy. Then stars burst in front of her wobbly, dizzy head. A nebula of a thousand flames ignited, and she was at that glorious climax where the body plunges into a boiling pool of endless delights. Her movements now were quick and frantic, as though she were trying to prolong her ecstasy forever. Her lover dug into her to the root and ejaculated his hot sperm in a thick column. Linda felt the influx of the liquid and she contracted her muscles in order to milk dry his spasming cock.

They had matched one orgasm against the other. They had come together, as though they had been doing this sort of thing for years.

Linda let her legs fall apart, and she was totally free from shame. Later on, this attitude so deliberate in its manifestation surprised her and yet gave her a peculiar and new sense of pride.

Robert lay on top of her, quite fatigued. He had emptied himself like a trouper and he sprawled disjointedly over the limp form of his naked cousin.

A few minutes passed by, long and slumbersome. Linda slowly returned to reality as she disengaged herself from post-orgasmic torpor. She opened her eyes and the first thing she saw was Robert's lips crawling toward her cheek.

"How was it?" He smiled and wriggled into a better position with his head on her shoulder. "The act of love isn't too bad, is it?" "It's marvellous," replied Linda, who had tasted its pangs and happiness for the first time. "I never thought it could be like this. It is so sweet and sensual."

She stretched like a young kitten and her arms locked at the elbows. Her hands joined at the back of Robert's neck where her fingers spread through his curly hair.

"You know it's funny," Robert grinned and pecked her on the forehead... "It's the first time you've made love, and it's the first time that I've ever made love... with a virgin. That's funny isn't it?"

Linda wanted to know what it was like. Perhaps he wasn't satisfied. She had not really thought of what it was like for him; she had just experienced a thrilling ordeal, topped with the cream of pleasure.

"Was it any different?" She tried to catch his eyes.

"I'm not complaining. But listen, my dear cousin, you'll have to watch yourself here, and be cautious." Robert looked seriously at her.

She put her hand down toward her pussy and tried to keep the thick mixture of blood and sperm from staining the bedspread.

"Be cautious? Of what?" She seemed puzzled and really wanted to know what on earth he meant by all this.

"Come closer and I'll explain..."

At that precise moment the door opened and the two moved apart as Lola tip-toed into the room. The dark-skinned woman looked half-amused and half-serious. Linda didn't know how to take her, let alone how to act or find words to mutter.

She had forgotten that Lola would come back and she was taken aback by the unwanted apparition. She tried to crawl into bed as though she were trying to hide some evidence. Of course, it was of no avail, for the evidence was undisputedly in front of Lola. Robert didn't budge and Linda was astonished to see how casually he treated the whole affair.

He simply turned his head nonchalantly and said to the mistress (for Linda imagined her to be one):

"You're right in time to accompany her to the bathroom. That's a woman's duty, you know?"

Lola helped Linda out of bed as though she were ready to spank a naughty child. As Linda scrambled to her feet, Lola teased her ironically.

"Come along. We have to clean up. Now, aren't you a bad girl, so terribly pressed for it... Tsk, tsk, tsk... Ah, what a family." They reached the bathroom and Linda was suddenly downcast and felt certain recriminations. Lola was less talkative and scolding, but managed to add a few words.

"We'll have to hurry. After I soak you, you'll have to get dressed quickly. Your uncle wants to see you and say... *hello.*"

chapter two

A half an hour later Linda was seated in the salon waiting for her uncle. Lola had left her there, for she was busy in the kitchen preparing the night's dinner. Robert seemed to have disappeared all of a sudden. And as for all that, Alice, the maid, was no where to be seen.

The young girl felt tired, her head swimming in the clouds. She didn't realize it but she was suffering from the fatigue of love. However, a smile mounted to her lips while thinking of what she had just accomplished with Robert. Oh well, her virginity was something in the past. She wouldn't be able to use *that* as a defense for many valuable reasons. But Linda truly didn't have any regrets, since she had made a discovery that was altogether agreeable.

She was a woman now – well almost. It would be better to say that she was on the road to becoming one. Her imagination got the better of her. She wondered when her cousin would make love to her again. Maybe he would come into her room that night? In that case, she would remember not to lock the door. *Perhaps it will be Lola who will start up again?* Oh well, she would just have to wait and see what would happen... Her reverie was interrupted by footsteps coming from the library. The door opened and a man entered the salon. He approached with a smiling, delightful air.

"Ah, Linda. How good it is to see you. How are you? I'm glad to see you among us."

It was uncle Arthur alright. Linda noticed quickly, as he strutted across the room, his elegant walk and perfect masculine bearing. He was tall, sun-tanned, athletic with steel-grey eyes and greying temples. Uncle Arthur was exactly the type of man Linda thought of as being the perfect seducer. She even remembered him from her younger days. This splendid hunk of manhood had not changed. And maybe he had even improved. She found him very attractive. She greeted him with a timid strained voice as she put out her hand to be grasped warmly by the distinguished Arthur.

But Arthur paid no attention to the outstretched hand and he took the girl by her shoulders and kissed her lightly on the corner of the mouth. Linda turned beet-red as she inhaled the lavender perfume emanating from the tall man, who despite her blushing, was only her uncle.

Arthur looked her over, his hands never leaving her shoulders. He smiled.

"Well then. It is really wonderful to see you. You've gotten quite attractive, you know? Well, well, well... How do you like our house?"

"Oh, it's fine," Linda exclaimed. "I met Lola and Robert and we... and we..." She didn't know how to end her sentence. Was it possible that uncle Arthur knew how they had spent the morning and early afternoon?

"Let's just say that you got along fine together." Arthur helped her disentangle the sentence and straighten her thoughts out. Little did he know she was thinking quite well. It was only manipulating in a proper manner that concerned her.

"Tell me Linda? I know this is unusual to ask, especially the day of your arrival, but could you help me out? Lola is busy and Robert, well that rascal can never he found when someone wants him. You won't mind will you?" He smiled graciously.

"Not at all. But I don't know whether I shall be capable of doing what you wish. What is it, may I ask?"

"Oh, there's no mystery to it. I'll explain. Just follow me into the library."

Uncle Arthur led the way into the library taking long sure strides. Linda followed obediently. The library was paneled by dark mahogany. There were many books in the bookcases which ran across the room. She knew Arthur was highly literate and intellectual and she felt that she should watch every word. The windows were large and bordered by red-velvet curtains with a strip of white mousseline running down the edges.

The curtains filtered the bright sun and the room bathed its few pieces of furniture, a great table covered with papers, a large ample armchair, a divan in a melody of soft brooding colours.

Linda noticed a ladder which led to the stacks of books on the upper shelves.

"We'll here it is. My hide-away where I work. All you will have to do is bring the books I name so that I shall be able to take notes. That's easy enough isn't?"

"I think I'll be able to manage that alright." Linda laughed, apparently at ease for the first time. She was beginning to find her uncle warm and pleasing.

"How will I go about finding the book you want?" she asked, glancing at the many many shelves of literature.

"I have a method so don't worry about it. All the cases are marked alphabetically."

They began to work and Linda found that the job was easy and not bone-breaking at all. The only thing that presented a problem was climbing up and down the ladder. She wished that she had worn some slacks. It was embarrassing for her to climb that ladder with her legs pinched together.

"I can't find it," she declared, leaning far to the right and then to the left.

"Wait I'll help you," Arthur said courteously, rising from his armchair and moving to where she was.

Linda continued to look for the misplaced book, while below, her uncle gazed up her skirt, which was large enough to give the spectator a languorous view. The girl turned around and pretended to still be searching for the book, but she felt the penetrating glance of uncle Arthur and this unsettled her nerves. She was forced to keep her legs slightly apart to keep from losing her balance.

"You're right. I think I left that book in my apartment in the city. You can come down now." Arthur helped her to the ground as his strong fingers gripped her waist. She felt a chill run up her spine as his hands slid up to her bosom. When she turned around, she felt guilty for having such a horrid imagination.

Uncle Arthur thumbed his chin and murmured a few words.

"You are very pretty, my lovely niece, and you were

particularly attractive on that ladder. I must admit that you have splendid legs. It makes me realize that you have really grown up. It's silly of me not to have thought of it before."

She was flattered, turned red and spun in a half-turn. Linda knew these gestures were unbecoming of a 'grown-up'. Yet the presence of her uncle so close and his constant attention instilled a new sensation far different from the one she felt with Robert.

Uncle Arthur moved toward his desk. With his right hand outstretched he indicated a chair.

"Sit down Linda."

He scratched his head and it was evident that another idea was brewing in his intellectual mind.

"Better yet. Come and sit on the arm of my chair."

Linda's head bobbed up at this strange request. She flushed crimson with timidity.

"Come along and be friendly."

"Do you want me so close?"

"Of course." Arthur's smile had won her over. She had no choice but to have confidence in this handsome man who was, after all, her uncle.

Once seated, Arthur put his arm around her waist. And before she had a chance to jerk away, he had another hand half up her skirt where he was patting her thighs. Linda was troubled and she stiffened partly out of surprise and partly out of fright.

"I think it would be better if I left now," she murmured entirely without conviction. The poor youngster didn't want to disobey and yet...

As though he had not heard her remark, her uncle exclaimed in a vigorous tone: "You're not comfortable kicking around like that."

He was peculiar. Linda noticed it for the first time. His lips screwed up and his eyes grew feverish and even to a young girl as youthful as Linda, she knew it was the outward signs of lust. He became eager and restless and his tongue rolled over the corner of his mouth.

She had found that he had greatly changed in the span of just a few minutes. He was a veritable Jekyll and Hyde case,

Linda's Strange Vacation

but there was something amazingly attractive about him. His golden tan flushed and gave him added colour. His grey temples marked him as very masculine and resolved. Arthur's sinuous and strong arms were commanding and sure, despite their unleashed nervous energy, in grasping and capturing the delicious morsel who had come to live in his house.

Linda felt his warm breath behind her neck, between her hair and running lightly down her back. His hand roamed under her slip and toyfully tickled her pubic hair. Linda sensed a great probing thing throbbing near her asshole. He seemed to be juggling her on his lap as though he wanted to rip through her clothes. His member was violently searching, and for some reason she pictured a madman with a hammer.

Uncle Arthur almost wrenched the breath out her with his forceful grasp. When she turned to express her disapproval, she met a pair of eyes that glittered with fierce heat. She was spellbound and strangely enough attracted by this new face she saw. Her uncle almost foamed at the mouth as his right hand busied itself with the task of unbuttoning his trousers.

Linda almost leapt up but she was held fast. When she looked down at his lap a huge penis, rigidly erect, poked in the air. She had never seen anything like it. It was twice as big as Robert's both in length and diameter. She watched the purple head of this proud cock, with its slight opening. It pushed itself towards her face as though it were a canon ready to fire. Of course, she instinctively moved backward, but her uncle held her prisoner in his armchair. A lustful smile, triumphal and wicked, crinkled his face.

"Well, what do you have to say now, my little one? It's big and handsome. Isn't it nicer than the one that you put between your legs a little while ago with that untamed rascal Robert? But, by heck, I think your afraid. Why? It isn't going to hurt you, little dear. You'll have it anyway, and you'll be so happy about it when we're finished that I even think you'll ask for more of it. What do you think of that?"

While he was speaking, he was already caressing the open mouth of the young girl. It appeared as though she had already abandoned any idea of resisting she might have had. Linda leaned forward and gently nibbled on the head of

Arthur's penis, which had a strong odour that excited her. Her teeth inspired her uncle to grow even harder.

She had *some* experience... just that bit from the morning. And Linda planned on using it all. She remembered that Robert told her to use her tongue first of all, which she did, spiralling around the massive prick in barber-pole fashion. Her uncle plunged his weapon in her mouth as though it were made of rubber. Poor Linda almost suffocated.

"You like it, don't you?" he asked, a rhetorical question. His mood and excitement were so great that his powerful thrusts had Linda's face all red and her eyes closed to keep tears from flowing. Never had she endured such a ruthless attack.

"Suck well, my girl. Go on, do it well."

Defenceless Linda could hardly breathe, let alone answer back to the rampaging adult who, horror of horrors, was her uncle. Try as she would she could not get all of that phallus in her mouth, but she found energy enough to take as much in as she could and licked it clean with her flickering tongue. With a tremendous effort she was able to stretch her lips about half-way down the thick shaft. One of her hands was then guided to the spot where bristling pubic hairs, black as night, hid a pair of balls as large as lemons. Her hand cupped the heavy testicles and her trembling fingers began to stroke and massage them.

With various movements of her head, up and down and from side to side, she began to masturbate her uncle with mouth and tongue. Linda felt the veins in his cock throb and expand. The sudden expansion excited the girl and she became more and more audacious. Her hand grasped Arthur's penis as though she had been acquainted with it for a long time, and her tongue darted around the purple glans, which was oozing a thick white liquid ever so slowly. Linda began to bite on it as though it were good enough to eat.

Then his cock began to pulsate with a sudden spasm, and before Linda could think of what she might do under such circumstances, her mouth was full of salty, burning fluid which drooled from her bottom lip. She looked up bewildered and flushed. Uncle Arthur placed his hand over her mouth, preventing her from spitting it out. So it went down swallowed, mouthful after mouthful. It was strange to see the girl brimming over with his hot jism – there must have been a pint of it, or so it seemed.

Linda did not seem unpleased with the taste of Arthur's come. She even went back to suckling the phallus greedily, trying to get the last white drops out of it. It was though she were a baby calf trying to get at the dripping remainders of mother's milk.

When her feast finally came to a halt, she drew back and took a good look at the man, who was dropping in his armchair with limbs akimbo and his eyes half-closed in delirium.

"Little wench. You had me in the stars for awhile. I had no idea you were so handy with that lovely mouth of yours. And did you enjoy it?"

What could she say? She blushed, her eyes could not meet his inflamed eyes and so they remained downcast. The act had been accomplished and words, she thought, were useless. However, she managed to utter a few wise ones.

"If it pleased you uncle, it had the same effect on me."

They sat quietly for a few minutes and then Arthur's hand began to wander up Linda's thighs in the same direction. This time he pinched at her bottom and his finger came to rest on the pink rim of her asshole.

"No, don't touch *tonton!*" She jumped up and ran to the window. "Please don't touch it."

Arthur wondered about his niece. What was this 'tonton' business? Did she have an anal complex? He planned on finding out. He strode over to the door and locked it. When he came back to the centre of the room, Linda was sitting on the table, her bare legs offering an attractive sight.

"And now my darling, you're going to see something that will perhaps shock you and rob you of that snippy and carefree attitude you have." His voice grew hard and his lips turned cruel with a mocking air.

When Linda saw him close the door and lock it, she had already suspected that something unpleasant was in store for her. She thought of screaming out, but there was no one who would come to her rescue. But on second thought, what more could he do to her? She was too nervous to appreciate the situation for what it was worth.

Her uncle did not even take the trouble of placing his drooping cock back in his trousers. He walked to the window and closed the curtains and then came back to her.

"I was told that you were 'devirginized' this morning. It was just what I wanted to do myself. I was counting on it – but one can't have everything. In any case, there are parts of you that are still intact, and healthy, and virgin. Robert wouldn't have operated in two directions. There is a limit to the young lad's experience."

He noticed that Linda didn't catch on to what he was saying. He quickly put his hands on her legs and pulled aside her skirt. Uncle Arthur was in complete control of himself this time.

"I am speaking, my dear cousin, in terms that you will understand better... I am speaking of your 'virginal anus'."

Linda put her hand over her mouth in an effort to hold back a stifling cry.

"My what?"

"Yes, exactly, my dear. And I promise you that you will not get out of this room before you have given me your little flower of a hot pink asshole. I want *some* sort of pleasure today. Quick, get undressed."

Arthur had already unbuttoned his shirt. He rapidly peeled off his pants and shorts, preparing for what was almost a daily practice with him in his adult life.

Her uncle revealed two strong legs and a muscular torso. His chest was covered with dark crinkly hair the same colour as that outlined his huge sex organs. As he eyed Linda, who was undressing slowly with a contorted expression on her face, his cock bolted up like a flag-pole. In a few seconds his prick had once more taken on the respectable proportions of the last half-hour.

Linda seemed drained of all thoughts, and had no pluck to fight back with. She was incapable of making a gesture. Arthur's fierce eyes burnt right through her while the same cruel mouth twisted in delight and terrible passion.

"Ah, you don't want to behave, is that it? Well, we shall see about that. I'll have you just the same!"

She had not as yet taken off her blouse and Arthur, with one fell swoop of his large hand, ripped it from her body. Her eyes almost popped out of their sockets when he then did the same with her bra. Linda's pert breasts quivered in the air. Wild and hungry, uncle Arthur pounced on her and mercilessly bit into those two ripe fruits.

Linda felt the teeth marks and she cried out in pain. The sudden burst brought him back to his senses and he let up for an instant, looking strangely at the girl who dared to defy him.

With a thrust of his hand he ripped off her skirt, then put his fingers around the elastic waistband of her panties and snapped the cord, ripping flimsy material.

Linda was now completely nude. Her uncle leaned heavily on her, forcing her to arch over the table.

His weight and extreme passion crushed her and she felt the jabs of the many items that were scattered on the table. Bites and kisses were bestowed upon her mouth, neck, and breasts. Then uncle Arthur backed off for awhile and contemplated his victim.

"She's well-made, my little niece!" He laughed, speaking to himself. "Is she really a woman now? Do you know what one does to delicious little girls like you?"

With one hand he pushed her legs apart, and stabbed a finger brutally in her anus. Linda squealed, but her uncle pushed harder with his finger, pushing into her.

"Now, don't scream." He rubbed his cock against her belly. It was as hard as a policeman's baton. "What are you going to do when you have *this* up there?" He emphasised his words by applying pressure with his buried finger.

Linda screeched an 'ouch'. She was horrified by the thought that his big instrument would pulverize her tender rosebud. Even a finger hurt as it went back and forth. What would an enormous piston like his do to her? The idea made her faint. She spread her legs wider apart to relieve the pressure of the thick finger. Pleasure mixed with pain ebbed in the cells of her lower body. The tickling sensation close to her vulva was undeniable, agreeable in some ways though it plugged up her very tiny aperture. "You're beginning to like it, aren't you? Very well."

He withdrew his finger and inhaled with satisfaction.

"Come here. We're going to do it on the divan." He led her by her rump, which she found embarrassing to say the least.

He lay her on the soft divan. Linda felt the rigid cock against her body and awaited the tormenting moment, the moment when he would penetrate. She was sure he would be brutal about it, and it would all come about when she was least prepared for it. He was jealous of what Robert had accomplished with her and he wanted to be one up on his loathsome nephew.

She sensed his preparation, his heat and his terrifying, throbbing member. Then he leaned over his niece and urged her to open her thighs. She obeyed and watched his face sink like the sun as it buried itself in her pussy. His hot tongue soothed her cunt lips, which had been bruised by the assaults of cousin Robert. It was the first time she realized that this area still hurt.

Then he put his mouth at her anus, and penetrated with the tip of his tongue. Uncle Arthur was full of improvisations. She hoped that he meant his tongue and not his thing. Linda prayed that he would reconsider his terrible plan.

What he was doing to her now proved to be entirely to her liking. He licked around the rim and then tongued slightly in the hole like a timid bee. It sent chills of warm delight up and down her spine. She even enjoyed the chiding bites on her rump that caused her to squirm. Linda wiggled her buttocks, spreading wider in order to please her uncle, whom she hoped would spare her.

Arthur was drunk with the intoxication of love. He began to lick her furiously. Both the vagina and anus were neatly combed by his unfailing tongue, but the anus was particularly favoured.

Linda started to moan with pleasure. It felt good, but really good. Squeals of animal delight issued from her wet lips.

"Do you like that?" cried Arthur, with his face buried

between her musky buttocks.

"Oh, that's fine," murmured the ecstatic youngster. "It's delicious. I love it so much."

The uncle remained spellbound as though he were contemplating two gorgeous hunks of fruit. He squeezed the buttocks as though he wanted to rip them off.

"And now comes the fun. We are going to see whether you'll like what I am going to do."

Linda's mind reeled in a mad attempt to ward off what might be a true disaster. A sudden thought occurred to her. Perhaps he would be less brutal if she pretended that she wanted it as much as he. He might lose interest. It was worth taking the chance, for she had nothing more to lose.

"Do what you like... You can do whatever you choose, uncle dear." Somehow her voice sounded unassured and weak.

He waited for nothing more. He had the permission – and even if he hadn't it would have amounted to the same thing. Arthur turned her over on her belly, and her head was quickly buried in between her knees. Through her spread out legs she was able to see the enormous cock wend its way toward her rump. It rolled around as though it were getting its bearing and then it stiffened in aim and finality of purpose. At that moment Linda knew she was doomed. She closed her eyes and breathed heavily. Instinctively she recoiled and tried to dodge his thrust, but it was too late. He had already lodged the head of his cock in the tiny wet opening. A tear fell from the cheek of the unlucky adolescent. Arthur noticed the whimpering of his child-like niece, but it made no difference to his operations. He attacked for a second time, lubricating the anus with more saliva and an adept finger, easing it open. "You see, little doll, you'll never be a real woman until you're deflowered right here. It may just as well be me..."

And he proved what he meant. With one heave he burst through that tight band of flesh and into the entrails of his beloved niece. Linda let out a savage howl. She had never felt such a painful sensation before. It was a profound suffering that caught in her throat. A staff of masculine flesh had broken through her sphincter with all the animal force needed to rupture a tiny, undefended aperture.

Thoughts spun in her broken head. *That's not the way one makes love. He's trying to kill me.* Her body remained pinned to the divan, with her thighs spread wide apart and her face tormented and crushed on the pillow. Linda was in a stupor. The only reaction and return to life she could muster up was repulsion toward her uncle's biting embraces on the neck and his teeth marks against her mouth. He was horrid to her, she mused. Who could have such a wicked, monstrous uncle?

Uncle Arthur was only half inside the small opening. He still had his work cut out, so to speak, and he was never one who shirked a task, whether it was literature or love. For this man both of them intertwined, and drained his very senses.

He plunged once more, only more brutally, more indecently. Stretching her red, glistening ring to breaking-point, he managed to bury his prick to the hilt in the stricken girl, who seemed to bob and remain paralysed with her neck stretching taut and her eyelids tightly closed.

The grey-templed man accelerated his thrusts while he played with the wet-lipped cunt of his lovely niece. Linda was unaware, due to the violent pain, that she had two rectal orgasms. Only during the second one did the element of pleasure begin to enter into play. A strange smile crept over her like a light veil of soft silk.

Her uncle rolled on her like a rough sea captain, his pleasure as immense as the ocean and as joyous as a sky of deep azure.

"Tell me, Linda, does it still hurt? I think you are beginning to enjoy it. You're as wet as a little puppy... Come now, own up to it."

"I... I... I do like it. Yes... It's good." Her voice was wavering with a sensual shrill.

"My little pup, pup, pup." Her uncle whispered in her ear and then pushed up into the heart of her bowels and laughed heartily as though a victory had been won.

Linda moaned with the new onslaught of pleasure that filled her body. This time she felt that she was on the verge of having an huge orgasm. Stimulated and primed, she wished to carry the fuck to its ultimate glory. She took the man's testicles and adeptly toyed with them. She even pulled on them, indicating that he should not spare the rod to spoil the child. Linda wanted him deep, very deep within her.

Arthur was getting his just rewards now. He reeled with the throbbing sensation of pre-orgasmic pleasure, roaring with joy and impulsively biting into Linda's back as he hammered away in her asshole with his huge prick.

Linda felt her orgasm creeping up bit by bit, and then, to strengthen her own climax, Arthur unleashed his spunk in three mighty spasms, flooding her seething rectum. The young girl shook and hissed with pleasure as white streams of come poured down over her cunt-lips, dousing the expensive divan. Her guts were wounded, but her body had ascended to an unknown paradise.

Despite the ejaculation Arthur's cock stood rigid, as though it refused to acknowledge its diminishing powers. It remained lodged in Linda's anus as though it wanted to ride forever in that new tunnel of love.

Arthur was proud of his performance. He had far surpassed his brazen nephew. He withdrew his cock, dripping with sperm and wet shit, and placed it under the nose of his still-trembling niece. It was covered with a mixture of white, yellow and brown slime.

"Look at it Linda. Isn't it magnificent, covered with the shit of your asshole?"

Linda didn't answer, but she took a chance and fondled the semi-stiff member.

"Now, chicken dumpling, you're going to suck on it properly and clean if off. You're quite capable of doing such a thing with that pretty mouth of yours, aren't you?"

Linda was in such a feverish sensual state that she simply couldn't refuse such a request. She took the phallus by the root and shoved it between her lips. She lapped and licked and sucked, and uncle Arthur was enraptured by the marvellous job she did. After a certain time, she felt it become hard again. Of course, this excited her all the more. She even felt disposed to renew the love session, any way uncle Arthur wished to suggest. But Arthur pushed her away. It wasn't a vicious push, it was gentle and he smiled at the young apprentice.

"Take it easy. You're going to swallow me alive! I can

see that down deep you're a real glutton for this type of sausage. You're even more famished than your sister Brigette."

Linda looked at her uncle in great astonishment. She knew Brigette had spent a good part of her summer vacation at the villa. She had hardly seen her sister, who was a year older than she and was enroled in another college. Linda didn't have a chance to talk to her and find out what happened at the villa. It would have been helpful if she was warned in advance.

"You mean that with Brigette... it happened as well?"

Linda lay still, breathing deeply. Arthur put his hand on her breast.

"Just telling that story makes me excited. I think that I'm ready to make love again."

Arthur fell into the saddle without any trouble. Linda was lying back spread-eagled on the divan, wet and waiting. Apparently the story had made its effects on her as well.

"You're sure you don't want me to take you by the anus, first of all?"

Linda looked up at him and then lowered her eyes, showing him that she was his humble servant.

"Later on," she murmured softly, her eyes still glancing at the floor. "It still hurts... I would like to try... the other way first."

"Alright then. Open your legs up wide." Arthur's hands rubbed up and down the young body, moulding its form.

The young lass opened her legs as far as they could go and Arthur aimed his great prick at her dripping cunt.

"Now be careful, because this time you're going to feel it. I mean business. Prepare yourself."

And in one slip of his magic wand he was in her, snug and warm. Linda had the odd sensation that she was being devirginized a second time. She felt she was being invaded for good now, and with a cock worthy of mention. The neophyte was performing a real task this time. She tasted the hardened cock as it pressed to the very depths of her cunt. She thought, she cried, she moved to and fro and caught the rhythm of the staunch piston that powered into her with all its might.

She even took Arthur by his hips and made him abide to a movement that was closer to what she liked. Finally they synchronized their pace and were soon in perfect bliss, building and building to the supreme moment.

Linda reflected on how good it was. She pinched Arthur's rump and with another hand she squeezed his balls and the base of his cock and it throbbed like a huge muscle, which it most certainly was, raw and alive with animal force.

Her uncle mounted her brutally. His weight crushed her and he beat her with his feverish body. Arthur's stomach pushed against her young lower belly with all the force of tidal wave. But Linda, pushed backward on the divan to the point where her head dropped off the edge, didn't mind the attack one bit. The girl ate it up. She had wild thoughts about a bull, a sturdy bull raping her.

"My strong, wonderful bull." These words issued from her lips and she couldn't prevent herself from muttering them several times.

"That's right. I'm a bull and you're a young calf. Why not?" Uncle Arthur bucked like one and renewed his thrusts to a punishing intensity.

Linda moaned and groaned without stopping. She no longer had to concentrate on her pleasure. Pleasure had consumed her and it was igniting holy fires within. She came almost without realizing it and her cunt juice cascaded between her shapely thighs.

"Oh, how good it is... It's so good..." She cried for the third time as a stronger orgasm gripped her loins, forcing her to tremble and shudder like a tree in a windstorm.

She felt her uncle's hot sperm shooting into her, and the two brought their respective orgasms to a wild, mutual climax.

Uncle and niece had harmonized well in their act of love – a brutal, ardent love that was only to be the beginning.

They moved around a bit. It was the aftermath and the languor of the immense passion that had stirred them. Then, tired and limp, the two buckled in silence. Linda could no longer move her arm. The calf had lost its footing.

"I'm dead," she uttered briefly.

Uncle Arthur didn't say a thing.

♦

Arthur lay there thinking of a future treatment to administer on his lovely young niece.

Until then, they had just made love. How boring it was for him. He was a real connoisseur and, above all, he was gifted with a superb imagination. It was his duty to take care of the girl and initiate her into the realms of love in the best tradition of the family.

He moved away from the girl and went to his desk. As the light darkened in his library, he brightened his table lamp and began to write a few words.

...I find that the younger they are the more susceptible they are to ruthless attacks. Since their imaginations are wildly alive, they combine the little experience they have had thus in their lives and apply it to the act. The act is briskly approved when it suggests the erotic and the implausible for them. Strange creatures, everyone. For Brigette, it was a horse, for she never forgot the huge equestrian animal's cock, hard and ready to function on the female who was grazing in the next pasture. For Linda, the bull. She was looking for the barrel-chested fellow who could snort and prove his valour against the odds of the sword... and then there was blood in her mind, signifying the deflowering...

Everything was clear in his writer's head. He pulled out a cigarette and casually lit it as he slumped back into his leather armchair.

A few circles of misty smoke helped him to tint the air around him and clear his thoughts. He hunched over his documents and read.

...The young 12-18 are ~~essentially~~ romantic. Reality eludes them and they have no intention coming to grips with this unpleasant monster. Reality is a spanking, a chiding, harsh words. Reality, for them, is morality, adult society, and the humdrum of social this and social that...

Later on he read a passage that made him take notice, and a smile curled his lips.

...Teach your child, father, teach him a good dose of it. There's the hairbrush, your belt. Don't use a newspaper, it's too

Linda's Strange Vacation

weak. Mix the blood in that child of yours and give him some hope for the future. Let his romanticism win over all in the final run, but first let him taste the sweet brutality of pain. Break his britches, or more delightfully, concentrate on your daughter, daddy dear. And if you don't have one, go adopt one quickly or you'll go mad. You're getting on and so is your mistress, perfumed and dry, trying so hard to be the flower she was and never will be again.

Punishment to evoke pleasure. Look into it.

It's worth a try. (Consult list of punishing devices in Vol. 13, pages 164–246.) Punishment, pugilism, power, precision, perseverance, plunder, positivism, pleasure, pulsations, probing, pleasure and pure pleasure. Is there any doubt that "P" – yes, standing for prick, pornography, and pimp – is my favourite letter...?

Arthur closed his book and crushed out his cigarette. He went over to the cabinet at the end of the room and unlocked it. He appeared to be checking its contents. After a swift glance, he closed it.

He tip-toed over to the girl, who was laying there crumpled and worn, and with his forefinger he traced a "P" ever so lightly on her bare back.

chapter three

When Linda opened her eyes, she discovered the pitch darkness of night. She caught sight of her uncle standing not too far away. Arthur had taken two glasses and a bottle from his private cabinet. He held out one of the receptacles half-filled with whiskey.

"Here, drink this. It will do you good."

"But, but – I don't drink," Linda protested. Her uncle seemed irritated and the two thin lines on his forehead furrowed with vexation.

"Now don't be silly. Drink it."

The young girl used her better judgement and did as she was told. Although she made horrible faces and the liquid truly burned her throat, she managed to swallow it all the same. In all her young virginal life it was the first time she had tasted hard liquor.

"Now it's my turn to drink."

He took his glass and approached Linda's cunt with a very serious expression on his face. Then he poured the liquid into her belly-button. With hungry lips he followed the alcohol as it ran down to her pubic triangle. Once more he poured the liquor and this time it rolled down her thighs. Rapaciously he drank from the roiling fountain. Linda hurled her painful cries. The alcohol was burning her tender sex. Arthur buried his thin, elegant head between her immaculate thighs. Above, he let drip the last drops of whiskey onto her curly bush and then slobbered away like a thirsty madman.

Linda soon felt less pain, due to the expert licking manoeuvres of her highly-skilled uncle. She offered her pussy without any precaution, happy to be attacked by this ardent flow of affection. His tongue searched and searched as though it were looking for a maraschino cherry. While his face plunged deep within her aching cunt lips, his other hand found the whiskey bottle. Without the slightest hesitation or further ado, Arthur aimed the neck of Haig and Haig at the girl's sopping anus. It plugged in with a slurping noise that shocked and embarrassed Linda. With a brusque effort he flipped the helpless lass over in the air and began to pour the whiskey down her entrails in a burning enema. Linda squealed her pain and fright, which were equally acute. The sudden flood of liquid, a powerful burning liquid at that, caused an eruption of suffering in the vicinity of the girl's over-heated sex. At last an uncorking sound came from the adolescent's rear, indicating that the bottle had made its exit as violently as it had entered.

Immediately, Arthur's head was there to replace the glass cock. He loved alcohol and adored sex, and he was a man who loved to have his cake and eat it at the same time. Arthur disdained the misuse of pleasures. He was proud of his delicate gourmet tendencies, and he gave a royal proof of his aristocracy and a rough account of his virility.

Linda's little snatch turned brown as she scratched her blistered anus. She whimpered and moaned as she prepared to voyage on the turbulent road of further erotic indecencies.

"The best of scotch mixed with the excrement of my fair niece Linda," Arthur howled with personal triumph, and his laughter was shrill and piercing. "What could be better than this wholesome aperitif? Haven't you ever been buttfucked by a bottle of whiskey before, my dear? Think what you've missed."

Totally mortified, Linda could not and would not respond to such an impossible question. Her uncle appeared to be completely drunk with his sense of power and amusement.

She thought of getting up and going to the toilet, but the eager fingers of her probing uncle forbade her to move. Suddenly she let go with a stream of scalding urine, which splashed mercilessly into Arthur's handsome face. Linda tried in vain to hold back, but the pressure on her bladder was too strong. Thus she squirted a yellow flow of steaming piss flush on her uncle's mouth.

But Arthur did not quit his post. He was inextinguishable. He gulped down the steaming fluid greedily, smacking his lips. Ready to receive the last discharge from either orifice, and already covered with shit and urine, Arthur created such an impression on the Linda's sensitive temperament that the poor girl turned half-way around and vomited.

Almost in a faint from the repulsive sight she had been witness to, Linda did not see her uncle scamper to the chair in which he placed his clothes.

Arthur slipped a leather belt from his trousers as he clinched his teeth. Briskly he hovered over Linda before unleashing a wicked blow which slithered off the girl's lovely back. She was so surprised that she held back the cry that hung quivering on her lips.

Once again Arthur's hand circled in the air and a second stroke came crashing down with such tremendous force that a red mark was tattooed immediately on the girl's pale shoulders.

This time Linda howled with pain and her body trembled with fear. She had expected the worse and it might have been terrible, but it all came whistling down with the third thundering swipe of the leather strap.

Linda rolled on the carpet, partly to ward off the pain and partly to escape the furious blows. But her uncle, who had not the slightest intention of letting up, reigned supreme dictator of his young captive. He aimed at her pale buttocks next, and a grid of livid marks was thatched there in the space of a few minutes. From there he worked upward to her breasts.

The young kitten jumped in the air, grovelled on the floor and desperately tried to hide under the table. Her twists and turns had one singular effect on Arthur – they excited him all the more. He redoubled his punishment under the stupefied gaze of the writhing, zebra-marked Linda.

"You little bitch. You'll have enough to be thirsty with. I'll skin you, my pet." He puffed and blustered his threats.

"Please, no more... Enough, enough!" Linda felt that she had *already* been skinned.

Then, from her anus, a dark substance flowed out. It wasn't her fault. The sudden emotion and fright, not to mention the enema of malt, had given her the 'shits'. Her brown, bubbling faecal matter soiled the carpet and the room was quickly filled with a nauseating odour of urine and excrement, mixed with fresh sweat and traces of come.

"I should saw you in half, my little animal beauty. What would you say if I made you eat all that? Aren't you ashamed – dirtying the carpet that way?" Arthur didn't quit his lashing one iota, even as he lectured the beaten captive.

Linda hung her head. At that exact moment and in that woeful condition she would have accepted anything. She no longer had any will and her sensations were a mass of confusion. She could not endure the punishment and yet, despite herself, she was now realizing violent orgasms provoked by the rapid belt-lashes her sadistic uncle was firing between her legs, the tip of the belt snaking in and out of her gaping pussy. What *was* she to believe, in her shell-shocked state?

Her uncle finally ceased his whipping. He glowered at the humbled torso spattered with red, blue and black marks. Arthur watched the broken body creep toward him on all fours. He stood motionless as a tombstone, gazing upon the crushed creature who was now hugging and kissing his legs.

The greying man felt his cock grow hard again, and the lively head of his niece ventured instinctively to the throbbing glans. She gobbled him into her hot mouth, sucking the erection like a child with a lollipop.

Uncle Arthur let the girl have her fun for awhile, but he had other intentions. He soon pushed the drunken youngster away, and addressed her in an a voice full of unbending authority.

"Come – we are going to take a bath together."

He made her get up and after crossing the large study, he opened a door, almost hidden from view. Arthur led his niece into a bathroom which was large and tiled in rose squares. The bathroom not only contained a large bathtub, but an equally large divan which was covered by a white drapery. There were other accessories in the bathroom and Linda gazed with horror at the medicine chest.

She closed her eyes and her mind drifted into the realms of wild imagination. Was she entering the domain of paradise or hell? "I'll prepare the bath." Arthur took little time to turn on the bathtub faucets.

Linda took a look around and found the object of her sudden desire. She reeled over to the toilet and straddled it without the least consideration of Arthur's presence. She farted and turned red as gouts of come, whiskey and shit spattered the bowl. Arthur smiled and his lips curved in contentment.

"Why you look very lovely in that position," he leered.

He tiptoed over to the sitting waif and presented her with his stiff prick. Linda, still straddling the toilet seat, took the cock between her teeth avidly. She felt two pleasures at once. At the same time as she was shitting, she had a full-blown, plunging cock down her throat.

In her wildest imagination she would never have dreamed all this was possible. It was only that morning that she had arrived, pure and innocent, just to spend a vacation by the sea. Never in her most daring fantasies would she have concocted these wild scenes and perverted sensations. And yet, reality had already soared beyond the most powerful hallucination.

Arthur, who was admiring the situation with the eye of a true libertine, licked his lips at each plop of wet shit that issued from the girl's angelic asshole.

"Stop. I don't want to come right now, since I have other pleasures in view."

Linda, who had finished her needs, leaned over to grab the toilet paper, but Arthur's hand stopped her from exercising any further action. Neatly he unravelled the roll of paper and wiped the insides of her buttocks clean himself. Then he bent over and carefully, fastidiously licked out his niece's pink and brown anus. Enraptured, she pushed back against his probing tongue until her sphincter was clamped around its tip, trying to milk his come into her burning rectum. For a while he let her impale herself in that way, then he withdrew.

"Come here, the bath is ready." Arthur led naked Linda by the hand.

They stepped into the over-sized bath at the same time. The water came up to their hips. Linda felt a prickly sensation caused by the tepid water, which soothed and burned her skin at the same time. She had recently been soundly thrashed and she was highly sensitive from head to toe. Little by little she became used to the warming effect of the water as she watched her uncle soap himself vigorously.

Then Arthur soaped his niece as though he were washing a puppy-dog, the stinging lather infesting the criss-cross slashes across her skin. Linda made faces and it was obvious that her wounds gave her much distress.

"Now, now..." Her uncle's voice grew paternal and debonair. "You're as dirty as a pigling and you squeal at a piece of soap. If you don't behave, I shall have to punish you – and you can just guess how I'll go about it." He meant business and Linda had no doubts about it. She didn't have to strain her imagination any more. Linda had been initiated and she now knew anything could happen. This bathroom scene was a far cry from being dispensed with. Surprises were undoubtedly in store for her. And, what was most surprising of all, she found herself welcoming the unexpected, the unknown with an almost voracious pleasure.

Her uncle stood up in the bathtub and spread the soap all over her fine body. She was soon covered with soap suds, particularly her fuzzy bush. Linda thought of the many times she had accomplished this same act with just a hint of the pleasure it might give if treated by some worthy hands. Reality supersedes fiction, and her uncle's hand spread her thighs in an effort to thoroughly soap her ass, belly and inner thighs. A delicate finger wiggled in her anus. Linda was careful to conceal her pleasure. She wriggled with satisfaction.

"Now we're going to buttfuck in a bathtub, my dear. Hang on to the railing and spread apart, darling mermaid."

Linda didn't have to be coaxed twice. She felt a small tidal wave encircle her pussy and the rippling sensation meant that a flesh torpedo was being well aimed at her foaming nether regions.

A direct hit. The penis slipped into her hungry rim like an oiled fist into a waiting glove, burying itself to the hilt. Meanwhile, Linda's cunt was being washed out by the warm soapy suds which welled with each thrust of Arthur's loins.

This time the young girl squirmed and squealed with pleasure. Never before had she felt the true value of her uncle's prick. It went in and out with all the relentless power of a piston. When she turned her head, she saw the foam floating on the water's surface, the turbulence of their two sexes in heated collision. She couldn't help gazing back at Arthur's face. He appeared transfigured as he took on the aspects of a demon and an angel all at once.

"It's magnificent. You're wonderful." Linda was sincere in her praise, though she suffered a bit due to the width of Arthur's cock. It was difficult to withstand his huge erection in her small asshole, and it was with both pain and pleasure that she soaked the erotic stimulation of this most novel bathtime adventure.

chapter four

The time had come for Linda and her uncle to withdraw from their soap-sud game. But they splashed with pleasure like two fiery animals at the climax, and a thick white substance, streaked with red and brown, floated gelatinously on the surface of the water.

Arthur was the first to scamper out of the tub. He took a large beach towel and rubbed himself dry as his niece bounced out of the bath dripping from head to foot. Playfully Arthur lashed out with a flick of the towel. The sting caught Linda right between her buttocks. The girl howled and tried to dodge a second whack that slithered off her thighs.

The helpless lass ducked behind the toilet stool for protection. And this is where she had made her mistake. Arthur smiled cruelly, and it was all too apparent that he had found a new method of entertaining himself. A wicked strike of the towel, cradling around the toilet lever, flushed the bowl and gave the girl a start.

Linda ran from her hiding place and found herself cornered along the tiled walls. Arthur tracked her down like a favourite hunt. The towel, partially wet, hummed in the air and caught the adolescent across the breasts.

"Please, dear uncle, no more." Linda had uttered the words that could only stimulated her enraged relative further.

"Here's some 'no more' for you, my sweet." His teeth glittered.

Several blows buckled Linda to her knees as she cringed in horror. What made matters worse was the wet skin, lashed by the heavy soaking towel. This caused red eruptions about her lower abdomen, breasts and nipples.

Arthur's penis grew large yet again, and it vibrated in the steamy pungent mist of the bathroom. The haze, combined of heat, sweat and humidity, hampered the ardent uncle in his task of taming a young vixen.

Furiously he threw the towel aside and dragged the limp girl to the shower. There, under the rain of the sprinkler, uncle Arthur buttfucked his lovely niece while standing. Catching her flush in the asshole, he tweaked the tips of her wet nipples with his dexterous fingers.

The immense flood of ever-changing thrills, mixed with the delights of orgasm, swept through Linda's body and her heart beat like a trip hammer. It was strange how pain, a pain which she felt she could never endure, turned into a magnificent treat whenever Arthur's cock plunged so deep within her. The man already loved to piston in and out of her cunt, and now that her asshole had also been broken in, a new level of voluptuous pleasure possessed her being.

Their movements were even more frenetic than the down-pour of water. Linda's bottom moved rhythmically forward and back while Arthur cupped her breasts and tickled her rigid nipples. Both of them, inflamed by the wonderful pressure and temperature of the water, performed like animals. Their moans and panting sounds were drowned out by the flooding shower, but when they finally climaxed an echo of ecstasy burst in the cell of the bathroom, crackling against the tiles.

Arthur, as capricious as ever, was the first to leave the shower stall. Evidently he was a master of his own acts, and was decisive in all his movements. He quickly closed the glass door on Linda, who naturally hollered to be let out. When she turned off the shower, she shivered and when she kept it running, the water temperature mounted at an alarming rate.

Arthur had a strange way of amusing himself. Luckily for Linda, Alice suddenly knocked on the door and asked for her uncle.

"What do you want? Go away." Arthur was indignant.

"You wanted me to wear that special outfit with the black tights and red bra." Her voice cooed with honey.

Arthur returned to the very pleasant reality of his present situation. It was true that he had summoned Alice for an encounter at six. She was as malleable as a child. For quite awhile, he had enjoyed a rare amusement with Alice and he was not going to be denied of his pleasure because of a wet niece.

He bundled himself up in his bath-robe and scurried out of the bathroom. Linda was free and relieved, although she at once felt betrayed and alone. It was the first time she had ever sensed the pangs of jealousy.

Curiosity mixed with lust guided her to the room in which Arthur and Alice were ready to entangle voluptuously.

Naturally it would take place in the library. Arthur negligently – or perhaps it was on purpose – left the door open. Linda had a perfect spot from where to take in the performance of the two professionals.

Alice was standing semi-naked in a pair of very high-heeled shoes. They were bright orange and gave her legs, which were sheathed in black lace stockings, a superb silhouette. The maid, who had seemed so insignificant before, was bewitching in her extravagant costume.

One of the odd accoutrements of the outlandish outfit was her red bra. She appeared uncomfortable with it, and she squirmed painfully when she had to make the slightest effort with her upper body.

The maid's face was painted up like that of a low-grade prostitute. Her lips and eye make-up were terribly exaggerated and her face was an invitation to new levels of licentiousness.

Arthur registered his approval. A snide smile crept across his handsome face as he squeezed Alice's two ripe breasts. The curvy maid let out a yell that pierced Linda's ear-drums. For a moment Linda imagined that Alice was having her period, but then she reasoned that it was something else, something that was on the inside lining of the bra. Later on, she found that she was perfectly right in her reasoning. Sharp little needle points caused the torture and humiliation of the unwholesome garment.

"Don't cry like that. You'll draw everyone's attention." Arthur was displeased with Alice and his hand pressed the girl's cheeks in a sign of admonishment.

Then the elegant man tugged down the young lady's panties and plunged his face into the grove of her pubic hair.

The perfume of her pussy was so strong that it caught the nostrils of the peeking Linda. The smell was nauseating. It reeked so pungently of unwashed come and cheap perfume that Linda held her nose for a few minutes. She was astonished at how her uncle was able to bear such a repulsive stench.

Meanwhile Arthur's mouth had gone unerringly to the very heart of the maid's steaming pussy. Alice's legs drifted wider and wider apart as she gripped Arthur's damp hair. Her knees began to shake as her lover gave his all. Linda remembered how superb Arthur was a pussy-licking, and she knew that Alice was having a riotously good time of it. Her legs and buttocks looked divine, raised high and spread open with the orange high heels raking at the ceiling, her lascivious posture due to the encouragement of Arthur's skilful tongue.

A whimsical moan trickled from Alice's throat, and Linda felt her own cunt becoming wetter and wetter as her youthful eyes drank in the delicious scene.

Her uncle's hands wandered up to the spiked bra and his two large palms squeezed the maid's tits. Alice turned faint and she bit her lower lip, drawing blood.

Yet she didn't complain. If she did, she knew she would receive nothing but painful abuse. She was shaken by pleasure, but at the same time she was forced to abide the suffering administered by her noble lover's hands.

Alice's fingernails clawed in Arthur's hair as she tried to relieve the metal massage on her breasts. The uncle, steady at his post, lapped away at her pussy and continued to abuse her tits.

The bitter and the sweet were combined as Alice ground her hips. She did not know whether to seek a haven of rest by pushing the man away, or enjoy the paradisiacal pleasures to be earned by sticking it out.

Thus Arthur controlled his victim – or loved one, depending on the point of view one wishes to take.

Linda later found out that Arthur had theories on sex that were declared 'revelational and astounding' by experts in the field. Arthur's books were not known publicly but they had a secret audience that cherished them far above the classics.

Well, at the moment the great sexologist was

performing his deeds on a paltry maid. He could have had the pick of metropolitan women, but he had his reasons. Arthur knew how to discriminate and above all he knew what he wanted. Alice filled the menu, and he was satisfied with his choice.

As the youngster reeled in a pathetic scene of torture and delight, Arthur slipped away and plucked a rubber dildo from his drawer. Swiftly he flew back to his purring cat, replaced his mouth in her bush and licked her out as before. Then, deftly, he plugged the dildo into the small opening of Alice's asshole. Linda was amazed to see how everything was regulated and planned.

Arthur pumped away with the instrument while his tongue ripped in and out of the maid's soaking vagina. Alice's eyes turned in her head like a slot machine. Slowly they came out cherry red and Linda knew Arthur was closing in on the jackpot.

With one great cry Alice unburdened her immense orgasm in the gentleman's mouth. He sucked her dry, drinking down torrents of hot thick cunt-juice, as he controlled his erection in order to keep from ejaculating.

The thunder of Alice's inarticulate moans excited Arthur, and he violently ripped away her panties. Brutally he slammed his swollen cock into the maid's cunt, while he continued to manipulate the false phallus which was reaming out her slippery asshole with amazing dexterity.

For a while, the two ground away in a deep vacant frenzy. They were like two violent dancers who were given to shaking voluptuously to their own inner rhythms in the centre of a grand ballroom, only this was Arthur's library, and the scene was intimate and warm.

Linda was inflamed by the expert movements of the two superb lovers, who were by now glowing in ecstasy. She began to masturbate, heaving with lust. Her middle finger went all the way up her cunt as her tongue fell out of her mouth. Saliva dripped from her lips, while a sticky substance trickled on the carpet from her dripping snatch. She had made up her mind to live vicariously with the two lovers. A secret desire gripped her, and she felt an intense need to bite into Alice's rump.

But she didn't dare, fearing the punishment, which would be perhaps...

Her thought was broken like a twig at the sound of Arthur's muffled voice.

"Linda – come here and join us."

Dear Arthur could not have given her a more pleasing present.

She was on the spot in no time. And Linda performed her functions like a trouper. With her teeth she pulled out the rubber dildo from Alice's asshole, and put her head straight between her butt-cheeks without even demanding permission from her notorious uncle.

While Arthur laboured in and out of the maid's sticky bush, Linda deeply penetrated her asshole with her thin, thirsty tongue. Occasionally she licked at Arthur's tight balls, and the base of his red cock as it thrust in and out of Alice's cunt.

Arthur, who was no novice in the giving pleasure, now gave up Alice's pussy for a dip into Linda's hungry asshole.

The man was dripping with come, although he had not as yet reached the supreme moment. He hammered his cock into the half-inch opening, giving Linda such a violent thrill that she redoubled her anal licking and lapping, much to the delight of Alice who was in seventh heaven.

"Is everyone happy?" Arthur asked, partly in pride and partly with self-imposed rapture.

There was no response. The two young ladies were too busy reaping the harvest of their vast pleasure ride. Alice suddenly felt a wave of gratitude which she felt she should deliver to her master, who was pushing the girls into the wall with his pounding. She abandoned her position to kneel at Arthur's rear, and started to chew at his rump, running her tongue down until it slipped into the musky crevice of his rectum.

The trio thus changed two or three times, without any unfavourable change or let-down in sheer pleasure and ecstasy.

After twenty minutes of intense orgiastic couplings, the threesome unloaded their come into the mouth and bowels of their respective partners and then tumbled to the ground in a heap.

Arthur was the first to regain his footing, after wiping the sweat from his brow. He smiled ironically as he gazed at the two limp torsos wrapped together on the floor.

"Enough is enough ladies," he laughed jovially. "We'll be at it again another time. Don't you realize it's after eight and dinner isn't even prepared? What kind of a household do you think I'm running anyway? Alice, get to the kitchen before you receive treatment threefold!"

That was all the spent maid had to hear. She scurried out of the room pale with fright, clutching her garments. Linda was rocked out of her slumber by the sudden departure of the luscious maid.

Arthur helped his niece to her feet. The first thing Linda did was to throw her arms around her uncle's neck, but he quickly pushed her aside, showing that he hated the idea of over-sentimentality.

"Now go and see what Robert and that tigress are up to. I have my ideas on the subject. Tell them to come down for dinner immediately after they've showered, I'm sure they'll need to be refreshed after their work-out."

He walked over to his niece and affectionately placed his hand under her chin. His handsome gaze met her large wet eyes and he looked deep within, as through trying to decode the secrets of her adolescent soul.

"Are you happy here, Linda?" He wanted the truth, and he was not going to settle for anything else.

"Oh, uncle... I don't know. I think so. You see, I never, never..."

He walked to his desk and picked up her words as though he had known them for a long while. "...Never expected to see the likes of it."

He tapped a cigarette on the back of his hand and his eyes suddenly changed. Linda detected a shade of grey darken in the sombre sockets.

"You'll find, Linda dear, that we have only just began to know each other. I promise you that a full-dressed adventure lies in front of you. So far we have just engaged in penny-ante affairs. Just wait, and you'll be astonished the more."

With these words, Arthur opened the door and Linda knew that she was to go and call his mistress and Robert. A flood of broken ideas crept through her mind like the quick fall of a spring.

She was lucid and careful to select the true value of the sudden inspiration that throbbed in her veins and heart.

All at once she turned beet-red. She felt ashamed, haunted by her acts. Linda knew that they would live with her a long while. She had been robbed of her innocence. *But what of it,* she thought. Her puritanism had always been a bother. It was better to be done with it once and for all.

Then on the other hand? No... There was no doubt about it – she came from a sensual, lustful family. There was no sense refuting hereditary. She was a member of Arthur's clan and she decided to be proud of it. However, she knew she was unlike Arthur. So much different than her uncle, that a sudden terrifying fear gripped her heart.

She climbed the stairs feverishly. Linda had an errand to perform and she made a noble effort to erase her morbid thoughts. At the end of the hall she tapped lightly on Robert's door. There was no answer. She heard a blend of strained voices. Linda opened the door and was not at all surprised to see Robert and Lola enlaced like two serpents.

"Fuck me in the rear, Robert honey. Do it good, you young whipper-snapper – or I'll bite off your cock."

Lola playfully nibbled on the boy's ear-lobe. Their bodies oozed sweat and an odour that was purely sensual and pungent. Linda didn't have the courage to intrude, and yet she had a mission to perform.

"Dinner will be ready soon. Uncle Arthur sent me to tell you to wash up."

She looked guiltily at the couple as though she were a real kill-joy, destined to spoil their fun. It was apparent that they dismissed her words disdainfully. Linda found that her throat was dry and she could not utter the same words for a second time.

Although she felt like running from the room, she was glued to the spot. Suddenly she became enthraled by Lola's seductively bouncing breasts. Robert had her from behind, and was jarring her with rapid plunges in the rear. Lola bucked forward with her hair wildly covering her handsome face.

Linda watched her heavy tits jiggle in the air. A burning urge to devour them incensed the girl, and in no time at all she found herself already kneeling on the bed sucking tenderly on the dark red nipples. Lola caressed Linda's head and she whispered in her ear stimulating words of love, her tongue caressing Linda's ear-lobe.

"Love them, my buttercup. Suck them well and nip on them as though they were ripe cherries. I'll make you queen, my dear. Take bigger mouthfuls, Linda darling. Come now, you've grown up my little one."

Robert had buried his throbbing cock in Lola's sweaty, voluptuous asshole. Through sheer determination he kept back his orgasm as he bit into the neck of the lovely brown-skinned beauty.

Linda no longer knew why she had come into their secret abode, but she relinquished all questions as she sank into the abandon of lust. Lola's breasts were so juicy and delicious that the girl felt she could suck on them forever.

Lola sweetly fingered Linda's pussy, and she knew every sensitive crease and fold of a young girl's cunt. Her long fingers caused a hot saliva to run from Linda's mouth. The trio pitched deliriously and the bed springs squealed with the burden of their love-making.

None of them had eaten for hours. They were all healthy and gifted with enormous appetites, but they had long forgotten dinner time. In their games of love, their concentration was on the fruits of passion and nothing else.

A sheet of condensation covered the windows as the three bodies smouldered with caresses and tonguings. Robert became purple with his tremendous effort to sustain his drive.

Linda and Lola certainly wanted the encounter to continue until doomsday. For the first time they had found out the real capacities of one another. Delighted to find that they were in perfect harmony, the two females bestowed their respective affections and art upon each other.

Then with a gust of wind the door flew open and uncle Arthur stormed in, as angry as a lion. Linda looked askance at the enraged man without letting a teat slip out of her mouth. Arthur's eyes turned violently red.

"So this is what you're all up to. Linda disobeys me first of all, and then of course Robert and my fair lady persuaded her to join them. Well it needs a lesson, this perverted act does."

Arthur brandished a whip that shook between his legs. Words flew hot and heavy.

"Lola you are a no-good bitch. I hold you responsible for the deviations of these children. Robert, if you continue to be as presumptions and aggressive in your manner, there will be no more use of the car and I promise you that I'll put that great cock of yours in a sling. Linda, disobedience costs dearly in my household and I will not allow it for a minute. You'll learn your lesson very shortly, my dear niece."

With quick sharp strides he came to the bed and hovered over the trio as if momentarily paralysed. Then his lithe frame went into action as his arm furiously wielded the lash.

A first punishing stroke whammed across Robert's back, driving his cock more securely into the sucking hole of mistress Lola's ass. A second blow encircled the threesome, who were literally moulded together by its force. It caught Linda on the buttocks and thighs and she winced, biting into Lola's poor breasts. The tigress howled as she felt the sudden teeth stab into her flesh.

Blow after blow rained down on the naughty trio. Arthur was truly mad and he intended to have everyone pay for her and his misdeeds.

Robert pleaded for him to let up, but Lola had a strange contorted look on her face. She was a victim of mixed emotions, and Linda was disturbed and astonished to see a whole range of facial expressions emanate from her lovely, sensual friend.

The whipping had achieved an opposite effect on Lola. She was writhing with a sickly sensual pleasure that would not diminish.

Her excitation became unbearable, and it produced an odd effect on Linda and Robert. The two youngsters weathered the storm of the whip and they too took refuge in a newly arisen pleasure. They scrambled together like hungry startled animals. Their sexes were wet and their mouths were bubbling with saliva as they renewed their orgy baptised in blood.

"Have it out, you three. Get it all out of your system. Tomorrow is another day and we will see what comes out of your misbehaviour. But you'll bear the marks of today's chastisement. Take that... and that... for your pleasure!"

Arthur was livid with rage. He refused to believe that his law and order had backfired in such a way. Lola had known the exceptional man too long, and she had stayed with him for very personal reasons. She knew how to come out on top even with an intelligent fox like Arthur.

Robert was the first to let loose and have a shattering orgasm. His prick spasmed in the Lola's majestic asshole as his balls emptied every last drop of semen into her bowels. He withdrew with a wet plop. A small trickle of whitish spunk clung to the crack of her ass, mixing with a brownish colour that emitted a bittersweet stench. The odour filled the room and not one of the four complained about it. They revelled in its musky allure, and Linda, driven wild, was the second to burst wide open, her cunt-juices showering everybody. She captured Lola in her arms and her mouth slipped from the breasts down to the belly button and then still lower to the gaping cunt. She buried her face in the rosy folds, tonguing away with youthful fire.

Arthur gave his whip up for lost. He was curiously taken by the mass of feverish flesh. Now he would teach them a lesson. Within warning, the elegant master plunged his stout cock into the dry asshole of his nephew, who bellowed in agony and seemed thunderstruck at this unprecedented onslaught.

"There, my dear Robert – a sudden surprise for your manhood. No one ever told you that a rear end is a haven not to be denied, whether it is that of a young lady or a young gentleman. Don't look so pained, my dear fellow. You'll come out of it alright. You're a wee bit tight of course, but that will be straightened out in due time."

Robert fled with blood pouring from his anus, crushed by the humiliating experience.

At dinner that night he was unable to raise his head and respond to the jibes of his uncle. Lola though admitted she had come several times. And when asked how many, she timidly lowered her eyes and calculated...

"Four."

Linda knew that they were big, exorbitant ones. She had witnessed at least two monstrous monsoons that Lola blew out of her womb.

When Arthur turned toward Linda with his usual calm grace, he didn't have to wait long for the answer.

"Three."

Linda turned red and she attempted to cover her blushes with the whiteness of the napkin, which only served as a definite contrast.

"Then everybody is content. Well, let's dig into the chicken and eat heartily. Alice has also prepared a steak for each of us. We've got to regain the energy we lost in our foolhardy endeavours today."

It was difficult to say whether Arthur had a smile on his lips or whether they were contorted by the an unintentional memory of the whip's vicious bite.

"Alice, you may sit with us tonight. After all, you had a workout as well. Come in when you're ready my dear. I want us all to behave as one big happy family."

They all ate with gusto.

chapter five

At dinner, Arthur became pensive and his mind was working at double time. He tapped his fingers together and stroked his chin. Although he no longer seemed to have an appetite, his tablemates were eating rapaciously.

"I hope everyone finds the dinner as it should be? I made sure that it was carefully seasoned. Pepper and spices help in restoring amorous urges."

Arthur watched Linda snap the leg of the chicken and pick it up with her dainty fingers. She blushed as she noticed his prolonged stare. Little did she guess her uncle's thoughts. How he would have liked to pluck this young chicken apart for good.

Lola looked ravishing in her new blue gown, while Robert ate like a college football player. He kept filling his plate with potatoes and disgusted the refined Arthur, who looked at him with disdain.

Alice entered with a second plate of vegetables. She was dressed in a scanty outfit that was daring and extremely sexy. Her bosom jutted out pertly and her little bottom wiggled tightly under a strange looking pair of panties.

Suddenly Arthur snapped his fingers. He seemed to have had an idea that he rather relished.

"I would like to see you after dinner, Linda. It's for a matter... let's say a certain *dessert* that I have for you."

Linda looked surprised, and she slowly lost her appetite due to a growing perplexity. Arthur on the other hand, renewed his hunger and now ate almost as rapidly as Robert.

Lola rubbed her hand along Linda's knee, and the young adolescent felt a warm sensation creep between her thighs. Lola's hands were truly remarkable. The mere touch of this exceptional beauty had a stimulating effect on the young girl.

Their slight display of emotions dwindled as Arthur clapped his hands, signifying that he was wise to the pair's antics. When dinner was finally over, Arthur requested Linda to follow him into his library. She obeyed, docile and refined in her gracious steps.

Once in the library, Arthur gazed longingly at his niece. He fingered a book and turned a few pages, just to practice his touch. Arthur was a man of much nervous energy, and he had the habit of wringing his hands.

"Linda, I'm writing a story about a girl such as you. She's an unusual girl who represents adventure to the fullest extent. Her name is Ancella. I named her after an Egyptian princess who died a strange death at the early age of twenty-two. As the story goes, the young princess was walking in the nearby forest some few hundred yards from her castle, when she spied a bush sparsely covered with orange fruit. Her protectress, a woman of some seventy years of age, forbade her to taste the fruit. The princess became inquisitive and she tried some anyway, against the pleading of the elderly woman.

Three days later the princess was taken by a series of convulsions and she suddenly became terrifyingly lustful. Heretofore, she had been a virgin of the purest order, but suddenly this strange transformation fell upon her.

At first many of the court thought she had inherited the whorish instincts of her mother, a court concubine, but later they found she was truly a victim of a sexual passion and hunger that knew no bounds.

The girl literally raped every young and old servitor of the king and queen. It is said that she was soft-skinned and extremely beautiful, and her response to the male population was met with applause and pleasure. Disorder broke out in the kingdom and a veritable City of Sodom ensued."

Linda watched Arthur as he minutely described the many details of the fascinating story. The man's eyes glowed and he appeared to see the many sensual events before him as he told the tale.

"The princess died of sexual and sadistic abuse brought on mostly by her own hands. I have often wondered if the myth of the fruit is true, or whether it was her own nature that destroyed her. At any rate you can see that the story enthrals me. And what about you, doesn't it have its effect?"

Linda had no idea of how her uncle wanted her to answer, but she decided to adhere to his enthusiasm.

"It is an astounding story, if it is true?"

"What do you mean if it is true? I am convinced that it is. Why there is even some documentation attesting to its validity. I am really surprised, Linda, that you think that it is a mere figment of someone's imagination."

Linda was quick to ward off a possible burst of anger spell that she felt she might have to endure. Words were her best protection, although Arthur was rarely fooled by rhetoric or perfumed and flattering words.

"Oh, I'm sure it has some basis of truth in it. I was just wondering whether *all* of it can be substantiated."

Arthur smiled and his hands tightly grasped the book he was holding.

"Linda, you're a wonderful little liar in your way. But I must admit, I am fond of you."

They exchanged smiles. It was difficult to say whether it was an exchange between enemies or friends. Their expressions were tinged by a marked ambiguity.

"I only told you that story to let you know that you have become the princess Ancella for me. There is no fruit here to offer you, but everyday henceforth you will taste an exotic dish of fruit which I have ordered. They are all different, but I am sure one of them will have an effect on you."

He laughed crazily and at first Linda laughed with him, feeling that Arthur was giving vent to his peculiar sense of humour. Then it dawned on the youngster that he was quite serious in his endeavour.

A shiver caused Linda to grow pale and contemplate on her fate, on the defence she would have to present.

Words failed the girl and the only reaction she presented to her merciless uncle were a few drops of bitter tears.

"Enough of that. It is not going to help matters. I've made up my mind."

Linda appeared crushed, broken in two. Her uncle placed his sinewy arms around her shoulders. He kissed her hair and her temple and patted her on her rump.

"What do you think of Alice, my dear?"

Linda was shaken from her depression. It was a surprising question to hear after such a tense quarter of an hour.

"Why, she seems perfectly alright to me."

"Well, my little one, I've prepared a treat for you. You've had everyone amongst us with the exception of our delicious maid. It is only normal that you see for yourself what delicate, sensual delights she may have in store for you, and I hope the act will be a mutual affair."

Suddenly Linda's thoughts swiftly turned to Alice. She'd had a soupcon of the maid's asshole, and she was a luscious little thing alright. She was much more peppery and juicy than Lola. But there was something common in her that made Linda pout, despite her desire not to give her reactions away. However, if Alice was good enough for Robert, and even Arthur, then she must have *some* saving grace.

"You two young ladies are going to perform in front of me in just a few minutes. You know we have no cinema here or ballroom, and we have to make up our own entertainment."

Linda was led over to a sumptuous divan cover with a purple fabric that was warm and soft. Arthur told her that this was to be the decor of their love act.

He went over to his bureau and pressed a buzzer. It was obviously for Alice. Linda noticed that there were a series of buttons and that all Arthur had to do was press one or any given number and his 'victims' were requested to answer.

In no time flat, Alice entered the room. The maid was dressed in lace that was as scanty as the attire of a newly-wed. Her sexual commonness was exaggerated, but far from unpleasant. She looked like a tart, with her high heels and her split crotch panties and peephole bra.

On a closer glance, Linda was able to detect that oddity of attire which gave the girl a peculiar allure – although Alice could never have looked more sexual.

The girl wore frilly purple garters attached to old-fashioned black-brown stockings. Her extremely tight panties were chewed away, as if by moths. A swathe of pubic hair stuck out at one end, and a part of the curve of the left buttock made its appearance as well.

Alice had full breasts and they stood at attention in the jet black and white bra that scarcely covered their bulging orbs, the lipsticked nipples poking out. Extra height was gained through the use of very high Italian shoes, that blended with the ensemble.

For the first time in her sexual life, Linda desired to be a male. She had a strange desire for Alice, and she couldn't decide whether it was the clothing, or rather the lack of it, or whether it was Alice herself.

Uncle Arthur was quick to see that everything pointed toward success. He went over to his private cabinet and extracted an instrument Linda had never noticed before. The girl was awestruck when she saw a perfect replica of a man's penis made out of plastic or rubber (as far as she could make out) and attached to a belt. But it didn't take long for Linda to catch on to its use.

Arthur burst out in a winsome smile when Linda took the stiff rubber dick out of his hand and stepped into the strange harness as though she had made use of one all her life.

"You learn quickly, my princess. You'll soon see what it's like to be a male. I want you tell me your exact reactions. Please don't hide anything from me."

Cradling the false cock as though it were made of china, Linda aimed it at the frightened maid. The schoolgirl backed Alice to the couch and then stretched her out in a technique that made Arthur stroke his chin inquiringly.

With one knee Linda forced Alice's legs apart. With her long fingers she stripped the girl of her panties by merely ripping on the elastic. The material burst under her savage pull.

Alice was perplexed to see Linda delight in the role of masculine prowess. She even noticed the change in her eyes. The young adolescent gave positive proof of a male side of her nature.

Linda grabbed her cock, just as a proud lover would encircle the instrument he treasures. The girl tickled Alice's cunt lips with the head of the prick, before stabbing into the wet mass of hair.

One of Linda's hands cradled the buttocks of the voluptuous maid, tickling her glistening asshole and demonstrating that she was aware of the fine art bestowed by expert male lovers.

"Excellent, princess, excellent. I couldn't have done better myself." Arthur cheered her on, although his niece needed absolutely no encouragement whatsoever.

Very soon the dildo slid rigidly inside the depths of Alice's cunt. The young maid let out a moan of enjoyment. She hugged tightly to Linda's neck and even bit her lover on the ear-lobe. Arthur went behind his desk and began to take notes. His eyes wandered from the love scene back to the written page. He noticed the manoeuvres and dexterity of his lovely niece as she brought Alice to the dizzy heights of orgasm.

The maid began to drool, and her eyes seemed to go dead all at once. Linda was hungrily biting one of the youngster's tits while a hand wondered up and down her feverish vertebrae.

"I love that... Oh, oh... it's good, so good... love, love, love it."

Alice began a magnificent chant to her strange lover. She murmured little nothings in Linda's ear. Although the words were incoherent, they spurred Linda on.

The rubber cock gained a milky shine as it slipped in and out, in and out of Alice's soaking pussy. Alice was completely stretched open, and she gave her entire being to the passionate thrusts of the phallic bitch who was servicing her so adroitly.

Linda was panting away and although she showed signs of flagging, it was apparent that the whole scene excited her beyond belief.

The two girls, svelte and superb in their lesbian abandon, paraded their sexual depravity before the lecherous onlooker.

Linda could no longer control herself. She ripped off the garter belt and had the diminutive maid practically naked and devoid of her clothes. She pounded the synthetic cock into

Alice's hole.

"Take her from behind," instructed Arthur, who was watching the scene while taking a flood of notes.

Linda did not have to be urged on. She pivoted the maid around and placed her dog-fashion on the divan. With one lusty plunge she managed to stick the enormous head of the dildo into her small but well-oiled anus. Alice groaned in pain, but she didn't protest to the sudden sodomization by her female partner.

A glossy sheen crept over Linda's forehead and it was evident that the girl was giving Alice her best. Linda's left hand was tickling her clit while her right was pinching and teasing her nipples.

Suddenly the two began to shudder and shake, and they screamed as they exploded in simultaneous orgasm, all their cunt juice spraying from their gushing pussies. A slow smear of brown trickled from Alice's anus. Alice was suffocating, crushed by the weight of Linda's hefty instrument. She had taken it from the front, and then succumbed to the terrible assault behind. But it felt so wonderful that she did not complain, indeed she pleaded for more pain, sweet pain such as only Linda was able to administer.

"Do it again. Please don't let up. I want it so badly. Again and again, darling!"

The two young kittens went at it with all their might. Linda did not spare her partner for one moment. After three more incredibly strong, consecutive orgasms, they both crumpled in a heap as if unconscious with ecstasy.

Arthur kept writing, and he failed to notice Linda's mouth creep slowly down Alice's body, her hot tongue lapping the sweat from her navel before plunging into the depths of her wide-open, come-covered pussy.

chapter six

Due to excessive fatigue, Arthur retired to his room early and left the others to their charming company.

Robert dozed off on the corner couch and when he awoke, he was not too surprised to see Linda and Lola interlaced in each other's arms. The young fellow threw his shoulders back and advanced toward the two women. An ironic smile dominated his features.

"Well, well, well. Aren't you going to invite me to your little get-together?"

Linda didn't know what to say, but Lola burst out in nervous laughter and exclaimed: "This young man is in need of something. Just look at him. He's holding us at gun point."

Needless to add that she was referring to Robert's cock, which stood at full attention, slightly twitching. He looked down at his proud tool like a hungry wolf and then his eyes wandered over the two nudes twined in their lewd coupling.

"What do you say, Linda? Shall we try his wares and see what he's worth?"

Robert didn't wait for an nod from either side. He approached the two and gave Lola's full thigh a slap with his left hand, Linda's marvellous breasts with his right.

"You'll see, my 'belles femmes'," he boasted. "Now to begin *there*..."

He jumped behind Lola and placed his handsome young face right between her two succulent buttocks, spreading them wide apart with his fingers. Robert began to lick her anus avidly, like a dog. Lola did not utter a word, but instead she backed into his mouth to facilitate the operation, opening her sphincter to admit his tongue as deeply as possible.

Linda felt abandoned. Something which she never liked before. She crept under Robert's legs and began to lap at the tip of his pulsating cock. Her lithe, moist tongue soon forced the erection to its highest pitch.

"Go to it cousin!" The young man's body contorted in pleasure. "Take it in your mouth."

Linda carried out the command and practically swallowed the hardened pole of flesh, sucking on it as hard as she could with her lips tightly round its root. Her tongue slipped over the entire length of his shaft, while his glans leaked strings of pre-come into her throat. The youngster caressed and squeezed his balls, and instinctively scratched his back with her wonderfully painted fingernails. The hand roamed slowly down his backbone and her forefinger, moist with saliva, slipped into his asshole.

She heard the wails of her two partners and from the corner of her eye she saw that Robert was not only licking out Lola's asshole, but her cunt lips as well.

Linda suddenly had an novel idea.

By stretching out on her back she could reach Lola and gain access to her delicious mouth. The tanned woman caught on immediately to the wishes of her younger companion. She complied at once, the pair sucking each other's tongues in deep, sensual kisses, and soon the happy groans of the threesome amplified in the warm air.

In a few minutes they were writhing, tonguing and fingering in rhythm, and their moans formed one large sound that seemed to emanate from one entity.

"Wait a second." Robert interrupted the session, turning toward Linda.

He withdrew his cock from the Linda's slippery mouth and directed the heavy tool toward the rear of squirming Lola, who seemed unhappy at the abrupt change.

"Just watch and learn, kiddo," Robert leered at Linda.

The bright schoolgirl watched with profound curiosity. She was looking at the scene in a topsyturvy position, which added to the sensual aspects and gave the picture an entirely new slant.

Lola backed onto Robert's prick of Robert like a hot filly, and she wiggled wantonly as she attempted to impale her pussy. However, Lola didn't forget Linda for a second, and her tongue was as active as ever. It felt like a soft silk sponge as it gobbled up the youngster's scented cunt juice.

"Now I'm going to fuck the great Lola in the ass. Just watch me, Linda honey."

"Yes... I see... Go ahead, buttfuck her. I want to look on. Robert, give her a good fucking." Linda was happy at her close-up view.

She had no idea what she was saying, she was so excited by her role. She even felt that she was the protagonist of this erotic operation.

Robert aimed his cock right at Lola's asshole and spread her cheeks apart with his big hands in his impatience to begin the lewd act.

Linda didn't lose sight of Robert's actions, and she was almost as excited as he was. She even got in a few last tongue strokes on her cousin's cock, then she helped Lola enjoy herself to the fullest by deeply licking her pussy with her hot mouth.

In this unique position she was able to watch the masterful workings of Robert's cock as it penetrated slowly into the magnificent brunette's rectum.

Robert was half-way inside when Lola began to let out a muffled cry of joy. Linda's mouth was full of sweet juice, cunt juice emitted by the gorgeous woman, who was loosing the floods of her passion by the gallon.

Still working with her tongue, Linda was able to watch Robert's balls knocking up against Lola's buttocks. She gasped as she saw that Robert had buttfucked Lola all the way in to the hilt.

"How nice that looks," she murmured ecstatically.

Lola was grinding her behind against Robert's belly and uttering unintelligible phrases.

Robert was incensed by the muttering and babbling of the lovely brunette. He plunged in and out of her tightly stretched anus like a madman. Linda was inspired by the furious attack, and her avid oral stimulation of Lola's clit drove the older woman into seventh heaven.

"Faster, faster, my pet! Go to it Robert. I want to feel it all the way inside me." Her head bobbed up and down as though she were riding a wild pony.

Robert responded with two or three vigorous strokes.

"She's a real bitch. She's never satisfied. Good old Lola never gets enough of it. We ought to get a donkey for her..."

Linda heard the infamous words and tried to imagine Lola getting screwed by a mule. She even seemed to see the enormous pizzle of the animal and she couldn't help thinking that such a wicked instrument would certainly give true satisfaction. Linda made a mental note to ask her friend whether diversions of a such nature were prohibited by uncle Arthur. Since he was a demon of the senses, why not indulge in that harmless erotic pastime?

Linda's head spun with curious and fantastic obsessions. She felt that she would never back out of even the most perverse type of erotic pleasure. Perhaps the seeds of the princess that Arthur mentioned were taking fruit.

Just thinking gave her the sudden urge to be penetrated by a fat cock. She wanted something hot, wet and stiff between her legs, and she wanted it quickly.

Desire heightened her perception. She attempted to draw Robert away from Lola. Lola would certainly forgive this ruse by her friend, and anyway she would be able to compensate her in another manner.

Linda disengaged herself from the couple and spread herself out on the bed alongside Lola. Flat on her back with her legs slightly apart, the girl played with the soft hairs of her sex, looking at Robert bewitchingly.

Robert suddenly stopped his movements and he was like a wolf who happened to spot a luscious chunk of raw meat.

"You little whore of a cousin. You want it too, eh?"

"Yes," Linda responded coyly and simply.

"I haven't two cocks, you know? I can't take on two at a time, that's simple isn't it?" Robert said teasingly.

Linda turned toward Lola and took her face and violently kissed her open mouth. Lola reacted to the flame of passion that was a mixture of tenderness, forceful love, and a game.

"Oh, Lola dear. Let me have him for a minute. I want it so badly. Honestly, I need it. It's itching so much. Lola, I do love you terribly – let me have it?"

Lola gave back a passionate tonguing and then looked at the young waif with irony and a storm of passion.

She signalled to Robert.

"Alright Robert, take the little tart. Can't you see she's dying for it?"

Robert laughed. He buffed and bellowed and briskly shoved his cock back into the bronzed beauty's asshole.

"What do you think I am, your servant? Do you think I have to obey you without having the right to choose for myself?"

Lola wasn't fooled by the play Robert put on. She saw that he was attracted by her cousin as she spread-eagled herself on the bed, panting away with lust. The boy just wanted to tease the girl and make her long for him all the more.

Linda was taken in by the game. In fact, she grabbed the boy's arm and pleaded with him hysterically.

"Please Robert, please... I want to be... I *crave* to be fucked by you..."

Robert pulled out his prick from the two cheeks of Lola's rump. Linda watched it as though she were spellbound by its movements. Hypnotized by this rigid snake streaked with shit and dribbling thick milky strands of come, she thought she would go mad with the need to have it inside her.

Suddenly she seized it with her hand and forced Robert to take the necessary step. Lola, who was on her side, pushed the boy by his buttocks toward the beckoning girl. Robert didn't wait any longer, and in a trice he managed to impale his cousin with his abnormally swollen cock. Lola her eyes inflamed, was delighted to watch the two writhe in heated pleasure.

Robert pumped away with force and unbridled passion, till at last he felt his balls exploding and he whipped his cock out of Linda's cunt, spraying great gouts of hot spunk onto his cousin's startled face.

chapter seven

A half-an-hour later, the three were stretched out on the bed. Robert was in between his two mistresses. Lola's and Linda's hands met while they tickled and stroked the balls and penis of the happy young man, who was peacefully reclined with his hands in back of his head. He let the girls do what they wished, while he closed his eyes and beamed contentment all over his boyish face.

"I really must say that this young scamp has a certain talent for his gangly age. Don't you think I'm right, Linda dear?"

Linda merely smiled and continued to caress her cousin's ball sac.

"Tell me Robert, when did you first make love? When was the very first time you properly possessed a woman?" Lola asked the boy questions because she was truly inquisitive. She had an admiration for the younger generation and their precocity, and wanted to know their ways.

"I guess I was fourteen. That's right, I remember. I wasn't more than fourteen. I did it with Edith, my sister. Do you know her Linda?"

"Yes. I saw her once at aunt Martha's in London about three years ago."

"Tell us what happened," Lola coaxed the lad.

"Well, we were by the sea near Atlantic City – Edith, Rita, my youngest sister and my mother. Edith at the time was nineteen and Rita was fourteen, or nearly fourteen. Edith was, and still is for that matter, very attractive with her brown tresses and her tigerish body. Her ass is perfectly formed and her teats are just as they should be. When she walks down the street she has everyone's head turning, men and women alike.

"One day I decided to take a long walk along the water-front. I think I wanted to be alone, because I walked a good deal. I headed for the little cabin we had near the north shore. For miles around you couldn't hear a living soul. Nearing the cabin I heard some noise.

"Being by nature quite curious, I decided to sneak up and see what it was all about. Through a small crack in the wood I was able to spy Edith, my svelte sister, stretched out on the floor completely nude. There was a man on top of her and I recognized him to be the young architect that had been flirting with her since we had come to the beach. He was looming over her in a lewd position, and Edith seemed to be enjoying the taste of his 'thing'. I watched for a few seconds and then drew away as softly as I had come. I hid in the nearby bushes.

"Ten minutes later the architect had left the cabin, apparently afraid of being caught by our mother. But I knew no-one was going to come before noon, and it was hardly ten o'clock."

"And what did you do then?" Linda asked, following his story with interest and awaiting a denouement to the intriguing tale.

"Once he had left, I went back to the cabin. I opened the door and I saw Edith still lying on the floor, obviously tired from her violent efforts. When she regained her senses and saw me, she tried to hide her nudity. She asked with surprise what I was doing there at such an early hour.

"'You made love quite well, sis,' I said, tossing it off as if it were the most natural thing to say. She looked at me with hate in her eyes. 'Get the hell out of here. I want to dress.' This was her vulgar response. I tried my luck and said, 'You don't have to get dressed for what you're going to do. If not, I'm going to tell mother the truth – and she is not going to like that, is she?' She was thunderstruck. 'You're out of your head.' Then with a little more conviction she called me a dirty little pig and pushed me away.

"I held my stand and told her she was nothing but a slut herself, and that if she would make love with me, I wouldn't breathe a word.

"Edith didn't say a word. She just stared at me resignedly. I undressed nervously, and then threw myself on her like a young lion. 'Take it easy, little brother. This is where you have to get in.' She took my prick with her hand and felt its hardness. Adeptly she slipped it into her wet vagina. Then she shifted around and made it all the harder. Her movements were so well-accomplished that inside a few seconds I came with all my might. My first thought was that it was much, much better than masturbating at the cinema. Several of my friends would hold a masturbating session when we watched a sexy film. You know, we would change around and masturbate each other, or suck each other off in the dark.

"It seemed that Edith had a penchant toward incest, because to my surprise that same evening she asked me to come up to her room and recommence the same business we had taken up that morning. She taught me the sweet pleasure of sucking and being sucked. We spent the whole night making love."

"And then what happened?" Lola wanted to know everything as she stroked Robert's massive cock.

"Afterwards, everything came naturally. I can even remember the first experience of this type that I had with Rita. One evening she was sleeping and I tip-toed into her room like a thief. She had pushed her covers aside and she was sleeping naked because it was a hot summer's night. I woke her by placing my hand on her pussy. She has that silken type of hair that curls gently, a bit like yours Linda. Naturally she cried out in alarm, but was less frightened to see her brother. She said she had been dreaming and thought it might be a burglar. I reassured her and told her not to be afraid. I told her a fib about losing my key and that I would have to sleep with her that night. I pretended to be annoyed at my misfortune. At first she didn't like the idea, but seeing that her brother was hard put (in fact, I was growing hard by the minute), she relented. Until then, we had the normal relationship between brother and sister and she wasn't in the least suspicious about anything out of the norm. She rolled over and covered herself, while I lay down by her side."

"My, you're slow getting to the point," said Linda, pressing and squeezing the head of her cousin's cock.

"A few minutes later, I began to caress her softly. She moved away and told me not too be so intimate with her. She was sure I was just teasing her and she played the part of someone annoyed. She told me she wanted to sleep and to keep my roving hands to myself. Suddenly I jumped on top of her and pushed her legs apart. My cock was ready and with a bit of effort I managed to penetrate her. In spite of her young age she wasn't a virgin. When she understood that I was serious in my endeavour, she submitted willingly. The little darling of a sister loved to be fucked, and the following nights she didn't fail to come to my room to get screwed in the many fashions that Edith had taught me. Even now when we see each other, we never hesitate in taking advantage of our feverish desires.

"Rita told me that she lost her virginity at thirteen. She was alone in the house one day when a man knocked on the door. He was a lowly butcher and she was ready to close the door on him after taking his package, when the man jumped her and forced her to the couch in the living room. Rita told me that in spite of the pain she found the whole act extremely satisfactory. She adored the manner in which he had violated her. I had always thought that Rita was a little devil, and this story confirmed my opinion.

"She told me that no-one but me knows about it. Since that time, and before I tried it with her, she had been screwed twice by strangers in brief encounters. All the boys of her own age irritated her, and she found no joy in being with them."

Linda couldn't help thinking of how Robert and his sisters were advanced for their ages, and how they made good use of their very young lives to taste the pleasures of fucking and sucking.

"So that's the way it is? You made love with your sisters in such a disgusting, incestuous way. What a family, what shame," Lola laughed, teasing the young man.

"And why not? If you had a brother with a prick that you liked, would you say no?" Robert got back at Lola with this slight chiding.

"I haven't got a brother, so I don't know how to respond." Lola tickled his balls.

"I think we ought to hurry up, if we want to take a bath before lunch." Linda took the initiative. An improvised after midnight feast was called 'lunch' in this strange household where every hour was a vibrant period of pleasure.

"You're right, Linda. We had better hurry," Lola chimed in.

"Wait a minute. You're not going to leave me in this state after playing around with my nuts for a half-hour."

Robert showed the two young ladies his powerful phallus, which had sprung up like a flag-pole while he was telling the filthy story of his sisters' antics. He waggled the tool under the eyes of Lola and Linda.

"We're in a rush. We don't have time to busy ourselves with your cause." Lola laughed uproariously on seeing Robert's cock twitch with frustration.

"Hey, I know what you can do. Both of you can suck on it at once, and that way it will be over quicker."

The two friends agreed with feigned reluctance, just to tease the lad, and then bent their heads toward his erection. Lola was the first to take in a mouthful, and Linda had to be content with the lad's balls, which were quite swollen with lust. Then they changed round and Linda eased her mouth over the hot cock while Lola nibbled at the sac beneath.

Robert let out a groan of delight and his two hands sunk into the girls' hair and he patted them on their excellent work.

He was obsessed with the marvellous idea of the two girls who were applying their art for his sole benefit. In his mind's eye he saw his two sisters working him over, and this intensified his pleasure as though he were being ravished by *four* lovely women of different ages.

"Quicker, my dears, faster... I'm co... I'm goingggg to come!" He shrieked out his ecstasy.

It was Linda who still had the fat prick in her mouth and she sucked on it with both force and affection. She ran her tongue along the shaft then flicked around the glans. Her cousin's stories had put her in a frenzy that she had never known before. The scene reached a raging climax, Robert moaning feverishly as he threw his head backwards and he ejaculated. She felt the hot spunk jet into her mouth, flooding her throat.

Lola wanted to get some of the juice, and she took

Linda's place in the dying moments of Robert's pleasure, sucking up the very last drops. The two bitches had taken an equal share of liquid and they both swallowed it at the same time, as Robert's eyes popped with floating, unutterable delight.

Then, to show how much they appreciated the young lad, they cleaned him out entirely with their long tongues, Linda washing out his anus with deep circular licking while Lola saw to the inside of his inflamed foreskin before grooming his pubic hair.

chapter eight

Early in the morning Linda finally went to bed, tired but satisfied. She spent the next morning at the beach with Lola and Robert, and then later on with uncle Arthur and Alice at the villa. They all ate together and then everyone went his or her separate way, except Linda wound up with Lola and Robert.

The day was spent in resting up. Lola drove Linda to the strand, a thin layer of beach, which offered a splendid view. Linda was able to admire the setting sun under the soft caresses of the tiger lady, Lola. When the two friends came back to the house, they were laughing jovially and appeared to be in an exceptional frame of mind.

"Good night, Lola." Linda gave the sentence an added twist in the hope of having Lola with her that night.

"Nighty-night," Lola responded, with an odd exuberant smile. She even added a mean phrase that was not at all warranted, but it was just Lola's way of taunting the girl.

. "Have fun, dear."

Linda felt sure that Lola was just being ironic, thinking that the young girl was going to masturbate before catching her beauty sleep. But little did Lola guess that the precocious schoolgirl wanted something else than the simple process of jerking off in her bed.

However, Linda was not discontent to find her room warm and snug. She undressed herself and walked over to the window for some fresh air and to admire the full moon that sprayed its light over the bed.

Then she heard the noise of several automobiles arriving at the villa, and she wondered who on earth could be calling at such an hour, when everyone was almost asleep.

With the curiosity of a cat she went to the door and heard her uncle greet the new arrivals.

Gosh, he's awake, Linda said to herself, almost out loud.

She opened the door a little to hear the conversation between her uncle and his friends.

"You're late," Arthur reproached the newcomers.

"We had trouble with the car." It was a woman who spoke.

The others, men and women, laughed at the seemingly inoffensive words. Linda put on a night dress and silently went to the foot of the stairs. She wanted to see what they looked like.

Luckily she was able to glance down into the living room, where she saw four men, one the age of her uncle and the others a bit younger. She also counted three women, two who were approximately twenty-five and a third who was no more than sixteen. The youngest was the one with the heartiest laughter. She had a vibrant, attractive body which was highlighted by the pullover clinging to her upper body and a yellow skirt that accentuated the curves of her torso.

Linda noticed that they all spoke informally, and she was sure that they were good friends of her uncle. Compelled to see better, Linda courageously descended a few steps. She watched her uncle, who was pouring liquor in their glasses. Then he sat next to the gamine in the yellow skirt and put his arm around her waist, which looked slim and firm.

"And you, Annie? In good form tonight?"

"Tip-top. And you, grandpa?" She was brazen and Linda didn't see how the girl dared to respond in this manner. Linda was then astonished to see the young girl put her hand between Arthur's legs. Arthur merely laughed and placed his mouth right on the nipple of the girl's left breast and bit into it sharply.

"Ouch! Edgar, your friend is a brute."

The man named Edgar drank his whiskey calmly and then put down his glass.

"Where's Lola, Arthur? Isn't she going to come down?"

"In a little while. Don't be impatient. By the way, we have another guest. My niece."

Linda instinctively perked up her ears and listened

intently.

"What's she like?" one of the men asked.

"You'll see her presently," Arthur said, unaware that his curious niece was quite present already.

They all began to drink one glass of whiskey after another. One of the two older women, a brunette who was rather tall and well-stacked, was reclining. Right by her was one of the four men, who caressed her legs pulling her skirt high up on her milky thighs. The other woman, blonde-haired and nervous, was seated in a large armchair between two men. The fourth man, named Edgar, remained alone in a leather armchair by the window.

At that moment Alice arrived with a tray of sandwiches. She came in barefooted with a short apron that barely reached her knees, and one could guess that she had little or nothing on underneath.

She put the tray on the table and came up to Edgar, who grabbed her by the waist and made her sit on his lap.

"Come, my little one. I want to make an exploration. Don't worry, it will be very personal and precise."

And he began to put his hands under Alice's apron. Alice pretended to run away and she broke out in a peel of laughter. But the man discovered her nude thighs and then unveiled her breasts, which jumped out as though they were expecting that treatment all along.

"Just look at these marvels, everybody." He held the maid up for all to see.

He leaned down and sucked on one and then the other tit, just to capture their warmth and flavour.

"I defy any of you women to show a better pair. Is there anyone who wants to complete?"

Annie perked up anxiously. She sprang to her feet and immediately exclaimed: "Well how about these, for example?"

She brusquely pealed off her pullover, and two splendid young teats popped out in all their gravity-defying majesty. They were firm as two coconut halves. The men applauded.

"Bravo!" Arthur shouted.

And he took Annie by force and brought her close to

his sinewy body. He placed his mouth on the nipple of one rosebud tit and tongued the sweet teenage flesh.

"And what about you others? Helen, Christine? We're waiting, and it isn't fair to keep us waiting, you know." Edgar was eager to see some action.

Helen, the large brunette, responded with a chuckle. The fellow who was sitting at her side put his hand underneath her blouse, while the other was already busy masturbating the pink-faced lady. She abandoned herself with half-closed eyes. The blonde, Christine, took up the challenge. She stripped down with an indifferent air and turned to everyone with a blasé expression.

"Don't you think we are all prudes? We are definitely wearing too much. Let's not be so ridiculous."

She let her dress fall to the ground. She didn't have a stitch of underclothing on. Linda, from her advantageous hiding place, thought – and justly so – that the women had prepared for the evening. It was bound to wind up in a real spectacle. Linda was feverish with excitement.

"It's our turn men. The evening has begun rather quickly tonight, so let's make the best of it."

"Alright fellows," another added. "Edgar, Nick, Stephen and Arthur – everything off."

And they all answered the call. The women were anxious to see the cocks of the four gentlemen, who were just as immodest as the females present.

Linda had her eyes bulging out as she watched the men undress themselves hastily. When they were all nude, she saw that the friends of her uncle all had a prick of gigantic proportions. She especially noticed Edgar's. His powerful brown weapon was menacing Alice. Linda tried to imagine the feel of such an enormous cock in her vagina. And she almost cried aloud when she thought of the same tool attempting to enter her anus.

The festival, or orgy, or whatever one wished to call it, was decidedly on the way. Linda observed the antics of the revellers. Edgar already had Alice on the carpet, having ripped off her flimsy apron. The little maid squirmed lasciviously on the plush covering like a mink in all splendour.

The petite servant girl showed her long svelte thighs in all their glory. Her two teats stood up and greeted her handsome violater and her smooth belly undulated like the ripple of splashing water. Her bush of curly pubic hair seemed electrified Edgar bore down upon her. The man's face fell upon her pungent pussy like a hungry fox, and he plunged his inflamed tongue deep within her lips of pleasure.

Annie didn't hesitate to duplicate matters, and even improve upon them. She knelt before Arthur and took his sturdy prick straight in her small oval mouth. The youngster emitted lewd noises as she slobbered away with the engorged cock plugged deep in her mouth.

The teenager had not as yet taken off her tight skirt, and it was Nick who took the initiative on unzipping the garment and pushing it to the floor. It was evident that he wished to have part of the girl for himself. Annie did not increase nor decrease her sucking. She just was concerned with her job and apparently she enjoyed it, from the look on Arthur's face.

The man who was called Stephen was still occupied with Helen, who was laid out on the divan with open thighs. The girl had a body that was meant to be sculpted. She resembled a statue with her fine muscular torso.

Stephen had the large woman on her belly and she arched up, enabling him to lick her asshole. Linda covered her mouth to keep from giggling when she saw how the young lady was grimacing at her awkward position.

Nick mounted Christine as soon as she was available. His cock was fat and rigid and the blonde girl was moaning with pleasure in no time.

Linda was watching the extraordinary coupling of partners when she heard footsteps behind her. Turning around, she saw Lola who stopped a few feet away from her. Undoubtedly she had been looking in on Arthur's guests too, for there was a sardonic smile on her lips.

Lola had put on her yellow pyjamas and she put her finger to her lips in a signal of silence. Then she tip-toed over to Linda.

"It's entertaining, isn't it? Have you been here for a long

time?"

"Since they arrived. Why have they come here?" Linda asked.

Lola laughed silently. She whispered in Linda's pretty ear.

"It's just a little party that your uncle has organized. But what we are seeing is only the aperitif."

"The aperitif?"

"I mean it is only the beginning. They're just warming up, rubbing against one another and lightly making love. But the best is yet to come. Naturally you're invited."

"Me?" Linda was surprised to hear this.

She glanced at the people in the salon and her eyes immediately fell on Edgar's prick. The young man was busy tickling Alice's ear. Linda was surprised at the sudden feeling that gripped her. She was envious of Alice and she would have changed places with her at the drop of a hat. Lucky Alice had that wonderful, juicy cock at her beck and call.

Lola was delighted to see that Linda took such pleasure in the party. The older woman was able to read the young girl's thoughts, and she made a proposition.

"Yes, of course, you can participate in the party, because you are the attraction that Arthur promised his guests. In one way, that's why they're here. You will be screwed and buttfucked by all the men. They will do what they wish with you, and you'll be happy to give in. Doesn't that give you goose pimples, just to think of all the hot cocks you'll feel in you?"

Linda trembled on hearing these words, but her eyes remained glued to the scene below. She secretly anticipated the delicious treats that were in store for her.

"I didn't tell you about the women. What a bunch of hot bitches in heat *they* are. They wouldn't hesitate to put their hands in their fathers' pants. They'll throw themselves on you like a pack of wolves. One month ago Annie, the youngest, brought her thirteen-year-old sister to one of these shindigs. She did it on purpose, in order to pervert her sister who she always loved and hated at the same time. The poor kid, although she was good-looking, was raped by your uncle and buttfucked by

Edgar. Then they all got in their licks. The girl must have been sodomized at least twelve or thirteen times. The morning after she could hardly walk and her asshole was bleeding. She had to stay here, after giving a weak excuse to her parents. But I suspect her of being a regular nymphomaniac, just like her sister. She doesn't let a day go by without flirting with any man she picks up. Once in a while she stalks them down in the street like a whore."

Lola spoke luridly, and her words excited Linda who was visibly moved by what the brunette had to say. Her eyes were filled with bright fascination.

In the living room, the scene had changed slightly. Arthur had put Annie on his knees and he was just starting to stick his cock into the girl's tiny asshole. At once, Linda saw the big dick disappear, in one gulp, into the red anus. Annie jumped in the air as though she had been stung by a bee. And Edgar was doing the same to Alice, but in a different fashion. He had the maid lie on the floor, point her feet to the ceiling and hang on to her ankles. Edgar dug underneath and met her anus with his beautiful prick. It seemed to Linda that Alice, who was normally used to such an operation, was not taking the huge cock as well as she usually did. Suddenly Linda realized that while she was watching Edgar and Alice go through the act of sodomy, she was idly masturbating herself. Nevertheless she continued, in spite of Lola's amused look.

Stephen made Christine submit by employing a treatment that usually has a good deal of success with young girls. He had her lying on her side and he slipped his slender cock into her vagina from behind. He had slyly unhooked a candle, and Linda saw that it was wiggling in Christine's asshole. The lucky girl was being serviced by two rigid instruments. Although she let out a piercing cry, it was apparent that she was enjoying herself by the smile on her face. She was even on the verge of coming, judging by the way her pussy was discharging its juice. Then Christine emitted a long groan, her pelvis and buttocks bucking, and she managed to be the first to come. Teenager Annie was next in line.

Linda noticed that she was extremely wet between the thighs. She had come herself, but she had so fixed her attention on the others that she had not noticed her own arousal. In fact, she was astonished at seeing the clear white liquid drip to the floor.

"Well, that isn't nice, is it? I think it's time for us to take part in the game, don't you?" Lola took Linda firmly by the arm and led her downstairs. The young girl was flushed. Lola went down the steps so rapidly that Linda almost lost her breath.

"Hey everyone! Here she is. The guest of honour."

Everybody looked at her, appraising her from head to foot.

Edgar was the first to break the silence, while he held on firmly to Alice who was snugly lodged underneath him. He said he approved of the guest, and beamed with delight.

"Well if it isn't our Lola, Lolalita. And the other must be the famous niece we've heard so much about. And, I might add, not without good reason!"

"Come along, princess. Don't be timid. Nobody here will bite you... yet." Uncle Arthur proudly took the girl's hand.

Linda pulled down her nightie, which just barely reached her knees. Lola pushed her toward the group and soon Linda found herself surrounded by the many guests.

"Well, what's the verdict, ladies and gentlemen? Shall we adopt her or not?"

"She looks like the kind who would go for our antics," Nick said with a scrupulous air.

He continued to masturbate Helen while the blonde sucked him off, ogling the newcomer. Normally she would be busy with Arthur's cock, which she loved.

Lola and Linda had arrived at the right time and they gave a certain enthusiasm to the group, who livened up and began to show their gratitude.

Nick unplugged his cock long enough to demonstrate its proportions to Linda, who could not take her eyes off it. It was covered with saliva and had attained a length that was quite impressive. He brandished it like a conquering hero.

"Let's see what she can do," Stephen hollered out.

Nick unbuttoned Linda's pale nightie. Soon she was nude and her nipples grew hard at once. Her little bush of hair glittered in the candlelight of the living room. The young girl

Linda's Strange Vacation

looked at Lola helplessly.

Lola was already seated between Arthur and Helen. They sat like three majesties on the divan, deciding the fate of the modest schoolgirl.

"She's kind of young." Nick offered his opinion as he brought the girl close to his nude, hairy body. "But I think she has promise. As for me, I'm ready to take her apart right now. Are there any objections?"

"Go ahead, my boy. But remember, I'm the one that is going to take her from behind," Edgar boasted, thumping his chest like a hunter.

Alice was somewhat jealous, and she dragged her buttfucker back to the position he had neglected while contemplating future delights.

Annie, the little nympho, approached Linda and fixed her on the spot with a cruel smile.

"I have a proposition to make all of you. While you two take her from the front and the back, she is going to lick me out."

Linda listened to all of this without even trying to get a word in edgewise. She was intimidated by the numbers, and she was too emotionally disturbed to offer any resistance.

"Let's have a little order in our meeting, ladies and gentlemen, if I may call you that." Arthur proved that he was the organizer and chairman of the whole affair. In his usual, amiable way he dominated the situation with his fatherly smile.

"Now, my niece is all yours, just as I had promised. And you can do as you like with her. But I am going to offer you a proposition. First of all, the men are going to treat her with their cocks. She'll be had from the front by Nick, and Edgar can have her the way he suggested. Stephen and myself will receive her best kisses. Don't worry about her youngish air. She can take all you fellows have to offer." He bade them on, and wished them all good luck.

Linda, still in the clutches of Nick who was feeling her up more and more, had her anus plugged by one of his fingers. She realised that it would be impossible to escape her fate. She had to face up to it. Her mission was to satisfy all the men and, probably, all the women in the group.

"And what about us?" Helen spoke out. Linda prepared for the worst.

Lola stripped down and she was lying on the couch next to Arthur like the queen of Sheba. A cigarette hung from her full lips.

"Don't be in such a rush, dear," Arthur laughed amusedly.

"I'll take care of her," Annie said with lust flaming in her eyes.

"Oh, no, Annie, we'll take care of you ourselves. You had your night a few weeks back. You must learn to give way to others. Egoism is a terrible sin, you know."

Arthur managed to keep the hungry women in cheek, but he was wondering just how long he could hold out with such a pack of she-wolves. He laughed heartily and it was quite clear that he was the master of his own household. He had to be diplomatic about it all, and he decided to use tact.

"Let's all be calm. I'm going to find someone who will be able to help us out."

Arthur had already spotted Robert coming down the stairs. The lad was nude and he had the same ironic and luxurious smile as usual. He saluted everyone, being familiar with the clan for many months now.

"I see that my cousin is up for the slaughter. Well, that's the way the big ball bounces. Good luck Linda, honey."

"Robert, sugar." Annie snuggled up to the young fellow and cooed in his ear with her best capricious, baby-doll voice. "You'll take care of me, won't you? Your uncle seems to forget all about me."

"Why you little liar! Just a minute ago I had my penis in your asshole, and you've got the nerve to complain. Well, that's a woman for you..."

"Let's stop beating around the bush. Do whatever you want all of you – but I'm going to start off with a healthy chunk. That delicious, pink asshole is all mine, gentlemen." Edgar was the first to start the ball rolling.

He disengaged his cock from Alice's rump. It was slick and steaming. The young maid received such a shock at this withdrawal that she remained non-plussed and gaping on the floor, waiting for someone to replace her lover.

Edgar approached Linda, who almost crossed her eyes gazing at his enormous, threatening prick. This was the man who had excited her imagination. With the gigantic proportions and the purple head sticking high above two testicles as large as tennis balls, the cock was ringed in brown matter all along the shaft. It was the shit of little Alice.

"He'll kill me with that thing if he puts it in my rear," thought Linda, who was turning green with worry.

Nick folded her legs back and made her sit on the floor.

"Wait a minute Eddie. She should be comfortable to get the best out of it." Nick carefully put the girl in the prescribed position.

Then he took a pillow from the divan and placed it under the girl's sweet buttocks.

"Isn't that better now, my angel?"

Edgar tipped his huge cock along the rim of the girl's mouth and then stroked her on both cheeks with the heavy glans. Linda inhaled the pungent odour of the soiled phallus. The horrible scent gave the girl an added thrill, and she slowly prepared herself for the double violation.

Exquisitely, her tongue nipped out and darted at the rigid cock. She closed her eyes and a smile brightened on her youthful face.

Stephen and Arthur came over, and Linda was soon encircled by four great pricks, purplish flesh throbbing in unison.

Christine and Annie came over to join in the fun. They watched the luxurious setting unfold and their lovely eyes rolled with excited curiosity.

"Everyone ready?" Nick set the starting signal.

"Just a second, Edgar. I'd like to lubricate her hole so that it will be all prepared for the feast."

Stephen bent down and licked the teenager's asshole. She rolled over in a wave of sensual agitation, pushing her anus back over his tongue. Christine turned red with envy.

"Get away from her. I'll do it."

"As you wish, *mademoiselle*, but do hurry."

"Say, what about me?" Helen's voice boomed out from the dark corner in the back of the room.

She came running over to the spot where the lascivious procedures were taking place. Helen and Christine gave curvaceous Linda the once over, and they didn't miss a point on her splendid body. The two women stuck to her like leeches. Christine rotated her tongue in the tight pink hole of her backside, while Helen expertly, slowly licked out her pussy. Every once in a while she would look up wide-eyed at the others, to let them know that she was enjoying herself. The others were vexed, envious and obviously becoming frustrated.

Christine began to cough because she had stuck her tongue so far up Linda's asshole. The anal vent was flooded with warm saliva and its sweet odour permeated the room. Helen was meticulously working on the front with the half-happy and half-indifferent air she usually presented. She made sucking noises as she rigorously tongue-fucked the swooning schoolgirl.

Linda flexed her muscles in pleasure and her head bobbed up and down like a cork floating on blue waters. The whites of her eyes showed to such an extent that all were wondering when her blue eyes would ever come back into her lovely head.

The men were growing impatient, and when their cries went unheeded they were forced to drag the girls away. But the females refused to give up their terrain and they fought the men tooth and nail. Arthur and Robert were obliged to haul them away by the roots of their hair. They took them into the parlour and satisfied them with various combinations of sodomy and cunt-sucking.

Alice and Annie joined them, while imperious Lola sat comfortably in an armchair, her arms folded and not the slightest expression in her beautiful bronze face.

The four men had managed to place Linda in the desired position, and Nick once more led the festivities. He swung one of her free legs in the air and lowered his head to the slippery, wide-open cunt. Nick decided that he would be more at home there with his cock, so he placed his hard-on at the opening. He groaned with satisfaction as the glans settled against her hot pussy lips, and then moaned his contentment when he slid deep inside the rose-coloured crevice.

"Are you ready at your end, Edgar?"

Nick was a good fellow, always thinking of others.

"Go on lad. Let's get down to work. You know the saying, talk is cheap."

Edgar slipped behind the delirious girl, who was prone on the floor but still managed an acrobatic half-turn to present her plump little buttocks, a sight which stiffened Edgar's cock by a good two inches.

Nick held her on her side while Edgar dipped down and fingered the anus. His large hands cupped the two halves of her gorgeous rump, pulling them apart, and he aimed his heavy penis at the shining asshole as it spread slowly open.

Linda jiggled for a second and then remained perfectly still, anticipating the penetration of her next lover. Then all of a sudden, she felt a human crow-bar burst into her tiny hole. Instead of riding the blow, she backed into it all the more and took the invading cock in full stride, sucking it deep inside her entrails to the very hilt.

Linda almost fainted on the spot. Edgar crashed into her asshole with his massive cock and Nick held fast, never giving more than a half centimetre of ground. The fainting schoolgirl was speared fore and aft, and the two men's cocks rubbed together on each side of her vaginal membrane.

A trickle of blood flowed down the thigh of the limp girl, and it was apparent that her asshole had widened by a good inch. She was half-unconscious in her struggle between pain and pleasure.

Edgar got all the more excited at the red streaks. He loved the tightness of her back-passage, but at the moment the young lady wasn't giving back any bumps and grinds. To liven her up a bit, he dug his shaft in to the hilt. Linda screeched in pain and then threw her cunt over to Nick, who ploughed into it with renewed gusto.

The two men felt each other pumping as they plunged deep within the confines of the schoolgirl's asshole and pussy. Due to the tightness and the compact structure of the girl's lower body, the two men were practically masturbating each other within the hot, wet hollows of her pelvis. Poor Linda felt blasted by the massive pricks, which were gaining momentum by the minute. She had a vague thought of how and where was it all going to end, but slowly she lost consciousness and the muscles of her thighs went dead as she sank into an unprecedented faint.

"What good is she? She can't take on two for a damn. Quick Arthur, get some smelling salts for your niece. The girl is croaking, old chap."

Arthur was too busy filling Helen's mouth with his prick to be bothered by such trivial incidents. The oblivious uncle hollered back his disgruntled feelings.

"Whack her a few times. She'll come around in no time."

Lola saw the distress of the two husky men and decided to take matters in her own hands.

From a drawer in Arthur's desk she brought out a thin flexible whip. She tapped Edgar on the shoulder with it, and he quickly got the hint. Both men leaned away, though they remained firmly buried inside the dazed girl. Lola unhooked some terrifying blows that brought Linda back to life in no time flat. The girl thought she would go out of her mind from the sting of the brutalizing whip. After a dozen well-aimed strokes, she gathered all her strength and tossed her body backward and forward trying to ward off the gnawing anguish of the lash.

But she was pinned by the two lovers who were tightly bound within. Suddenly, as the sting of Lola's blows connected with the raw nerves of her engorged orifices, she received a shock of pleasure which ran up her spinal cord.

Linda bucked and spun along the tickling carpet, as she started to grind away with her two lovers. For the first time, she gave way to the growing enjoyment that burned at her insides. Nick pistoned in and out of her pussy and then Edgar picked up the rhythm with his anal thrusts, and all three fused into a mass of pulsating flesh. Meanwhile Lola kept up her punishment and even wielded her strokes on the luckless men. The didn't seem to mind though, and it even appeared as though the flogging was pushing them on to new heights.

"Now you'll have me, my darling, just like you were

supposed to. Come on honey, grind away and do it properly. How are things on your end, Nick old boy?"

"Just fine, Edgar."

Linda relaxed and more than enjoyed herself. Her full lips gasped out moans of delight as she sucked away at Nick's earlobe. She winced with crazed sensual ecstasy as Edgar tongued her back and bit into her shoulder blade.

"Oh darling, gouge me out. You're big, my lover, and I love it. Oh, how I love it. You'll never know."

Her little pussy spasmed in synchronized rhythm as the two men gave all their energy to the luscious flesh which bound them.

It was a rare sight to see the young girl with her innocent asshole stuffed with a full-sized cock, while at the same time her snatch took a battering which threatened to split it apart.

Stephen and Arthur had come back, and they were insisting that the two fellows who were doing such an excellent job should now give up their turns. Nick and Edgar were reluctant to do so.

They were screwing and buttfucking Linda furiously, and besides, they were right in the swing of things. There was no good reason why they should relinquish their rights.

"Shall we pull out, Linda? Others are waiting and they don't seem to like the idea that we are getting all the honey."

"Tell them to go to hell." Linda responded vulgarly but justly so, for right at that moment she felt her pussy swelling with the pangs of a huge impending orgasm.

"Stick with us baby, and we'll fuck you to the stars." Nick was full of filthy talk as he prepared to explode.

Suddenly Linda thought she was going to suffocate. The two men crushed her between them and she felt their muscular bodies stiffen in an effort to retain their colossal climaxes.

"I think I've had it, Edgar! I'mm commingggg... There it is – Ahhhhhhhhh!" Nick unleashed his hot spunk into the far depths of Linda's cunt.

Linda jiggled up and down, and noticed Lola watching the proceedings with those panther-like eyes of hers. She wondered what the woman was thinking of as she felt the warm wave of come invade her lower belly.

In the meantime, Robert had come over and like the spoiled lad who was, stuck his cock straight into Linda's open mouth. She only had it open to breath better. But Linda didn't complain. She felt that it was just an added gift of male flesh, and should be consumed with gratitude. She started sucking on it as if it were a stick of candy, running her tongue up and down the shaft.

Meanwhile she refused to let Nick out of her pussy, and she milked his cock with her cunt muscles, keeping him semi-erect. She felt Edgar still slithering in and out of her soaking asshole.

Her mad tongue rolled around Robert's cock, which had grown to amazing proportions; the youngster was on the verge of a premature orgasm – much to his shame.

All at once, Robert blew out his sperm and it forced Linda's mouth to swell like a balloon. The girl valiantly kept the cock in her mouth as she gulped down the hot liquid.

Robert shook like a young lamb at a slaughter. His head flung back, he bellowed his approval while digging his fingers into Linda's wild silky hair.

Edgar was next. He didn't come all at once, but instead he throbbed out his white jism like a machine gun issues bullets.

Every time he let loose, Linda's rump expanded. The girl was in the throes of her third orgasm, and the deliberately slow manner in which Edgar was holding back gave the delirious girl hope of a fourth.

"You look like a perfect little angel," Lola said, and then howled with laughter. She had to hold her hand over her mouth to keep from startling everyone.

Suddenly Linda began to hiccup. Perhaps it was out of guilt, or perhaps it was due to Lola's mockery. Robert was inclined to believe that she swallowed too much of his sperm. Half of it had already gushed down her throat, while the rest of it was overflowing from her soft lips.

Nick finally disengaged his thoroughly tired prick from her sodden pussy. Robert followed suit when he saw that Edgar was reaching back on the small table to get at a cigarette. His limp cock fell from Linda's asshole, which was distended and overflowing with red- and brown-streaked jism.

Linda, completely fatigued, crawled over to where Lola was sitting.

"How was it, lovie? You seemed to be having a whale of a time."

"You'll never know. Oh, Lola... I lost count. Was it four or five?... It was unbelievable... just like a dream. I'd have never thought that it could be like that."

Lola patted her head and glanced at her peacefully.

"There are no complaints, then. But we've only just started. Much is yet to come!"

Lola took Linda by the hand and led her back to the group. Robert was trying to buttfuck Alice, while Arthur was getting in his best strokes on the spread-eagled Helen. He was pinching her teats while he plunged his big prick into her well-lubricated asshole. They were both on their way to having silent, powerful ejaculations.

"They haven't finished yet. I don't think we should disturb them, do you? Besides, it doesn't look as though they will be detained for long." Lola laughed playfully.

"Let's get started with the second half of the show." Edgar rubbed his hands.

"What second half?" Linda asked, looking somewhat puzzled.

Lola laughed and tapped her on the shoulders. "Don't be impatient. You'll see, and you'll *feel* much better about it."

Lola seemed to be having her private joke.

Linda watched the woman's face in its multiple expressions. She wondered just what surprise Lola had in store for her, and why she was chuckling like a wicked witch.

chapter nine

Linda gazed at Lola's bewitching belly. She watched the curly hair wind up from the crotch, and then she caught Lola's glance.

"May I?" Linda asked humbly.

After the terrible assault by the male members of the party, Linda was happy to return to the sanctified domain of womanhood.

Lola spread open her thighs and Linda's head lowered to meet the sweet-scented pussy. The young girl began to lick at the cunt-lips and clit like a puppy.

"You're a love, you know?" Lola whispered to Linda's bobbing head.

All the men present stood around and watched the two lascivious ladies. They were tired and rightfully felt that Lola's patience merited some consideration. Then they sank in the chairs and on the sofas, each one showing signs of his recent fatigue.

Annie was the first to perk up and make suggestion.

"Let's dance. I feel like moving around a little. Come on, don't be a bunch of stiffs."

"Come here and move around on this." Stephen tapped his cock and roared with a hoarse laughter.

"A little later darling. First of all, I want some music. Something that will give the place atmosphere and mood."

She went over to the phonograph and chose a waltz. This gave Edgar the opportunity to dance with Linda. He graciously took the young girl in his husky arms and they stepped elegantly to the bursting pleasure of music.

Linda felt his prick hard and ready for action. She clung to him like a ship-wrecked victim. Soon they were not the only ones who were dancing. Arthur held Annie in his arms, while

Stephen tripped the light fantastic with Lola. Nick picked up Helen and Robert had his hands wrapped around Christine's plump bottom.

All the men appeared ludicrous, with their pricks sticking up almost challenging their partners. Several of the women danced with their hands gripping or slowly pumping the members of their companions.

After a few spins, Arthur took Annie by her rump and raised her in the air. He continued to dance and at the same time he slipped his massive cock into her pussy. Without losing a step they continued to waltz, Arthur holding Annie by the buttocks so her cunt remained clamped over his cock.

"There's a good-looking couple for you." Lola indicated Arthur and Annie in their feverish embrace.

She didn't have a chance to elaborate on her opinion, for Stephen wheeled her to the floor (she was a bit too heavy to hoist in the air), bent her over and, after a few quick licks of her asshole, began to sodomize her on the spot. The others playfully called them obscene names.

Lola retained her excellent humour and chuckled with delight while she slid her long fingers along the back of Stephen's neck.

"No, Stevey darling, I want to finish this waltz. We are making a spectacle of ourselves in front of everyone."

However, the man would hear none of her useless pleading. He was right at the point of ramming his cock to the hilt inside her gorgeous asshole, when the door bell rang.

Everyone stopped dancing. They all looked astonished, and perhaps more than one entertained the thought of the police.

"At this hour? What in the world do people think? That they can break a party at any time?" Arthur appeared angry.

"Don't open the door, Arthur. It may be... and, oh, if my mother ever found out."

Linda fidgeted in her new fear. Lola took advantage of the occasion and freed herself from Stephen's clutches.

"I know who it is," she confessed to everyone. They all seemed to be greatly relieved.

"You're not going to open the door completely nude,

Lola. You're out of your head." Nick warned.

The others waited without saying a word. They were all expecting a scene of some sort and showed their apprehension by shuffling about aimlessly.

Lola opened the door and called to whoever was outside.

"Oh, there you are. Finally. You know, you haven't come too soon. It is terribly late."

A young lad, who couldn't have been more than twelve years of age, entered timidly. He was dressed in country attire and he gazed at the naked women with hungry eyes bulging.

He gathered up enough courage to move a few steps toward the centre of the room. Then he became aware of the unusual setting and stepped back.

"Oh... I... I..."

"Don't be afraid, little one. We aren't going to eat you alive. Now have you brought your friends?"

"Yes, they're outside..."

"We'll call them in. What are you waiting for? You can see that everyone has been impatiently staying up late for you." Lola winked at the group, who as yet had not caught on.

"Come on in..." The boy shouted.

"That's it. Tell them to hurry... Quickly... By the way. What is your name little fellow?"

"Gus, miss." He turned red all over.

The boy jumped out of the door and a few seconds later he came back dragging a cord.

"Whoa, there. Come on, Ben, come on Jos."

Everyone let out a nice round 'oh' when they saw the surprise. Two small donkeys appeared on the end of the cord that Gus held in his tiny hand.

Lola followed the young lad and his two 'friends' into the living room.

"Well, my friends. Here it is. The surprise I had in store for you."

"But what in the world?... What does it mean, Lola? It's some kind of a joke, isn't it?" Arthur tried to clarify matters.

"Here they are. Two little donkeys, Ben and Jos. Just as talented as they can be."

Linda's Strange Vacation

Lola took control of the evening with her imposing posture and laughing air.

"Where did you find them, Gus?" She stroked the boy's hair and he turned crimson once more. "My boss runs a small circus outside the city. He said I could have them for the night if I would feed them properly," Gus explained timidly.

Lola patted Ben on his hairy mane and then spun around to tell her listeners the story.

"I've known Gus for a few days now. He told me the secret about these two stubborn donkeys. You'll see that they aren't just ordinary donkeys, but that they come from the best society."

"And what may I ask is so extraordinary about those two mangy beasts?" Stephen let his curiosity get the better of him.

"Ben, it is true, is the one I prefer. He knows how to mount a lady with all the delicacy of his art. You should see the way he gets on top of Jos – who is incidentally a lady, and we should all call her Josette."

Lola gave Ben a big kiss.

"Josette knows how to interest men as well. Isn't that so, Gus dear?"

The lad looked down at his feet and couldn't respond from embarrassment.

Helen wrapped her arms around the youngster, and the warmth of her nude breasts in his face didn't help matters any.

The boy apparently loved it, but kept his head bobbing from side to side.

"He's a real cutey. I wonder how big he is? In the raw, naturally."

Helen evidently found Gus to her taste.

Annie detached herself from Arthur and skipped over to the two small animals.

"But what about that famous dick everyone talks so much about? How is it supposed to appear?"

"Some patience, sweetie." Lola wagged her finger at the impetuous teenager.

Lola took Ben and Josette by the cord and led them to the very centre of the room.

"Annie, you are going to suck Ben here. But will you remember that he is a donkey and not a man?"

"You'll see how I can make anyone sit up and take notice. Just let me at him."

Lola lifted her hand and pushed the girl back for a second.

"No. We will have our pleasure, make no mistake about that. But first of all, we should have some consideration for our guest of honour. Ben is prepared to shoot off at least a dozen times. I think we should start the fun off by giving him to..."

Everyone turned around and practically shouted in chorus:

"Linda!"

"Who, me?" cried the girl.

"Bravo! A better choice could not have been proposed. You have my blessing, my lucky niece." Arthur led her over to Ben as though she were some charming princess being betrothed to her dashing prince.

"Just think of it – my niece shall be buttfucked by a donkey in front of my very eyes. Now *this* is what I should like to see when we get together. Thank you Lola, for your pleasant surprise. I hope *all* of you will come up with a little something before summer is over. Just a little imagination, that's all it takes."

Arthur was extremely happy. In fact, he went back to his desk and started to take notes.

During the little respite, Helen took Gus over to the divan. The big brunette was noted for her love of initiating newcomers to the clan. The lad let himself be had with his mouth wide open.

"Come on, sonny. Take off your clothes."

"Take off my clothes?"

"Of course. Do you wish me to help you...?"

And before Gus had a chance to say yea or nay, Helen was helping him off with his shirt. Soon he was completely nude. He was slightly built, but quite sturdy for his age. Between his thighs, which lacked the first signs of hair, stood his little prick. It wasn't all that small, and Helen was surprised to see the proportions of such a young and innocent-looking lad.

Helen began to tickle the youngster's balls with an air of avid concentration.

"Tell me, honey. Haven't you ever licked off a woman before?"

Gus looked up at her completely abashed. He swallowed and failed to respond.

Finally a few words squeaked out of his heart-shaped mouth.

"No. Honestly, I never have."

Helen was delighted to see her young lover squirm as though he were at the dentist waiting to get his tooth pulled.

"Well, I imagine that you haven't. If you had, you would have been unfaithful to me. And you would not want to be unfaithful to this pretty thing, would you?"

She led the boy's right hand down to her pussy and he nervously fingered the wet lips.

"No, ma'am."

Suddenly, with one brisk movement, Helen took the lad by the scruff of his neck and buried his face in her cunt.

"Go on, Gussy. Pretend it's ice cream. You like ice cream, don't you?"

Perhaps the suggestion registered, because Helen had her mouth agape with pleasure in no time.

"Oh, the little devil..."

Judging from Helen's reactions, Gus must have learned his lessons quickly. Helen, of course, was turned on by thinking of the fresh virgin she had between her legs.

But the grand spectacle was in the centre of the room, around the two donkeys. Linda, who had refused, conceded her turn to Annie.

The little glutton wasted little time in getting underneath the animal. She licked his belly and then pressed her hungry mouth against the animal's genitals.

In a few seconds the animal's pizzle popped out, red and powerful.

Annie continued to lick it while she took it in her two hands because of its enormous size.

"It's enormous," Christine confirmed.

"It's beautiful." Alice seconded the notion.

Linda was speechless. She just thought of the moment that it would bludgeon in her like a flagpole. It was going to be bad enough just accepting its size in her pussy, but how in the world would she take it in her butt? He would certainly rip her open.

"We'd better prepare Linda. She looks as though she is ready to pass out," Nick told the fellows close at hand.

"Afraid? Cut it out. Why, I'll bet the little bitch is as wet as a ditch just thinking of that engine pounding into her. Am I not right, Linda sweet? I'll bet you want that beast all over you. Confess honey, we're all behind you."

"No, no. I don't want him. He's too big!"

Lola came to her side and comforted the shaking girl by placing a friendly arm around her shoulder.

"Now, now, my love. It'll be marvellous."

"By the way, Lola, have you had the pleasure of tasting this lovely animal and receiving it in the you know where?" It was Stephen who asked.

Lola smiled with her famous superior air.

"Of course. Do you think I would subject my friend to such a thing if I had not attempted it myself? Ben is just great, and I advise that some of the men present take notice of his efforts. They will learn a good deal, believe me."

"Don't tell us that it was Gus that helped you in your... efforts, my dear?" Helen was writhing under the caresses of little Gussy.

"No, my darling, it was his boss. The man is Italian – and well you know the rest."

"Alright girls, don't fight. It's not worth the trouble. If you want to have it out over Benjamin later, then we can get the whips out and fight it tooth and nail."

Arthur had a way of settling all arguments tactfully. The two women had become catty over their prized possessions.

Nick was curious, and continued to bombard Lola with questions.

"And the boss participated, eh?"

"Alright, wise guy. I'll tell you what you want to know. We started off by having Ben do it cuntwise and his owner,

Emmanuel, doing it from the rear. Then he got the dreadful – but wonderful – idea of having Benny stick it in my butt. I coolly accepted the proposition, while Emmanuel permitted himself to be sucked off. I might add that an agreeable time was had by all."

"I'll bet," Edgar snickered.

"That Italian is six-four and as strong as Hercules. I'm not sure who is the bigger, Benny or Emmy. And you can judge from the size of our tail-wagging friend that Emmanuel must have been somebody. I still can remember when he tossed me on the floor and said, 'Now both of us will slip in our bananas, my treasure.' Those were his exact words."

Lola was deep in a reverie, and she finally blinked her eyes and came out of it.

"Come on Linda, don't worry about a thing."

Linda stumbled over to Lola. The poor girl was shaking like a leaf. She still wasn't convinced. It was obvious she needed more than words to get her calm back.

"I ... just... can't."

Lola winked and once more calmed her down by telling her she would soon know what paradise was like. She showed the girl how to pass underneath the animal. She had her head right against that of the donkey with her arm around Ben's torso.

"Put your legs on the floor and keep your knees wide apart. Don't worry about a thing, we'll take care of the rest."

Linda obeyed and remained in the indicated position. She could feel the strength of the little mule, and the musky odour of its genitals washed over her.

Suddenly she felt a veritable snake stiffen against her body. It was more than a cock. It was a baseball bat.

"My gosh. It really is huge," Nick remarked. "Do you think she will be able to take it?"

"She'll take it alright, and what's more she is going to love it. Just wait and see if I'm not right."

Lola took Benny's great pizzle and lodged it at Linda's orifice. The young girl jumped back at the contact.

"Ah, then you feel it?"

"And how," said Linda.

The animal, which before seemed to be indifferent to the whole thing, gave a leap forward as though he were impetuous and wished to enter the girl. The end of his pizzle gouged at her pussy and it made Linda cry out with a frightened howl.

"I think we need some vaseline." Lola signalled to Robert to go up to the bathroom for some of the lubricant.

Robert scampered back in no time, and Lola smeared great swathes of it over Linda's cunt-lips and then deep inside her pussy.

"Now that should do it. Ready Linda honey?"

"I'm all set," the girl retorted, really not at all sure of herself.

Everyone was down on his or her hands and knees to watch the penetration. Annie was getting the biggest thrill out of it, and she masturbated without letting up.

"Go to it, Benjamin old fellow," Arthur cried, chewing on his pipe. "Let her have it."

Lola put the prick back in position and the donkey, used to this sort of situation, pushed forward. This time his pizzle disappeared, inch by inch, into Linda's swollen pussy and up into her womb. Her eyes opened wide and she wanted to ask if she had not been ripped apart.

Instinctively she spread her legs wide apart to ride the blows. Already she wasn't thinking of avoiding the huge member, but instead she made every effort to facilitate matters, raising her buttocks off the ground and thrusting forward with hips grinding.

Everyone watched Linda as though they were hypnotised. The young teenager had been a virgin just a few days ago, yet now she was being raped by a donkey. It was like a dream. And for Linda it was a dream come true.

Uncle Arthur began to take notes. He carefully steadied himself on his knees as he wrote furiously on his ink pad.

Annie approached Ben with her tongue outstretched. She was dying to lick the donkey's balls.

Lola aided Linda by pushing her into a more favourable position.

"He's a doll, isn't he Linda honey? Let him get all the

way in and you'll see what he's capable of."

"He wants to ride on top. It's no fun unless we can really help Linda to the heights of pleasure," commented Alice.

"I don't think I can stand any more of it," gasped Linda.

All at once she turned white. "He's going to kill me!"

Annie began to lick the frustrated beast's balls. This caused Benjamin to wiggle his prick further into Linda. A few drops of blood fell to the floor, showing that the mule had penetrated deep inside her.

Soon Linda's thighs were covered with streaks of blood. Ben started to let out a thunderous animal cry, and everyone guessed that he had spurted. But Lola insisted that the donkey was just getting to like the sport. Then he began to snort and buck, as though he were on the verge of a great orgasm. And lo and behold – he was. His thick donkey sperm flooded the near-unconscious girl's cunt and womb.

It was Lola who came to her rescue. The bronzed beauty dragged her backwards, disimpaling her. The bloody sperm left its thick trace on the carpet as it dropped in gouts from Linda's gaping pussy. Linda's stomach was spasming back and forth as she expelled the last drips of spunk out of her entrails.

"Now *that* was something. Lola, you're a genius. How did you ever think of it?" Stephen scratched his head.

Someone interrupted with a shout. It was Helen, who was right in the middle of a gigantic rousing orgasm brought on by the twinkling head of little Gus.

It was easy to see that Gus was excited about his position, because his little prick stuck up proudly, its tip leaking clear fluid, all the while his face was buried between Helen's tightly crossed thighs.

"Just look at that, will you. That bitch Helen couldn't wait to get hold of the little tyke. It's just like her to be greedy for newcomers." Arthur let his comments be heard by all, and in particular by Helen, who tossed it off lightly.

Christine threw an ironic smile over toward Gus and Helen, who were going through the final strains of their cunt-sucking lesson.

"And I thought he was a virgin," she exclaimed.

Once Helen had attained her pleasure, she raised the boy and up hugged him to her breasts. She permitted him to taste her cherry nipples. It was the kind of nibble the youngster richly enjoyed. He no longer remained timid. Gus bit into the teats as though they were made of cream cake.

Helen then cradled his prick in her fist, slowly pulling his wet foreskin back and forth over the glans, and the little fellow slobbered gluttonously over her nipples.

"Of course he is still a virgin. He's much too young to be otherwise. But *I'm* the one that is going to take it away from him and give him something else in exchange. After all, you've all amused yourselves with the donkey!"

She fondled Gus's head as though he were the most skilful of lovers.

"Don't be so possessive Helen. Wouldn't you like to feel Benjamin in you? I guess you prefer children's pencils to the crowbars of beasts."

Everyone laughed, and that included Helen. But she didn't let go of her boyish lover.

"Go on have your fun. While waiting my turn, I choose to remain with Gussy and teach him some things. None of you are against my plans, are you?"

Helen looked pleased with herself.

"I'll start with the pencil and wind up with the crowbar in due course."

They all nodded their approval. Now, another candidate was needed for the donkey's prick. Annie and Christine were very impatient, and it was finally the youngest who got into the act.

Annie had much more experience than Linda, and she rapidly got into the desired position. Instead of the vaseline, Annie was licked out properly by Alice, while Christine moistened Ben by sucking on the end of his great pizzle. She had quite a time with the sperm that still trickled around the beast's balls.

"It's delicious. I've never tasted anything like it. Look how hard he is getting already."

"Hurry up and get him inside me. I'm awfully hot and I want him badly," Annie squealed.

Linda watched attentively. She lay on the carpet leaning on an elbow, observing the scene. She realized that the pain she had endured was only secondary to the pleasure. When she felt her crotch, she gathered up her own come mixed with Benny's ejaculation and some drops of blood. The act had been savage, but she appreciated the marvellous after-effects. She scolded herself for not having behaved better.

Now Annie was possessing that wonderful prick that only a few minutes ago had stuffed to the core her with its animal heat and immensity. She was proud that Benjamin had come inside her with all his donkey fury.

Alice and Christine continued to lick the beast's testicles. They soon managed to get his pizzle in perfect working order for feverish Annie. The teenager was spread apart impatiently, wiggling and begging for the enormous prick to split her.

"Come on now, damn it. Let me have it. I know how to manage him. I'll do it by myself."

She flew onto the great pole of flesh like an acrobat, deeply impaling herself. An outsider would have said that she had done it many times before with Benjamin. At the first penetration, Annie flinched with pain and let out a sharp raspy cry.

Ben had entered with a kick and was stuck fast in the forefront of the youngster's pussy.

"Oh, it's great. I've never had anything like it between my legs. It hurts, but what the hell. It's terrific... but sensational... Go it, Benny, darling!"

Annie moved around like a fish out of water. She had Benjamin almost leaping in the air. Inch by inch the donkey penetrated her. Then, Annie started to shudder with noisy gasps and moans,

"Oh, oh... I feel it... coming... I want to come with him..."

It was almost as though the donkey had known what she desired. Benjamin began to bray and kick up his hind legs as though he wanted to dig in deeper. He started to shake and buck as if struck on the head. All at once he let loose. A stream of thick white cream shot into Annie's pussy. She rolled into him, trying to milk every last pearl of the sacred juice.

Then the girl crumpled to the ground, completely exhausted. She had a happy smile on her face.

"Hey, I'm next." Christine made her presence known to all.

"Let Benny have a rest," Stephen pleaded on behalf of the poor beast. "After all, he's not a machine. He's a genuine screwer like us, and he needs a rest once in awhile."

"He'll be able to rest up after I get through with him. I have a way with animals you know," Christine bragged.

Christine bent down to suck the dripping, half-hard pizzle. Although it was slightly soft, it retained its sizeable proportions. Christine took the prick in her mouth and rolled her tongue around it, cleaning off the blood and come.

She sucked avidly on the gobbets of sperm and washed the animal out with deliberate skill to make him hard again.

During Benjamin's star turn, the men in the room found that their activity had dropped off suddenly.

Arthur approached Josette and tapped her on the rear. The little she-donkey looked at him.

"I've tried everything else. This little bitch of a donkey has love in her eyes. I think I'll rip into her behind. It will do me good and I can chalk up another pleasure in my carnet."

Edgar, Stephen and Nick gathered around to watch this daring exploit.

"Why not? The girls are going wild over Benjamin. We should have our share of fun with Josie here."

"And I'm new at this type of game. I've got to admit it fellows, I've never buttfucked a mule before," said Nick.

"I did it to a goat once." Arthur revealed his intimate secrets. "It was a few years back, while I lived in the mountains. I was with three friends. During a walk we met a splendid little creature, a white goat. It was tied to a tree. All three of us screwed her. It was an amusing experience."

Edgar approached Josette and pressed his cock, which had grown remarkably rigid, up to her flank. The beast did not budge. She was evidently used to such attentions.

"In order to penetrate with some ease, I think it would be better to stick on a little vaseline. Josette's anus appears awfully small."

"I think you're right, old chap. She seems as tight as a virgin. Better try some."

Arthur helped Edgar lubricate his cock. Once again Edgar aimed his weapon at Josie's asshole. This time the great head of his prick entered without any difficulty.

"How is it?" Alice asked as she approached the group.

"It's hot as a furnace," Edgar replied.

He moved about trying to get a deeper penetration. He then began a to and fro movement.

"Is she better than mine?" Alice asked in a sweet tone, obviously trying to gain a comparison.

Edgar didn't answer her. He was too busy giving Josette his best strokes. The man sighed away as though he had never tasted a similar treat. And in fact, Edgar, with all his earthly experience, had not.

Alice wanted to watch the achievement close-by. She decided to lap her tongue around the rim of Edgar's anus. Good-naturedly she went to work, pulling his buttocks apart so she could get her tongue right inside his sphincter, which was already oiled with the musky sweat of his exertions.

On the other side of the room Christine had Benjamin in a fine state. The animal was foaming at the mouth and it was apparent that he preferred Christine to the others. Christine was right when she told everybody she knew how to handle the animal.

She kept talking to Benny as though she had made love to him all her life. Christine played with his balls while she hypnotised him with her feverish eyes.

"Maybe he just likes blondes," shrugged Stephen, trying to find a reason for her success.

Christine kept telling her friends of the marvellous effects. Arthur ran back to his desk and started taking notes.

The girl tried to open Ben's mouth and deep-kiss him, but the mule wouldn't have anything to do with her.

"He'll only French kiss with Josette, Christine. After all, the two are quite attached you know," Nick teased.

"He'll forget all about her when I get through. Look at the fire I've stirred in him already."

"You're going to look rather silly walking down the street with a donkey as your lover, dear," Nick jibed once again.

"The dirty beast. He wants to gouge my stomach out. I can feel his cock hammering in me like a steamshovel. What a monstrous prick this one has... Oh how it burns... It's like a bar of fire... When he trembles inside, there isn't a man living who can thrill me like that. This little donkey is... a real satyr, believe me."

Christine pressed herself up to the little donkey as though she were clinging to him for life, forcing her pussy further over his pizzle. She rubbed her lovely breasts against the skin of the beast. And all present could have sworn that Ben got hotter by this passionate treatment.

Christine must have come more than once, because she was panting like an exhausted sprinter. Her thighs were covered with her cunt-juice mixed with the donkey's own discharge.

"Since I've had someone like Benjamin, I can't settle for anything less. I'll go to any lengths to have something like this. Oh, it's good... but *really* good."

The others looked on and listened, surprised and admiring at the same time. Christine didn't put on any brakes in her exhibition. She let her real, sexual self come out and take charge.

Meanwhile, Helen was avidly teaching young Gus the techniques of expert love-making. The little fellow had his cock in her anus and was pumping away with mad frenzy.

In the meantime his mistress turned to talk to him as he plunged in and out of her tight asshole.

"Do you like that, Gus, honey? Are you about to come, kiddo?"

Gus couldn't answer back. His emotions had gotten the better part of him and he was swallowing all the wind he could muster in order to hold on. There was no doubt that he was feeling something that he had never known before.

The atmosphere of the surprise reunion was getting into full swing. Christine had hardly time to be released from the fidgeting donkey when Lola started to suck Ben's red dick. Lola wanted the beast now and she took an aggressive action in showing just how much she desired him.

The men in the room were overwhelmed by the sudden sensation of desire and abandon. They were partly mad at the women for their over-attention of a mere mule. They decided to get even by taking some healthy whacks at Josette.

When Josette proved what she could do, the men soon forgot all about the women and concentrated on the delightful animal.

Nick had already come three times and was trying to fight off the others in an attempt to stick it out for a fourth.

Once the girls became aware that they had been abandoned, in true female fashion they hovered over the males to try to lure them away from the wondrous beast. It was just too evident that they were jealous of Josette.

The donkey glared at them haughtily. When Ben saw that things weren't going the way they should and his Josette was bored with mere mortal sex, he four-legged it over to his whinnying companion.

Nick stepped aside and permitted Benjamin to show the men just how Josie liked her sex.

The two animals went at it hammer and tongs. It aroused everyone, and Lola soon found that she was being buttfucked by Stephen.

Nick dropped Linda on her back, whipped her legs right over her shoulders and drove his red, swollen cock deep inside her succulent anus.

"You liked what you got from that crazy donkey. Well here's something else you won't forget." Nick pushed into her right up to his balls. Linda didn't utter a solitary cry. She liked it and wasn't in the least bit afraid of anything now.

Ben's gigantic phallus had opened new vistas for the girl.

Uncle Arthur was sucking Helen's tits at the same time she was preoccupying herself with Gus. Arthur was somewhat jealous, and he was finally forced to give the youngster a swift kick in the backside to dislodge him from Helen's rectum. Arthur then jumped on the beautiful brunette and scolded her.

"Aren't you getting tired of dicks the size of little fingers? Here, try a thumb for a change."

Helen began to laugh uproariously.

"You're talking about Benjamin I suppose. You aren't going to compare yourself to him, are you?"

Everyone was in a gay and playful mood by now. Annie had Edgar on her shoulders and Stephen was busy with Alice, and the maid, at the same time, was sucking off Robert.

Little Gus remained in the corner sheepishly while Arthur fucked the daylights out of Helen.

Lola was the happiest of all. She was underneath Benjamin and taking his huge phallus in her pussy like a trouper. Nearby Linda was being sodomized by Nick.

There was a profound silence in the living room. The couples were on their last lap, slowly sighing into a limp drowsiness. The first to speak was Lola.

"The festival isn't over yet, folks. Let's refresh ourselves with some sandwiches and beer."

Annie and Alice went to the kitchen and prepared a snack for the group.

"Good idea Lola. I was beginning to get hungry," Edgar yawned.

"Why don't we play a game in the meantime?" Christine suggested. Everyone chimed in with his or her proposition.

Finally Lola piped up with something that appeared to fit the bill.

"I know a game that is rather amusing. You have to guess what I am thinking..."

"What do we have to guess?" Helen quizzed.

Lola smiled and then continued.

"It's not complicated. One of us will lie on the floor with her legs apart and her eyes covered with a scarf. Then she'll have to guess who is the man on top. If she's wrong, she'll have to suffer an atrocious whipping. I know some of you girls are dying for it though. If she's right, she gets a bonus."

"Not a bad idea," Edgar agreed.

"First of all let's eat. Then we'll begin." Uncle Arthur was very considerate of his guests.

Alice and Annie came in with a platter of food and drink. They even had something for Benjamin and Josette.

Lola hoisted her glass of beer and offered a toast.

"To everyone's sexual health."

They all gathered around Benjamin and poured beer down his throat, while the scandalous little Annie tried to suck him off once more. Benjamin responded by sending a great jet of piss down her throat, and she drank it all down as if it were lemonade.

Lola clapped her hands.

"Let's begin our game."

"Who is going to be first?"

"How about Linda?"

"I was sure of it," said Christine.

Linda didn't hesitate. She took the position her elders desired and she permitted her eyes to be covered by a perfumed handkerchief, which belonged to the voluptuous Lola.

Lola waved Stephen over. He knelt down and stuck his penis deep in the blindfolded girl's asshole.

"Who is it?"

"I'm not sure..," Linda responded.

"She's just doing that on purpose. Maybe she can't feel any more."

"Be quiet Annie, and give her a chance," Lola scolded.

Stephen warmed to the task, plunging his cock into Linda's already stretched anus. He pistoned in and out.

"Who is it?" Lola questioned.

"She's just putting on an act to get more, the little rascal."

Stephen dug his prick deeper into the luscious asshole, which felt as wet and warm as a pussy. He tried to keep from moaning his pleasure so as not to give himself away.

"Do you know who it is, Linda?" Lola questioned.

"No. Not yet... Let me feel him a little more..."

"But of course," Annie chimed in. She certainly was dying to be in Linda's place.

"She's just putting on the dog. The little whore couldn't ask for anything better."

Stephen now had his cock deeply embedded in Linda's rear and he started to poke her brutally. The girl, mistaken as to the width of the member, shouted out in a raspy half-happy, half-painful voice.

"It's Edgar, isn't it?... Edgar?"

The others were gleeful to see that she was wrong. Linda would have to pay the price of sucking each and every one of them.

"No, take a look. It isn't Edgar. It's Stephen. You'll have to pay the penitence, dear."

Arthur was wondering whether his niece did this on purpose. He questioned whether she was that vicious. Perhaps she really was gifted with the libertine family traits.

Stephen was forced to give up his masterful performance. He wanted to finish what he had started but he was out-numbered and had to abide to the rules of the game.

"Let me be the first," Nick piped up.

"No, first of all she is going to lick out all the women. And then suck their assholes... And then after..."

"And then after?" Annie's eyes were as big as stars.

"Then she will have the unique pleasure of being sodomized by Benjamin."

Everyone applauded Lola's brilliant proposition. They all imagined the immense delight that was awaiting them. The women lined up. Annie and Christine, naturally, were the first to proffer their wet snatches.

"She better give her all, or she'll see what I'm capable of."

The warning came from Christine.

Linda knelt down before the excitable Christine, who dug her fingernails into Linda's scalp and forced her head into her bush.

"Get in there and suck, sweetie. Do a good job, or it'll be the whip."

Christine had a reputation for not playing around. Crisp and cool, she needled Linda into a frenzy. Soon Linda was slobbering in the soaking folds Christine's pussy.

Annie jumped into the game as soon as she saw that Christine was on the verge of coming.

"Damn you, get back before I thrash you. I haven't come yeeeeeettt..." Due to the adroit licking tongue of the schoolgirl eating her pussy, Christine barely managed to finish her sentence. And at that, it was on a very high note.

Linda's Strange Vacation

After Annie, who tried to come twice after concealing her first orgasm, Helen almost suffocated the poor little dear.

Alice made Linda work very hard. The skimpy maid was terribly blasé over the whole thing, acting like a royal duchess. Her cunt still reeked of cheap perfume and come.

Real love was demonstrated with Lola however. Linda stuck her finger up Lola's behind and then put the finger in her mouth to mix the two, the come and the shit, to induce a real sensual pleasure. Both girls sucked the mixture, and Linda kept her finger embedded in Lola's asshole while she licked her clit until she came.

Once the women were content, everyone flocked around Benjamin. He and Linda were the star for that night. Arthur promised everyone a repeat performance some other time.

Nick took one of Ben's front legs and Robert the other. They lifted the beast in the air, while Linda sat on her knees. Lola informed her things would go better if she would put her buttocks high in the air. The girl listened attentively and had enough confidence in Lola to heed her warning.

Once Linda's pink, dilated asshole waggled in front of Benjamin's slow-growing prick, Helen took hold of it by the root and aimed it at Linda's orifice. The odour coming from her orifice inflamed the beast, and he rammed his pizzle home. Linda yelled like a martyr. Yet she held fast, and once the donkey's prick was fully up her asshole and the worst of the pain subsided, she began to relax and appreciate the fantastic sensation.

The mere thought of having such a tremendous organ in her bowels made Linda proud, not to mention turned on, and she was in form to give everyone what they came for.

The girl bucked and ground her hips like the best of professional belly dancers, only she was presenting her asshole. Her glistening sphincter, stretched to near bursting, cinched around the root of Ben's pizzle, milking the first drops of hot come from his balls.

Benjamin was delighted. He let out a few 'hee-haws' that gave all a few laughs. The mule kept driving home in Linda's boiling asshole.

"This is one of the better shows you've put on Arthur, my lad. Continue the good work," enthused Edgar.

It wasn't long before Benjamin rammed his cock in so far that Linda froze halfway in the air. "Ahhhhhhhh!" The girl cried as a golden smile crept over her lips.

Linda had reached a divine climax, but still the donkey rammed home. Christine came to the rescue by sucking on Ben's balls.

The animal's voice grew harsh and hoarse. Then with a bellowing, rough cry he let out his explosion. Linda was shot forward as though she were being fired from a cannon. Christine was pinned underneath the hind legs, which had given away.

Everyone applauded.

"Bravo!" Nick and Helen shouted in unison.

Linda fell forward in a stupor as the donkey's prick slowly withdrew from her asshole in a spray of jism, blood and shit.

The party had reached its denouement successfully. The guests, as well as the hosts were content.

When the bunch left that evening after having another round of food and drinks, Arthur felt proud and placed his arm over Linda's shoulder. The girl was dog-tired. She smiled bravely and excused herself for being such a slouch at the beginning of the evening.

The gang hailed her as an excellent newcomer, and Nick invited her to his home for the get-together the following weekend.

Arthur heartily shook Edgar's hand and the friends patted each other on the back.

"You're a real champ, Arthur, believe me. Give the girls some more for me." Edgar waved goodbye as he parted with the rest of the sated, delighted guests.

epilogue

Late that night, Arthur came into Linda's room. His strange eyes grew grave and insisting. Though tired, Linda was happy to submit to her uncle's lust. She felt the hour was perfect, three in the morning, and that her uncle, with excellent taste, had wakened her in the middle of a most erotic dream.

The man violated the girl. He bit into her ear lobe, her calf, her behind. Arthur, completely thrown into a peculiar state of lust, sucked at the girl's pussy as though it were the remains of a dried lemon.

Linda was driven to passionate heights as she licked and sucked on Arthur's majestic prick. The two ransacked each other for the delights of the flesh, and it was evident that they had achieved a perfect unity.

Suddenly Arthur leaped up and put his thin fingers on Linda's shoulders.

"Linda. I believe I'm in love with you."

"But uncle, what about Lola? You have been with her for a good number of years. It wouldn't be fair to her. She is so fond of you."

Arthur tumbled out of bed quite naked. He began to rub his hips. The man was clearly bothered by the thought of Lola.

"Lola doesn't mean a thing to me now that you've come into my life. You are the perfect fuck. She will just have to resign herself to it. Besides, Lola doesn't care about anyone but herself. She is mad with lust and hasn't the slightest notion of what love might be."

Linda stretched her bruised side, still sore from the powerful grasps of her uncle.

"Uncle Arthur, isn't our relationship incestuous?"

"My dear little nymph. It has been from the beginning.

The only thing I hadn't counted on was my love for you. My love for Linda, the princess I wanted to create. Well, you're the creation. And I have become a luckless Pygmalion."

Uncle Arthur came back to the bed and took Linda's hand and placed it on his cock, which was half limp.

Uncle and niece gazed into each other's eyes and saw love. For Linda, it came as a shock. She couldn't really say whether she was truly in love with her uncle or not.

She was very, very fond of him, certainly. Her love for him was much more in the vein of respect for an elder, although she now had a craving for him sexually.

In her confusion, Linda placed her arms around Arthur's neck and squeezed tightly.

"Oh, uncle Arthur. I don't know how I feel really."

Uncle Arthur, still sitting close to the girl, pushed his stiff prick against the cunt-lips of his sweet, sentimental niece.

"This time, my dear, we are going to make love slowly and with... *feeling.*"

He slipped his cock into the schoolgirl's hot, hungry gash. She arched back and accepted the full length of the handsome organ.

Arthur's hand crawled up and down her spine and finally came to rest on her buttocks. He squeezed and then sighed.

"How I love your backside, darling." He stuck his finger in the crevice between her buttocks and tickled her asshole.

Linda put her long tongue deep inside her uncle's mouth. Their tongues entwined in delight and their salivas mixed together lasciviously.

They embraced for several minutes, unaware that the door to Linda's room was slightly ajar.

Arthur crushed the girl to him and his cock drilled into her pussy.

"Can't you feel me, dear. I'm as hard as a rock. I want to last a lifetime with you. Buck a little, Linda, and show me your grace."

The girl obeyed and demonstrated her talent as a fully-fledged lover, her movements drawing him nearer to climax. Suddenly the door burst open and Lola, red-eyed and with her hair mussed and agitated, strode into the room.

In her hand she brandished a horse-whip. Lola had fire in her eyes. Her hand nervously gripped the ugly weapon.

"So Arthur. This is what you plan on doing to me. No more shall we pass the small hours of the morning making love. You've found someone else. A girl who passed as a friend at first, and now look at her. A tramp. Well, I'll get my vengeance."

She let the whip crack at the bed-post. It made such a loud crack that Linda had to blink from the noise it made.

"The donkey wasn't enough for you was it Linda? Well maybe we can give the evening some variety yet."

A wicked blow caught the girl around the neck and almost strangled her. When Arthur got up to protest, he was met with a vicious whip-lash that got him around the mid-section. The man doubled up in pain.

"Lola, you... you've gone out of your mind. What are you trying to prove?" The man spoke in pain.

Another sting of the lash caught him directly on the back and took the wind out of him for several seconds.

"Go ahead Arthur. Suffer a bit. It will do you good. You've been the great lord here. Everything you wanted was placed at your feet. How does it feel to get a taste of your own medicine?"

Lola swiped the whip down on the man's left foot. He yelped like a dog writhing in pain.

Linda came to the protection of her uncle. But she was met with a rain of blows that cut into her breasts and buttocks. Lola was trying to drive the whip into her asshole.

"Lola, put down that whip or I'll never forgive you. You've lost your head." Arthur just managed to puff these words out. He fought to regain his breath.

For a moment Lola hesitated. She knew Arthur's wrath, but this time she was definitely going to face it all the way. The tigress was determined to fight her man to the last breath.

By a glance of daggers, the two former lovers declared war. Linda began to whimper. For the first time since her visit to the villa, she became afraid, truly afraid.

With back-swipes and overhand blows, Lola let fly with

that horrible lash. Instead of seeking cover, Arthur crawled toward her. He had the disadvantage of having the frightened Linda clinging to him like a leech.

"Wiggle on the carpet with your princess, you worm. I'll have you both as striped as bloody zebras!"

Linda bit her lip and when she cried the pain caused by an excess of breathing made her dig her nails into her uncle's torso. Arthur struggled to get to his feet and stumble forth in search of the whip. He tried to ward off the blows with his elbow, but to no avail.

Within a few minutes, Lola had them both bleeding. Arthur bled from the mouth as though he had suffered internally. His back was streaked with red bruises. Linda matched him with her stripped, blood-flecked body.

"Now, you know what it is like to cheat your mistress."

Lola's eyes were like two red flames. Linda had never seen the bewitching woman in such a state of emotion as this before.

"You'll remember me Linda, won't you? Especially when you make true love to that bruised, beaten body."

Lola, who had her back up against the door, was suddenly thrown forward when the door was pushed open by Robert.

"Grab her, Robert boy."

Robert, realizing that a scandalous fight was taking place, obeyed his uncle and locked the woman's arms to her side. This gave Arthur a sufficient amount of time to stagger over to the furious whip-wielder.

With his remaining strength he slapped her across her proud and aggressive face. His next move was to snatch the whip from her hands. Arthur threw the weapon to the far corner of the room.

He met the defiant eyes with a backslap that caused Lola's head to bob up and down. Her eyes returned to meet his. Linda was surprised to see how brazen her friend was. Linda still felt that the rude intrusion was just a bad dream. But when she rubbed her tender bottom, she was quickly restored to reality.

"Now Lola, it's my turn to get even. And you know

when I get angry, it isn't very much fun."

Uncle Arthur meant business. He signalled to Robert to come close for instructions.

"They've all gone home by now, I suppose. We let Gus sleep with his donkeys in the garage. Robert, I want you to go down and get Benjamin. We haven't finished with the little mule yet. Our dear Lola is going to find out what Benny's really like."

Arthur let out a cruel laugh that slightly took Lola aback. Even Linda tried to plead with her vengeful uncle.

"Don't you think she has suffered enough for the evening? I'm sure she'll apologize and then everything will be alright. Please, uncle Arthur."

"No, Linda. I have no intention of letting her get off so easily. She must learn a lesson, here and now."

Arthur ripped off Lola's pyjamas and twisted her left nipple. Lola just gritted her teeth without uttering a cry. Arthur slapped her across the mouth.

"You are a proud bitch aren't you? Well, I've got a new mistress now and you will serve me in the most docile way. I'll tame you, my ex-darling."

Arthur put his hand to his chin trying to think of a million and one tortures to bestow upon the hapless brunette.

All at once Lola ran over to Linda and clutched her arm. She spoke to the girl in a terribly intense voice.

"Can't you see how he is? He will treat you like dirt one day and cast you aside. Think what you are doing, Linda. You will only be a princess for a short while, and then he'll give you up as he is doing with me."

Linda felt that Lola was right, but she could do nothing about it for the moment. She was surprised to see that Arthur was paying little attention to them. He was apparently lost in his own thoughts of cruel vengeance.

"Linda, go to my room and in my blue dress on the bed you'll find the keys to the car. Put on any clothes you can find and leave this terrible place."

Linda was pushed to the door. Without any hesitation she ran to Lola's room. Uneven in her thoughts, she questioned herself as to whether she was doing the right thing.

Once in Lola's room she searched for the keys and found them in the blue dress. Then she went over to the wardrobe and grabbed a rose dress and a heavy overcoat.

As she was hurriedly putting on the dress, she heard some foot-steps behind her. She turned around startled and frightened. Arthur and Lola barred the doorway.

Linda was taken aback at the sight of the two together. They had evidently patched up their quarrel.

"So you want to leave me just like that, Linda? What, you prefer the cold night to your warm tender uncle?"

Linda was speechless. She gazed at Lola for help, but the tiger woman was indifferent and languidly smoked a cigarette.

"You fell into our trap, Linda. Arthur wanted to see how faithful you would be. We planned that sham together. You didn't suppose for a minute that Arthur and I would leave each other for a mere child, did you?"

Linda's mouth dropped wide open. Their ruse fell into place. *She* would be the one who would have to pay the terrible price. It was difficult to imagine the games those two adults were capable of playing.

Once again the door flew open and Robert entered, dragging the obstinate Benjamin. The donkey seemed thoroughly wide-awake for such a late hour.

"If you have eyes to see with, Linda honey, you will notice that Benjamin has just had a shit. Like all men animals, he has an asshole too. You will kindly step up and lick Ben there, and properly. If not, I assure you that the consequences will be tenfold."

Linda felt so helpless that she unthinkingly walked over to the animal and knelt so that her head bumped its flanks. Ben's furry balls swung in her face and he brayed horribly.

Arthur pushed her by the neck, and her nose almost stuck in the animal's rear-end. The odour was horrible and sickly. Linda swallowed to keep from throwing up.

"Alright Linda, now lick the shit out of Benny's asshole. It may be quite tasteful. You never know."

Linda, with tears streaming down her face, tongued delicately at the mule's behind. Benjamin had recently had a shit alright, and animals usually don't get a chance to wipe out their rears.

Soon Linda's mouth was encrusted with a brown sticky mess. Lola kicked the poor girl on the rump and goaded her on.

"Come on. You can do better than that. Benny has a disdainful look on his face."

Linda steeled herself and burrowed her tongue further into the slippery asshole. The odour was nauseating, but somehow it affected the girl's senses and she wound up by almost enjoying the horrifying, but excitingly taboo, act.

"Well, well. I think she is winding up by liking Benjamin more and more. What do you say we adopt Benny for our household, Lola? We could always make good use of him. Needless to say, Linda would adore him."

The young girl turned crimson, and with the lumps of Ben's shit around her mouth, she looked quite a sight.

"I can't go on, uncle dear. Please, I'm feeling terrible."

"Just get some of the shit that dripped down along his legs. Then tongue him deeply and sincerely, and we will let you go. Have no fears about it, dear."

Linda did has she was told. She leaned down to the sturdy little hind quarters and lapped up some of the brown matter that had trickled there. Then she came back to the anus and tongued it as deeply as she could for a few minutes. She imagined it was the asshole of her lover, and towards the end of the second or third minute, Linda was so dazed with pleasure that Lola had a hard time dragging her away.

"Why the little bitch enjoys it. Look, she's coming. Just look at her thighs. They're covered with cunt-juice."

"What do you expect? After all, when I said she was my princess, I didn't mean to exaggerate. This girl is open to all callings. Why Lola, in no time we shall have her doing the most splendid sexual feats imaginable."

Linda was doing such a good job of cleaning out Benny's behind that the young mule had worked up an erection. He was helped along in his sexual urges by Linda's skilful manipulation of his balls. Her fine fingers worked from one testicle to the other.

"Go ahead, Lola. I see what you're after. You can get it all in your mouth – but open wide dear."

With great dexterity, Lola slid down under the animal and wielded the baseball bat-sized prick toward her hungry mouth. She slobbered it up. The force of the cock almost completely distorted her face. Lola inhaled deeply and sucked longingly on the gigantic pizzle.

"Uncle Arthur, can't I take Linda from the rear? She's just dying for it. Look at the way she is waggling around and dripping. Come on uncle, be nice."

It was true that Linda was giving someone the come-on signal; her youthful buttocks were swinging from left to right and then slowly grinding in the humid air.

"Go to it, Robert. But you better knock it home. This girl is very, very special and we want to handle her with care."

Robert leaped on Linda's back and drove his twitching cock deep into her distended anus. This only caused the girl to bury her head deeper in Benny's behind.

Arthur wanted to take a picture for his archives. The setting was delightful and the scene was elegant. He mused and thought that if he did take a snapshot, nobody would ever believe it. They would think it was a posed shot. And yet it was happening, right there before him.

The good uncle felt his cock rampant and burning with lust. It was almost purple with feverish engorgement. Arthur rushed over to Lola and dragged her from the donkey's penis by the roots of her hair.

"Lola, work on this for a while."

While the donkey brayed its discontent, Lola gluttonously poured her saliva over Arthur's hot cock.

Robert plunged away into Linda's precious asshole, while the 'princess' licked out Ben's backside with the most professional of oral agility.

As Lola crouched in front of Arthur, sucking him with all her skill, he barked orders to Robert to step up his speed.

"You little wretch. Let her have it with your best punches, Robert. Why the devil can't you have any appreciation for female bodies? All you ever think of his shooting your load. I'll have to teach you a thing or three."

He bounded away from Lola, who spat out a few drops of burning come. She was taken aback to see the man rampage about without considering her ultimate pleasure.

Arthur pushed Robert away and straddled the behind of the fair Linda. His enormous cock ripped into her gaping asshole as she continued to lap clean the donkey.

"This is the way it is done, Robert fellow. Roll around a little. Then go in and out. And then... all the way in. Make it... really good and deep."

Linda attested to the effect of this brand of action. She groaned her pleasure like a she-wolf howling to the moon.

"Get it, Robert? In... all... the... way... and then out slowly. Then tickle her cunt-lips with the head of it. Don't you see how she backs into it for the sheer love of it?"

And, indeed, Linda was backing into Arthur's fat prick. She wiggled her behind into a perfect position and at the same time she never lost a stroke with her tongue. Benjamin was dripping his spunk onto the expensive carpet.

Lola came to his rescue and placed her insatiable mouth around the animal cock. She siphoned out the hot white liquid and her eyes rolled with a mad joy as she swallowed it by the pint.

In the meantime, Robert was so hot and excited that he had to masturbate. At the last moment he bounded upon Lola and exploded his rigid cock into the beauty's anus.

All four were having a ball, but the one who appeared to be enjoying it the most was Benjamin, the astounding donkey. His eyes closed and he must certainly have entered a real animal paradise. He drooled at the mouth and brayed his delight.

The heat that the four created could be seen by the condensation on the window pane. The odour of Ben in particular caused the foursome to devote their very best efforts to the action at hand.

Inside of a quarter of an hour, the bedroom stank of shit and ejaculations. But this did not stop the couples from going into their third or fourth orgasm.

"I swear that I love you, Linda my darling princess."

Linda didn't care whether her uncle was sincere or not.

She just kept up the hip-pumping movements which were bringing her closer to another juice-spraying orgasm.

She turned from the donkey's rear-end and responded to her uncle's caresses.

"I love you too, Arthur."

"Then you'll be my princess for life. You'll wait on me hand and foot, and I'll lead you to the finest sexual thrills that can be had."

"Yes, uncle dear." Linda squinted with the joy of his fat prick plunging deeper and deeper into her.

From the floor, Lola agitated around the donkey's belly. She seemed annoyed with Robert.

"You're no damned good, you little stinker. You've come twice already and every time it goes flat. I guess it's your age that makes you so impetuous. I prefer Benjamin to you, my dear boy, as much as I regret telling you this."

Robert didn't give a damn. His appetite was grand and he decided to make the best of a special occasion.

"Just think of what Annie, Nick and the others are missing. And Alice is fast asleep in her little nook. This is tremendous. I could go at it all night."

"Just don't try it. It will probably kill you. Let me alone with Benjamin. He is my true lover, since Arthur has left me limp and flat."

Linda heard these infamous words, and this time she wasn't deceived by the ruse. She really didn't give one drop of 'donkey shit' whether the woman was serious or not.

"Linda, promise me that you won't go back to school without my approval. After all, you've learned much more here with me – and just think what more is in store for you."

Linda was set back by this unfamiliar proposal. She still had two years to go. And it was true, however, that in the course of a few days she had learned more about 'life' that she could ever have picked up in school.

However, she wanted to go back and put her knowledge into practice. It was difficult to make a decision at such a crucial time. Arthur spread her legs wide apart and over his shoulders as he penetrated deeper than ever.

"I'll do whatever you think best, uncle dear. But don't

you think my education will be neglected?"

"I'll get a tutor. I have just the one for you. He is known to be the finest lover in all of Europe. His name is Paul and he has a penis that is a foot long, no less. And it creates the strangest sensation inside, the women tell me."

At that moment Linda was consumed with a burning climax that coursed through every nerve of her body.

"Ahhhhhhh..."

The girl came and came. It was hard to tell whether it was due to her uncle or the mention of the name of a lover, Paul with the fabulous phallus.

Arthur pistoned into the girl with his most violent thrusts. He grew hotter and hotter as he felt the girl's discharge burn his swollen prick.

"Now you've really excited me, Linda. I think that I too... am... comminnnnng!"

Arthur clenched his teeth. He turned suddenly white and his head dropped on Linda's left shoulder. The man had just released a veritable tidal wave of jism.

Benjamin brayed for the fifth time. And Lola received a flood of hot spunk in her gorgeous mouth. It poured out of the corners and dripped down her neck.

Robert renewed himself by masturbating frenetically, like a deranged monkey. He made another attempt to leap upon Lola, but she would have none of it.

Arthur, limp as a rag, tried to compose a sentence. But due to his fatigued state, he failed to find the right words. Suddenly he regained his senses. He fondled Linda's soft hair and bit her back.

"My princess..." he uttered weakly.

Linda had rolled away from Benjamin and fell lifeless on the carpet.

When she opened her eyes she saw Arthur leaning over her. He had a strange humble look in his eyes. Linda almost thought it was the look of love.

Then of all things, she witnessed a tear that rolled down her uncle's cheek. His eyes blurred and his mouth gently sucked her teats. Once he returned to the surface he met her stupefied glance.

With a flood of tender words he sang a hymn in her honour, then he slid down to her feet and kissed then passionately. First the right, and then the left.

Arthur stretched his tired body over his niece's belly. Once more he had grown stiff, and was searching for the hot young pussy that he so cherished.

"Oh Linda. Allow me to be your... your *prince.*"

www.creationbooks.com